The Ark

Laura Liddell Nolen grew up in Hattiesburg, Mississippi. She has a degree in French and a license to practice law, but both are frozen in carbonite at present. She lives in Texas with her husband and two young children. *The Ark* was made possible in part by a SCBWI Work-In-Progress Award. Laura can be found on Twitter @LauraLLNolen. This is her first novel.

The Ark

LAURA LIDDELL NOLEN

Book One of The Ark Trilogy

HARPER
Voyager

Harper*Voyager*
an imprint of HarperCollins*Publishers* Ltd
1 London Bridge Street
London SE1 9GF

www.harpervoyagerbooks.co.uk

This Paperback Original 2015

1

First published in Great Britain in ebook format by Harper*Voyager* 2015

A catalogue record for this book
is available from the British Library

ISBN: 978-0-00-812069-6

Set in Sabon by Born Group using Atomik ePublisher from Easypress

Automatically produced by Atomik ePublisher from Easypress

Printed and bound in Great Britain

For Will

For Alli—

Thank you!

♡

Laurel L Nolen ☺

One

On the last day of Earth, I couldn't find my hairbrush. That probably seems like a silly thing to worry about, what with the imminent destruction of, well, *everything*, but my mom was always after me about my usual ratty ponytail. Normally, I'd ignore her. Or, if I were having a really bad day, I'd tell her what she could do with her hairbrush. But like I said, it was the last day of Earth. And I figured, since it was the last time she'd ever see me, I wanted it to go smoothly. I wanted her to remember me, if not fondly, then at least without anger.

A girl can dream.

I slipped out of my cell as soon as the door swung open. I'd done the same every day for the past month, and my family had yet to show up. Their OPT—Off-Planet Transport—took off in eighteen hours, so they still had time. Barely. I couldn't blame them if they didn't come. It wasn't hard to imagine that they'd rather escape to the stars without so much as a backward glance at me, their big disappointment. Even my father's influence couldn't persuade the government to give me a spot on an OPT.

Turns out, when humankind is deciding which of its children to save, the last place it looks is in prison.

But I was pretty sure they'd come. West had said as much in his last transmission. The thought of my younger brother actually halted me mid-step, like one of those punches in the gut where you can't breathe for a few seconds.

"Looking for something?" The lazy drawl floated out of the nearest cell.

Against my better instincts, I turned to see Cassa lying on her bunk, her arm draped across Kip. My Kip. Or at least, my ex-Kip. Whatever. In twenty-two hours, I wouldn't have to think about him anymore.

See? Silver lining. And they called me a perpetual pessimist at my last psych workup.

They barely fit next to each other on the flimsy mattress, but that wasn't the weird part. The guys' ward was separated by a substantial metal wall. We were kept apart during evening hours, for obvious reasons. Not that anyone cared anymore. The med staff had been the first to go, followed by the cleaning crew, followed by the kitchen crew. To show you where girls like me fell on the government's list of priorities, there was still a skeleton crew of guards lurking around, despite the fact that I hadn't had a real meal for going on a week. The guards would be gone soon, too, and then there'd be no one in here but us chickens.

I figured either Kip had a key, or the guards had left already. A key could be useful. My curiosity got the best of me. "How'd he get in here before the first bell?"

He cocked an eyebrow. "I got some tricks you ain't seen, babe. Why don't you join us? End of the world and all."

The guards were gone, then. I felt a small trill of anxiety deep in my chest. If the guards were gone, my family was even less likely to show. But it was never smart to show fear. "The Pinball could be headed *straight* for this building, and

I still wouldn't be desperate enough to touch you. Oh, wait. Guess you don't have to take my word for it."

I turned to leave, but he continued. "Now is that any way to treat your dear ole partners? Be nice or I won't give you back your stuff."

"Ugh, you were in my *room*?" I flexed my shoulder blades, making sure my gun was still tightly secured between them.

"Don't worry, Char. I didn't handle the merchandise. Didn't want to wake you up. Just lifted me a few keepsakes." He pronounced my name the way I like: *Char*, as in *charred*. Something that got burned.

I wasn't sure what Kip and Cassa were planning, but I knew I wouldn't like it. They were thieves and liars. I would know. I used to be one of them. That was before the last job, when Cassa had attacked an elderly man in the home we were robbing. She'd kicked him until he stopped fighting back. Kip had called her off after a few licks, but I just stood there, staring. The old man looked at me, like right at me, while we made our getaway, and my stomach twisted into a knot so tight that I tasted bile. That was the moment I knew I wanted out.

But by then, no one believed me. Or, if they did, no one cared. Except for Kip and Cassa, of course. They'd taken the news pretty hard, to put it lightly.

If I lunged for the box, I could probably grab my hairbrush and get out of there. I wouldn't have time for more than that. Then again, I'd be doing exactly what they expected, and I didn't have time for delays. My family could be in the commissary any second now.

"Ahem. Seeing as it's your last day of life, I might let you have one thing back," said Kip.

"In exchange for what?"

3

"I'm hurt. All our time together, and you still don't believe in my inherent generosity. But now that you mention it, I've got a hankering for some peanut butter crackers."

"Sorry, Kip. I'm fresh out of food. Kinda like everyone else."

"Nice try, *Charrr*." He drew my name out, as though tasting it. "I saw them yesterday. Figured you were hiding them under your pillow when I couldn't find them last night."

"You figured wrong."

All I could think about was my brother's face. And how I had this one last chance to apologize to my parents, for everything. I shrugged and turned to leave.

That was probably a mistake.

About five steps past Cassa's cell, an enormous weight tackled me from behind. My chest and face hit the dirty concrete. My anxiety over my parents leveled up into near-panic territory. I could not afford to deal with this right now. I flipped onto my back and jerked my knee upward, and Kip let out a groan.

But Cassa was already there, standing over us. She kicked my head, and my arms and legs quit obeying me. I was vaguely aware of the dispassionate stares coming from other cells as Kip and Cassa dragged me back to their room.

"Now, now, love," Kip murmured. "That was no way to treat your old friends."

"She's gone soft. Must have been distracted." Cassa wasn't British, but she had the intensely annoying habit of using a fake accent. Not all the time, either. Just with certain words or phrases. In my opinion, that made it even worse. It was probably an attempt to impress Kip. Or to prove to everyone she spent a lot of time with him.

They propped me up against the wall, and Kip began tying my wrists with a twisted black cord he pulled out of nowhere.

"Screw you."

"Is that any way for a lady to talk?" he said cheerfully, slipping his hand up my shirt. His fingers were like ice, and I winced. "Aha—found them." He removed a packet of crackers and waggled them in front of my face. Those were going to be my last meal. I bit back a curse. Wouldn't have made much difference in the end, anyway.

I didn't fully panic until they tied the ends of the cord to the exposed pipe of the sink.

"Wait, no. My family's going to be here. I have to get downstairs."

"No one's coming for you. And even if they were, do you really think they want to see you?"

Cassa grinned down at me. "But me and Kip, that's a different story. We're busting out of here."

"Figured we'd do a bit of traveling in our twilight years. I mean, hours. See the world, that sort of thing. So we need all the supplies we can get. And no one has supplies like you," said Kip.

Cassa spat. "And if you hadn't rolled on us, we might be bringing you along. Think about *that* while you wait for the Pinball. Alone."

I kicked at them, once, and Cassa responded by plopping down on top of my legs. Normally I'd have been able to deal with that, but nothing about today was normal, and I had to settle for growling at her. Somehow, that made me feel even more helpless. My face was abruptly hot, and I gave myself temporary permission to hold my breath. If I cried, I'd never get over it.

I didn't breathe until I had to. Gradually, my head cleared. "Don't tell me you're going hunting for the Remnant. They don't exist."

Cassa paused, just for an instant, and Kip gave me a hard look. "She couldn't possibly know that."

"She's friends with the Mole."

Kip rolled his eyes. "*He* couldn't possibly know that. He doesn't know everything, Cass."

"You sure about that?" I said. "He knows the way out. He wouldn't still be here if they exist. If there were even a chance."

Cassa bit her lip, but Kip ignored me and continued his search. He was a bit rougher than before. "Ah, what have we here? Little blade-stick-doohickey?" He pulled a makeshift knife from the leg of my pants and twisted it in his fingers. "Fair enough. Not your best work though, if I'm honest."

"Hello, what's this?" Cassa yanked me forward and pulled my shirt up in the back. There was a tearing pain as she ripped the duct tape off my shoulder blades. "Bingo. Char, you never disappoint."

Kip held the gun up to my face and grinned while peeling the remainder of the tape from the barrel. It had been my finest moment. The guard I stole it from never saw it coming. I consoled myself with the thought that, in a few short hours, I would never need a gun again. The thought was a lot more comforting than it should have been. It was probably the only silver lining I would cling to, in the end. No more guns, no more eternally disappointed family members. No more pitying glances from judges or lawyers or parole boards. Or West.

"I believe our work here is done," Cassa said. She couldn't get away from me soon enough. "Time to make our way in the world."

"Good luck with that," I muttered.

They stood to leave, but Kip stopped at the door. "Here," he said, pulling my shoebox off the bed and tossing it to the ground in front of me. "For old times' sake."

And then they were gone.

Two

My panic disappeared quickly. First of all, it never does any good. Years of burglarizing high-level targets taught me that. And secondly, Cassa had actually kicked me pretty hard. I leaned back, letting the cords on my wrists support some of my weight. I barely felt the pain that spread through my forearms. I closed my eyes. The harsh light from the ceiling collapsed into a crescent, then blinked away. It felt good.

But I couldn't let myself sleep. Not yet.

The usual noise on the block was gone, replaced by an eerie, soundless vacuum. I had been on lockup for so long that I was no longer at ease with total silence.

In her haste to leave, Cassa had missed the blade in my sock. Not that I could blame her. None of us had showered in a week. My leg was heavier than it should have been, but I managed to kick it up toward my mouth. I bit down on my shoelaces and yanked the knot out, then kicked off my shoe.

The blade itself was trickier, and it was several minutes before I had it between my teeth. From there, cutting the cords was nothing. I pulled on my shoe, leaving it untied, and took off for the commissary.

The only thought in my mind was West. West would come for me. He would smile for me, and it would be a sad smile, but it would belong to me. And I would tell him that he had deserved a better sister, and that I had always been proud that he hadn't turned out like me. And that I would never forget him.

And he would say that he would never forget me, either, and I would know that I wouldn't be forgotten. That I hadn't already been forgotten.

I threw open the door to the commissary and was greeted by a total rager. People jumping on tables, singing, laughing, sobbing. The air was sour with the smell of liquor, which some kind benefactor must have brought in for our final hours. This was no place for my little brother.

My parents must have had the same thought.

When I finally saw them, huddled in a corner, backs pressed against the wall, they were alone in a sea of dirty prison scrubs. West was nowhere to be found. My father had his arm around my mother, but I could tell they had been fighting. Her arm was clenched across her chest, and her face had that blankly pleasant expression she used in public when something was wrong.

My tongue grew thick as I pressed my way through the crowd. When I was close enough to my parents to touch them, my mother cringed, and my father tightened his grip on her shoulder, pulling her hard against him.

I cleared my throat and forced my tongue to move. "Mom, Dad. It's me."

Dad's brows deepened, and his eyes slid away from my face to focus on a place behind me, as though his real daughter might still emerge from the crowd.

"Where's West?" I asked.

"Your brother couldn't be here." My father's voice was strange, like listening to a once-familiar recording that had grown warped with time.

"What happened to your head?" My mother's voice was exactly as I recalled: piercing and unhappy. "You're bleeding. Let me take a look at that." I flinched as she reached for my face, and she echoed my reaction back to me. "I'm not going to hurt you. It's going to get infected, the state you're in."

"Not if I die first." My words had the intended effect of shutting her down, but it didn't feel like I wanted it to. Regret and fear crowded together in my stomach, and I looked away from her. "So, why couldn't West be here?"

"For Pete's sake, Charlotte," my father began, but Mom cut him off.

"His OPT had to leave."

"You're not all on the same one?"

"No, we are," Dad said, and it was Mom's turn to look away. I stared at her anyway, trying to figure out how they were all going to be together, but West wasn't here. In this room. "It's been hard for him," Dad continued. I flicked my eyes up toward my father, still confused.

"Michael," Mom whispered.

"It has. It's been hard for all of us. She should understand that."

"It's just not the time." She turned to me. "But he wrote you a note, sweetheart."

My mother had not called me sweetheart since I had called myself Charlotte. Dumb, I stared at the torn envelope in her hands. I snapped back to my senses when I saw the attention it was getting from the rest of the room. They were definitely watching us.

My father noticed it too, and stiffened. "We can't stay here any longer. You were ninety minutes late, anyway."

Mom wrenched herself from my father's grip and wrapped her arms around me. I fit my face against her collarbone, exactly like I had as a child. Her voice in my ear was no louder than the slightest whisper. "I never gave up on you. I should have told you that." Her arms moved down my back, and her grip tightened. "I'm so sorry, Charlotte."

Everything I had planned to tell them—everything from *I never meant to hurt you* to *please don't forget me*— curdled into a cold wad in my chest, and died in my throat. I tried to breathe in, but I heard myself make a sound like a gasp instead. "Mom. Please don't leave me here."

She jerked a little, as though something had knocked against her, and I didn't feel her breath going in or out anymore.

"Excuse me, Senator," a voice barked. I opened my eyes to peer over my mother's shoulder. An armed guard stood a few paces away.

My father reached around my mother, so that for the briefest instant, he was holding me, too. But then he closed his fingers around her wrists, and pulled her arms away from me. "Goodbye, Charlotte. I can't help but feel responsible for…" he began, then stopped.

I watched them leave, feeling numb, like floating under-water, before sliding the folded paper out of its nest. It was my brother's handwriting, but not as I remembered it. He'd be thirteen now, not seven or eight, as I always thought of him, so it took a moment to confirm that the lighter, sharper letters were his.

*

I'm sorry.

Yeah, I thought. *Me too, kiddo. Me too.*

No one stopped me on the way back to my cellblock, and I was doubly thankful to find it as empty as before. When I slipped West's envelope into my back pocket, my fingers closed around something sharp and hard. My mom must have put it there.

I pulled the object from my pocket as soon as I was sure I was alone. It was a dark metal card with a single silver band across the top. Raised symbols covered the band, and in my stupor, I ran my thumb over them twice before I realized that they were words.

Stamped across the top of the card was the phrase "North American Off-Planet Transport—Admit One."

Three

My whole life, I felt trapped. I hated the constant pressure to maintain the appearances that were so crucial to my parents' lifestyle. I resented every choice they made on my behalf: stuffy uniforms at private school, mind-numbing ballroom lessons at junior cotillion, forced smiles at charity events. No matter where I was or what I was doing, I was never where I wanted to be, and nothing I did made sense, even to me. I baffled the hell out of my parents. But all I wanted was to feel some kind of freedom, some kind of escape. Escape never came.

So my first stint in juvy, at the ripe old age of twelve, was hardly a big adjustment. It was actually more like a relief.

For the first time, I was surrounded by people who didn't care what I did with my hair or who I hung out with or where I was going, which was always the same answer: nowhere. I was a lost cause, and in here, no one questioned that or tried to change it. Once I got in the system, the only life I could ruin was my own. And everyone here was fine with that.

I knew for a fact I wasn't the only one who felt that way. Why else did I see the same kids coming in and out of here, for so many years that we had our own holiday traditions?

Heck, last year, I had a Secret Santa. I had given myself a name, and they called me by it. So don't tell me I didn't belong here.

Except that now, I had to get out.

Standing on the floor of my block, dwarfed by the rows of cells above and around me, I felt, for the first time, like a rat in a cage. And the cage had become a death trap.

I pressed the starpass deep down into my shoe, inside my sock, where no one could lift it off me without my knowing it, and tried to think. There were no more guards to bribe or threaten. After the meteor was discovered, and the Treaty of Phoenix was signed, everyone who enforced it, from soldiers to street cops to prison guards, was guaranteed a spot on one of the five Arks. Keep the walking dead from rioting, and you get to live. I could hardly blame them; it was a brilliant solution. How else could you get nineteen billion people to die quietly while half a million others escaped to the stars?

I didn't exactly have a key to the outside, since like I said, getting out had never been a big priority for me. But I knew someone who might.

Isaiah Underwood was a year older than I was, but it might as well have been fifty. He was legendary in our circles, not because he was the only juvy we knew who had escaped, which he was, but because he came back. Deliberately. I vaguely remembered the day he'd gotten out—alarms, total lockdown, the usual drill. Normally the missing prisoner was just hiding someplace halfway clever, like the laundry or whatever. But when Isaiah left, we stayed in our rooms for two straight days, and they never found him. They finally had to concede defeat and let us out.

I was between stays when he came back, but I'd heard the story a hundred times. Months had passed. Someone else had been placed in his cell. Everyone on his row was at lunch, and he just strolled into the commissary like he'd been in the john the whole time. Isaiah was back, except he wasn't. First thing you noticed was his eyes, or rather, his lack thereof. It was only when you talked to him that you realized something else was missing, too, but you couldn't pinpoint what it was. He was more thoughtful, less happy. Older.

We called him the Mole after that.

I took off in a dead sprint, hoping no one would see me. Running was an excellent way to make trouble for yourself. The walls smeared past in a blur of blue and gray, and even the barrier to the men's quarters didn't slow me down. It was wide open.

The Mole was sitting on his bed with his white cane across his lap. A book lay on the blanket before him, its precise rows of dots skating underneath long, careful fingers.

"A visitor." He smiled a white smile, and I raised my hand to greet him out of instinct.

"Hi, Mole."

"Charlotte Turner. You want some company? It's too late for that. They say we all die alone, but you can read my book with me until then."

"No, I—thanks, though. I was actually here because—"

"Charlotte, baby. Have a seat. You know what book this is?"

"No." I sat next to him on the bed. Another moment brushed past us both, too quickly.

"*Pilgrim's Progress*. I reckon we all have a journey to take. My journey's about over. You're out of breath. Don't want yours to end just yet?"

"That's why I'm here. Mole, I need to get out."

"We all want out of something."

"Not you."

"Even me."

14

"Then help me get out of here. We can go together."

"My prison's made of stronger walls than these."

I paused. "But you could help me leave mine, if you wanted to."

He turned his face to me, as though he could still see me. "You were a beautiful child. Someone should have told you that. A small bird in a big cage. I haven't seen you since you were thirteen."

"Tell me the way out."

He sighed and sagged, as though carrying something heavy. "You don't want to go out there. Ain't no good out there for folks like us."

"That why you came back?"

"It's all the same. Doesn't matter where I go. Only difference between us and them is that they don't know they're broken."

"Look, I get it. You're angry. And it burns you, like all the time, and sometimes that's the only thing you can feel. And you think that if you give up, if you stop fighting it, then maybe it won't hurt anymore. You think you've found peace because you believe that you belong here. But what if it doesn't have to be this way?"

He didn't answer, so I played another card. "What if the Remnant exists?"

The Mole leaned back against the rail of the bed. Something about his easy posture made me feel exposed, as though he knew what my future held. "Even if they did, there's nothing out there for me, *Charlotte*. You remember when you first got here?"

"Of course. Everyone remembers their first day in."

"You told me you didn't care whether your family missed you."

"They didn't."

"Mine didn't miss me, either." His voice was so soft, I wondered if I'd imagined it.

I didn't see what that had to do with anything. I had to get him to help me. "They say your old boss did that to you." I waved a finger at his eyes. He couldn't see, but he knew what I was talking about.

"Is that what they say?"

I nodded. "They say he couldn't stand you being out of the game. So when the Treaty was announced, he blinded you. He knew you'd never get a spot on an OPT if you were disabled."

The Mole gave a short laugh. "It wasn't my old boss. Turns out, he didn't miss me either."

"Who, then?"

He was quiet for a long time. "I was young enough to enter the lottery. Did they tell you that?" He was referring to the lottery for OPT spots, which was open to "all citizens of upstanding status under the age of forty, with no physical, mental, or moral infirmities." If you'd been convicted of a crime, you were no longer eligible, unless you were under the age of fourteen when the crime was committed.

I shrugged. "We all were. Until we weren't."

"My last conviction was under the age cut-off, so I didn't lose eligibility. Even if I'd come clean about breaking out, I had a few months to spare."

"So?"

"So, I'm trying to warn you, little bird. My boss didn't do this to me. He had bigger fish to fry."

"Then who did?"

He closed the book slowly and laid it on the retractable shelf near his sink. "I broke my mother's heart. You might know something about that."

"Surely your mom didn't—"

16

"Didn't want to deal with me in space. I reckon she would have, though. Mothers are like that. But my brother, that's another story. He was sick of watching me hurt her."

That took a long time to sink in. I shuddered. "Your own family."

"They made sure I'd never see the Ark. And now, my family is the one in here. So's yours. The Remnant doesn't exist, you know. Fairytales. Hope keeps people sane."

I leaned across the book and placed my hand on his, mulling over his story. His nickname seemed cruel now.

We were still for a moment, but my breathing didn't slow. His, by contrast, was as steady as the waves of the ocean. I wanted his calm, his acceptance, but I knew I wouldn't find it here. His thumb flicked up to touch my forefinger. Every instinct I had told me to keep the starpass a secret, but it was the only play I had left.

I pressed the silver and blue card into his hand. "Isaiah. My journey doesn't end here."

He ran a thumb over the letters, and his dark glasses couldn't conceal his surprise. "Alright, little bird. I'll show you how I did it."

Minutes later, we were standing in front of the walk-in freezer in the kitchen. Isaiah heaved the door ajar and waited for me to step inside.

"Back there." Isaiah indicated the far wall with his cane, and I climbed inside. The cold hit me immediately, but the pleasure of a momentary chill faded when the frigidity coated my skin. Thanks to a raid several days earlier, the shelves around me were bare. There was a sucking *pop* sound as the door closed behind him. "All the way back."

"Wait. It's dark."

"Always dark for me. Leave it closed. Don't want to be followed. Go on."

I stumbled forward in the cold. A few steps later, a pale green pin of light came into view on the back wall of the freezer. When I got closer, its dim light fell on the things around me—shreds of cardboard boxes and my own outstretched hands.

Isaiah's hands appeared a second later. He slid a flattened palm across the wall before us until his fingers met a seam. This he followed to a screw, which he loosened with a thumbnail, then twisted until it dropped into his outstretched hand.

I shivered as he repeated the process three more times.

"Here we go." Isaiah took a slow breath and heaved the panel onto the floor. "Watch your feet."

A gaping hole yawned in the wall in front of me. "What is this?"

"Used to be the vent to the air conditioning. My guess is the workers didn't much care about fixing it up when they installed the freezer during the last renovation."

"How did you find it?"

"I was always looking, back then. Always searching for my way out."

"Wish I could say the same."

"You follow this to the outside. Leads to the south gate. You can't get to it any other way, so it's not as secure as the rest. I got out by climbing the old unit and hoppin' down the fence. Here."

He shoved an industrial-sized kitchen mat into my arms, which he must have picked up at the entrance to the freezer. "I had to take this with me, when I made my journey, so that they wouldn't know how I did it. Won't much matter now whether you leave it there or not."

He was right about that.

"What's it for?"

"Razor wire on the fence. Won't stop 'em all, but you'll make it just fine. If you want to come back, in the very end, I'll be here."

I stood facing him, paralyzed by the moment. "Isaiah, please. Come with me. I already got one starpass, maybe we can figure something out. You can't stay here."

He smiled again and shook his head. The green light shone against his teeth as they swung back and forth. "It doesn't suit you, you know."

"What?"

"Your name. Char is the end of the story, the cooked goose. Maybe you were right, and your story's just getting started good. But look at me. I'm blind. They'll never let me on the transport. And if they see you with me, you'll have the same fate. And then you *will* be Char." He chuckled, a soft, deep sound that swallowed the steady hum of the freezer. "But don't think that this will be your freedom. You may find nothing but a bigger cage."

"Or maybe I will fly."

"Maybe so. Maybe so." He grasped my arm, briefly, by way of a farewell.

A door slammed, its sound muffled by the walls of the freezer. I hesitated, one foot in the vent. "Did you hear that?"

"Kitchen. People want food."

The freezing air made me suddenly aware of the tiny beads of sweat on my forehead. "No one here thinks there's food in the kitchen."

A series of methodical *clangs* danced around us. "Someone's looking for something else, then," Isaiah whispered. Cabinets were being slammed open. A louder bang announced that one of the pantries had been searched.

"It's Kip. He's going to find us."

I expected Isaiah to protest, to say that I couldn't possibly know who was out there, or that Kip had surely already left the prison by this point, but instead, he said, "Better go, then."

The bangs were getting closer. I knew, without any doubt, that it was Kip, and that he would find me. "He must have waited, then followed me. They're looking for the Remnant. They knew I'd go to you. Isaiah. Come with me."

"Ain't nothing for me out there. I'll stop him."

"You can't. You can't stop Kip. You haven't seen him when he's... You can't stay here."

"It's the only thing I *can* do."

"Take my hand."

His hand was warm and firm, and a lot stronger than his final protest. "Charl—"

"Come on. We're leaving. Your journey doesn't end here, either."

The duct was warm, but relatively ventilated. My hands shook as I replaced the grate. Normally, my hands were as steady as paperweights, no matter the stakes, but I was always unpredictable around Kip. It wasn't the first time my body had betrayed me in his presence.

I wore the mat on my back like a cape, clasping it in place with my left arm while holding my right arm in front of my face, so that I wouldn't run into anything. Isaiah followed at a short distance.

Almost immediately, my hand swiped into another wall. I panicked momentarily, sweeping my arms all around, before finding that the passageway had turned sharply and narrowed to a crawlspace near my right foot. I dropped to my knees and pressed into the darkness, trying not to think how very like a rat I was in that moment. Trying especially not to think about the possibility of other rats sharing the tunnel with me. But as soon as I heard a noise I couldn't assign to Isaiah, I surprised myself by hoping it came from a rat, and not Kip.

I don't know how I knew it was Kip who was following us, but I was absolutely certain that he'd find the grate. That was what he did. He found me. He pulled me back, no matter how much I wanted to get away.

I had crawled maybe ten yards when the gritty texture of the vent glinted into view, so I had to be close to the outdoors. Sure enough, within minutes, I could make out the slits of a grate, and beyond that, the green of grass and the dark gray of the prison walls.

I ran my fingers across the slatted panel for an instant before deciding that my best bet was probably to kick it out. I lay back, bracing myself with the mat underneath me, and slammed my feet into the thin metal as hard as I could.

The grate went flying through the air and landed four feet away.

Isaiah's muted laugh floated out of the tunnel behind me. "I should have mentioned that I never screwed it back into place."

Was this a game for him? I bit back a sharp response. "Did I mention he has a gun?"

"I know. I heard it scraping the ground when he started crawling."

Kip had reached the tunnel, then.

I popped out onto the grass, squinting in the sunlight, and stood up next to the old air conditioning unit, turning to help Isaiah. I got the impression that he needed a lot less help than I'd expected, but perhaps more than he realized. The afternoon air was only slightly cooler than the warmth of the ventilation shaft, but infinitely more pleasant. Full of hope, but tinged with my rising panic.

The ancient gray air conditioning unit was tall and thick, with its far edge positioned about a foot from the prison wall. I grabbed the mat from inside the vent behind me and threw it up onto the first ledge I saw. From there it was a matter of climbing as efficiently as possible without dropping the mat. I created a few frantic footholds by bashing in whatever ventilation slats I found, and before long, I stood on the top of the unit, my back to the prison wall.

"Okay, we have to—"

"Jump over the fence. You first." He waved a hand near his ear.

"I-Isaiah. I can't. You first."

"Afraid I won't follow? Not to worry. I'm right behind. Got me all fired up, now."

I sucked in a breath. We were pretty far off the ground, but my knees were about level with the top of the fence, which was several feet away. Thick coils of razor wire spun across its top, adding three more feet to its height. I slung the heavy mat over the razor wire, and, stepping back for a head start, leaped onto it for all I was worth. The wires gave slightly under my weight, and I never quite caught my balance. Almost as soon as my thighs touched the mat, I was falling face-first into the ground nearly twelve feet below.

I scrambled, limbs flailing against air and rubber, and managed to shift my upper body backward, so that my feet were beneath me when I began to fall in earnest. Time swung by in a single, heart-stopping arc before I hit the ground, hard. My legs buckled, and I threw my weight to the side, absorbing the secondary impact with my hip.

I breathed in, trying to contain the pain, and consoled myself with the knowledge that, where I was going, gravity wouldn't be my problem.

It was several seconds before I stood shakily to ascertain the damage. Something dark in my peripheral vision caught my attention, and I realized with a jolt that my entire left arm was bright red with blood.

My throat made a noise like a long, low groan while I searched for the source of the blood, which turned out to be a slash along the side of my left hand. I must have grabbed the edge of the mat during my mid-air acrobatics, leaving the skin exposed to the razor wire.

The blood coated my forearm and blotted onto my prison scrubs. This, combined with the rest of my appearance, was not going to fly at the OPT facility. Assuming I made it that far. I removed a sock and tied it as hard as I could around my hand. That would have to do for now.

"You ready?" I shout-whispered at Isaiah.

"As ever," he said back.

"You're about ten feet from—"

"I remember." Isaiah sent his cane sailing over the fence. He followed soon after, pausing only briefly atop the mat. He landed next to me, allowing his body to hit the ground once his legs had broken the fall.

"Okay, I'm impressed."

Isaiah smiled.

We began to jog directly away from the prison walls, Isaiah's cane sweeping the ground in fast-forward, but I quickly slowed our pace. I was weak from hunger, and from getting kicked in the head, so anything over a brisk walk was not on the menu. I turned back once, to say my final goodbyes to the prison that had been my home for years. As I watched, the grate popped out again.

The goodbyes didn't take very long.

A thicket of trees spread before me, and I pulled Isaiah behind the first one we reached. I remembered from the stories that a town lay behind them, populated mostly by prison staff and their families. In ages past, an escapee sought refuge here at his peril, but I doubted there were a lot of people left in town, since all the guards had spots on an OPT. We moved from tree to tree, hiding our path until we were deep enough into the trees that no one could see us from a distance.

Then it was full speed ahead. Or as full speed as we could manage.

The second house we came to had no lights on. Perfect. Probably belonged to one of the guards, and he or she would be knocking at the gate of the OPT launch site by now. I let myself in through a back window and paused only a moment to take in my surroundings before turning to assist Isaiah. Again, he needed my help a lot less than I expected. We headed straight for the kitchen, but I stuck near a window, keeping one eye out for Kip. When I was satisfied that he hadn't seen which house we entered, I relaxed slightly. Our best move was to stay here until he assumed we'd moved on.

I wanted a shower, but first things first. The house was old and small, with cheap linoleum on the kitchen floor that had begun to peel at the edges. I wondered how much Isaiah could ascertain about his surroundings, then noticed that the house smelled old and small, too.

The icer was stocked, though, as was the pantry, so to me, it was Buckingham Palace relocated to upstate New York.

Two ham-and-jelly sandwiches for me, three ham sandwiches for Isaiah, and then we broke into the potato chips.

"So good," I mumbled, not caring that the crumbs were sticking to my face.

Isaiah raised an eyebrow. "Didn't your mama ever teach you to chew with your mouth closed?"

"Sorry."

We climbed the narrow staircase, and I hopped into the rickety tub for the greatest shower of my entire life, leaving Isaiah to explore the other rooms.

I had no idea whose OPT pass I carried, but I knew they wouldn't look like an escaped prisoner. So I ignored the fluttery, urgent feeling in my chest and took the time to blow-dry my hair. A raid of the bathroom cabinet revealed lipstick, deodorant, and moisturizer, along with a dried-out tube of eyeliner. I applied the lipstick quickly, grateful to my mom for the second time that day, since she had spent the better part of my time between stints in juvy forcing me to learn how to wear makeup. Or trying to, anyway.

I ran the eyeliner wand under the tap for a few seconds, swished it around in the tube, and swiped a thin line across my eyelids. The result was a lot more responsible-teen-headed-to-the-mall, or wherever it is normal teenagers go, and a lot less bruised-and-bloodied convict.

The cabinet under the sink produced Band-Aids, a bottle of rubbing alcohol, and a worn-out, empty makeup bag. Gritting my teeth, I ran the alcohol over the cut on my hand, which had opened back up in the shower, and taped it shut with a Band-Aid. I used a wad of toilet paper doused in alcohol to dab at the cut above my eye from Cassa's shoe. Then I threw the toiletries into the makeup bag and headed for the bedroom, stark naked.

The first room was a bust. Granny panties, nightgowns, and a drawer full of bras big enough to wear as hats. No thank you.

I hit the jackpot with bedroom number two. Whoever lived here was about my size. I found vintage-looking lace underwear in the drawers. I pulled on a set and stuffed a second into the makeup bag.

The closet was even better. Crisp brown pants, flowy blouses, and smart-looking dresses hovered over a neat row of shoes for every occasion. This girl really had her act together. I had never lined up a pair of shoes in my life.

I selected a blue skirt and a heavily tailored sleeveless top made of the same material and paired them with camel-colored heels. I had no idea what one wore on an OPT, except that almost everyone there would either be super smart or super rich. My mom would probably tell me to find some pantyhose, so I returned to the underwear drawer with a sigh. I reflected that there probably weren't seasons in space, either, so I selected an additional outfit: a black, long-sleeved cotton shirt, black boots, and a pair of black pants.

I was just about to leave when I noticed a brown leather satchel-style purse slung over one of the coat hangers. A quick search of its contents turned up a wallet and ID. Magda Notting, born 2015. She'd be nearly fifty years old, then, much older than I expected, based on what I had seen of her clothing. She'd also be ineligible for a spot on one of the Arks. I wondered where she was. Probably waiting it out at a friend's house, or something. I hoped she wasn't alone.

I worked the black clothing into a roll and pressed it into the top of the satchel. I never considered putting the starpass into the bag. It went under my shirt, secured to the skin just below my collarbone with a series of Band-Aids. I took a final glance in the mirror and forced myself not to think about how we'd get Isaiah onto the OPT with only one starpass. I didn't know if I was the kind of person who'd sacrifice my life for someone else, and that scared me as much as anything else. I clopped my way out the door and down the steps, uneasy in Magda's heels. Uneasy in general.

"Isaiah?" I called. "You up there or down here?" Maybe he'd stepped outside. I was halfway through the sitting room, and maybe five feet from the door, when a rush of ice spilled down my spine, and I stopped short.

Someone was in the room with me. Someone with a rifle pointed straight at my chest.

Four

"Hold it right there, Missy." The gravelly voice paused long enough for a wracking cough.

I raised my hands as slowly as possible. In my experience, there were two kinds of people who point guns at other people. The first kind weren't going to shoot you unless they had to. Suckers, we called 'em. Suckers made it easy to get away. Sometimes you didn't even have to give their stuff back, as long as you started running before they got too jumpy. The second kind were just looking for an excuse to pull the trigger. As I was sizing her up, she chambered the cartridge.

This was definitely the second kind.

I made my voice as small and feminine as possible. "Look, I didn't mean any trouble. I thought you were gone."

"Doesn't give you the right to steal my stuff."

I turned around, slowly. "Really, I thought the house was abandoned. Please don't shoot." The woman in the corner was elderly and heavyset and sucking hard on a nicostick, the kind the government had approved the year they banned cigarettes. I had no doubt this wasn't the first time she'd handled a .30.

"Just what do you think you're doing, anyway?"

"I was hungry," I whimpered. "And I needed clothes."

"What for?"

"For the OPT."

"I saw them clothes in the bathroom. You don't belong on no transport."

I breathed out for a moment, and sniffed, and realized that my tears weren't actually fake, even though I had planned them. "I know."

"But you're going anyway."

If I spoke loudly enough, maybe Isaiah would hear me. Would he try to leave, or try to help me? Would he even be able to help? "I have to. My family went, and I was in lockup, and they left me there."

The rifle sagged to point at the ground. "Okay, alright. Don't cry." She continued to stare at me. "It's my daughter's clothes, you know."

"M-Magda?"

"My Magda. She died thirty years ago. You look a little like her." She jerked her head toward the wall beside me, where a series of yellowing photographs showed a happy family. The youngest, a girl, did indeed have dark hair and light eyes, but I thought the resemblance ended there. Not that I planned on pointing that out to my hostess, who still had two hands clenched around the rifle. Its butt folded into the ample flesh over her ribcage. I bet she wouldn't even feel the kick, with padding like that.

"Had a son, too. He worked at the detention center. Kellan Notting. Maybe you know him."

I shook my head. "He's on the transport now?"

She mirrored my head shake while taking another drag on her nicostick before answering. "Not anymore. Now he's on the Ark. Left a couple weeks ago. He drew the European one." She blew out the vaporized tar and glanced back at the photographs. "They called this morning to tell me he made it."

"I'm glad," I said, and meant it.

"So what are you in for?"

I coughed. It was a delicate situation. If I lied to her, she might shoot. But if I told her the truth, she'd probably think I was lying. Everyone else had.

"Robbery. I didn't do it."

The rifle twitched, barely, then she jerked it to her shoulder. The shot came an instant later, exploding into the wall above my head, louder than I thought possible. The carpet was suddenly coarse against my hands, and I found myself struggling not to scream. The anger on her face was terrifying. This was a woman who had no games to play. Whatever she wanted, she was determined to find it, and fast.

"Do I look like a fool to you?" She must have been shouting, otherwise I'd never have heard her.

I couldn't see why she cared what I said, but I was far too shaken to think it over. Everything came spilling out. "I mean, I did! Before. But not this time. I was out, and I had my family back, even though they still acted weird around me. Even that was getting better. So I told the gang I was leaving, but they didn't let me. They needed me to get into the best houses." I knew I was barely coherent, but I could not stop talking. "I broke up with my boyfriend, but he tricked me. I went out to meet him, just to talk, you know? And he drugged me and I woke up in this house, and everything was broken. The cops were already there. I never wanted any of it. I thought I did, but I missed them. My family. And then it was too late. Please. Please don't shoot."

I clamped my jaw shut, finally silent.

There was a long pause. Too long. But then she nodded. "Alright, get up. I'm going to help you. Needed to decide once I'd met ya."

I nodded, shaking, as though I totally understood the thought process there.

"I'm Meghan," she croaked.

"Char."

"Not anymore, you're not. You're Magda Notting, now. Best remember it. They're definitely going to ask. You won't get far with an expired ID, but it's better than nothing. They can't afford to look too close tonight anyway."

In my opinion, they couldn't afford not to, but Meghan continued. "Now, where's your friend?"

I started.

"I seen him come in with you."

"Um. I don't know. Shower, maybe?"

There was a slight rustle on the stairs. "I'm here," said Isaiah.

"You-all come with me. You're gonna need a car."

I stared at her. She might as well have told me I'd need a parakeet. "Wait, you're … you're giving us a car?"

"Sweetheart, it's eleven hours to midnight. You know they close the gates at midnight, right?" She shouldered into the door on the other side of the kitchen and stepped into the garage.

I followed, numb, stealing little glances at Isaiah, who looked equally surprised. "No."

"Well, you do now. And you've got a ways to go. And you're not the only one who's headed that way, either." She pressed the car sensor into my hands, pausing to activate the thumbprint scanner, and looped a state-issued grocery bag over my arm. "Was that ham and jelly?" I nodded, and she made a face. "Whatever rings your bell. I made a few more while you was changing clothes."

31

I stood next to the car door and stared at her.

She coughed nervously. "I figured you was hungry, coming from that place. We hear the stories. It's a crime, what they done with you. Now *get in*." She nodded approvingly as Isaiah climbed into the passenger seat. "You know how to get to Saint John?"

I looked from the car to Meghan. "I think so. Thank you, Meghan."

"Yeah, okay. Car, I'm authorizing this driver."

The car blipped on, and a warm female voice acknowledged the transfer. "Authorization accepted."

I slid into the seat and forced my hands to grip the wheel. I was still recovering, either from the gunshot or the conversation itself. I gestured toward the nicostick. "Any chance I can get one of those?"

"You know they don't let nic addicts on the OPT."

"How about that rifle?"

Her eyes narrowed. "Now don't you make me regret helping you, Char-whoever-you-are."

"No. I'm sorry."

"You best make it on that OPT, and all the way to the Ark. You best make it all the way to that new planet they're gonna colonize. And when you do…"

Meghan paused for another cough, this one so long that she bent forward, and I looked away.

And missed the door opening behind her.

I knew it was Kip before I saw him. It was a familiar, queasy feeling, like missing a rung on a ladder when you're way up in the air. My hands jerked tight against the wheel as though I needed to catch myself from falling. I met his eyes through the windshield unwillingly.

He kicked Meghan's wrist, and the rifle skidded across the concrete floor of the garage. When she straightened, her head came into contact with the barrel of his gun. My gun.

A smile twisted across Kip's face. "I knew you could do it, love. All I had to do was wait."

Cassa appeared behind him, and my throat went tight. She held my gaze, but spoke into Kip's ear, her lips an inch from his skin. "Looks like you were right. She can't go a day on the outside without robbing a house." Cassa turned to me. "We definitely owe you one, Char. We'd never have gotten out without you."

I peeled my hands off the steering wheel and raised them slowly. The thought hit me that I could just leave. I could duck down and drive the car in reverse, blind. By the time we hit the street, Kip couldn't kill me through the windshield. He probably wouldn't even try. Probably.

It was tempting.

"It's Kip and Cassa," I said. "They have a gun on Meghan."

Isaiah did not respond.

"We could leave. Make a run for it."

"We could," he said, his tone neutral.

Meghan stood still, arms at her side. There was a wild, helpless look in her eyes. She was afraid.

She's going to die anyway, I thought. If I left, I'd be saving Isaiah, too.

Kip cocked the gun and pressed it into Meghan's temple. "Get out of the car."

I took a breath. I needed a strategy, but what popped into my mind instead was, *She made us sandwiches for the road. After we'd broken into her home.*

Maybe it was better to leave, because then Kip and Cassa wouldn't make it to the OPT.

33

My stomach twisted. Kip wouldn't even *have* the gun if I hadn't stolen it from the guard. He spoke again, this time in a slow, schoolteacher voice, every word enunciated. "Get out *now*, or I. Will. Blow. Her. Brains. Out."

I looked back to Meghan, who thought I looked like her daughter.

"Okay, okay. I'm getting out."

Five

"Good girl." Kip turned the gun at us. I noticed that it never quite squared with my chest. Instead, it swerved toward Isaiah, then over my head and toward Meghan. "Stand over there, all of you."

While we huddled into the corner of the garage, Cassa swept up the rifle. "I still don't see much of a plan here, Kip," I said. "It's not like we have starpasses."

"Shut up." Cassa chucked the rifle into the front seat and slid behind the wheel. "Car on."

The car answered dispassionately. "Authorization necessary."

Cassa blew a breath through tense lips. A limp hank of blonde hair lifted, then collapsed back against her cheek. She climbed out of the car, and Kip waved the gun at Meghan.

"Authorize another user."

Meghan moved forward, then stopped. "No."

Cassa crossed the space between us in three enormous strides. In an instant, her free hand was around Meghan's throat, dragging her toward the hood of the car. "Stay back," she said to me.

Meghan's face hit the car, and she grunted in pain. *That was the wrong move*, I thought. She'd been afraid, earlier. Now Cassa was making her angry.

Angry people are harder to manipulate, unless you were subtle about it. Which Cassa wasn't, ever.

"Authorize me."

Meghan gritted her teeth. "No."

Cassa slammed Meghan onto the hood again. Kip moved in, and his gun bore into Meghan's cheek, stretching the loose skin taut. "This is your last chance."

I'd heard that tone before. Kip was deadly serious. He cocked the gun slowly, for effect, and Meghan froze.

"Wait," I said.

They looked at me.

"If you let her go, I'll drive you. Let her go, and let Isaiah ride with us."

"You can't exactly afford to negotiate here, Char," said Kip. At the same time, Cassa said, "No way."

"Look at her. You can tell she means it. I'm your only way out," I said. Kip looked toward the house, and I read the look on his face. "No family. Her son's already on an Ark. She gave us her *car*. She's ready to die, Cass."

Cassa glared first at me, then at Kip. "Kip, *no*. We talked about this. Char stays."

Kip sighed and clucked his tongue casually, as though trying to decide which pair of pants to wear. Finally, he shook the gun at us. "The Mole stays."

He was right: I couldn't afford to negotiate. But neither could he. "No deal."

Another moment passed, and Kip broke into his carefree grin. "Oh, all right." He circled the gun in the air. "One big happy road trip. Mount up, as they say. Time to go."

Cassa stared daggers at the back of his head, but eventually straightened and released her grip on Meghan. "All aboard. Quick like bunnies, before we change our minds. You two in front. Wouldn't want Isaiah to miss the scenery."

I wasn't much for goodbyes, and definitely not hugs, so it was a moment before I spoke again. I paused, almost to the driver's seat. "Meghan... thank you."

She only nodded. "Give 'em hell."

"Yes, ma'am."

Isaiah settled in next to me. We slammed the doors shut. I tried to relax, knowing that in a moment, I'd have a gun to my neck. Kip made a show of settling into the back seat, smiling indulgently, like a father giving a small child a piggyback ride.

Cassa was taking longer than I expected. When she opened the door, I forced myself to relax again. I focused on Meghan, who was still looking at me. She seemed satisfied. Almost happy.

She was still watching me when Cassa shot her.

Cassa was a fair shot, and this was close range, a direct hit to the head. Even knowing it was over, I couldn't stop myself from lunging for the car door. Immediately, the burning barrel of the gun pressed into my neck. Cassa was already seated behind me. A scalding sensation spread up into my scalp, and I screamed. Before me, Meghan's body hit the ground.

"Drive. Now," Cassa said into my ear.

I made an awful, whimpering sound, and Isaiah's hand slid over mine.

"He's next," said Cassa, moving the gun to point at Isaiah.

Isaiah squeezed my hand. I drove.

The silence stretched out like tar. It was a trick I learned my first week inside: how to cry without making any noise. Every soul in juvy had it down cold.

Isaiah's hand was warm against mine, his skin dry and soft. Every so often, he'd give me a little pat, or another squeeze, and the road would blur until I blinked. I held my hand still, afraid that any movement would cause him to take his hand away. He couldn't have known how much I needed it there.

After a moment, Kip's pale, icy fingers touched the spot on my neck where the barrel of the gun had been. I shivered hard.

"There, there, love. She was practically already dead anyway."

I forced my words through clenched teeth. "Then, *why*?"

Kip shrugged, and his hand mercifully left my neck. "Have to ask Cass that one."

"Because he came back for you," she said. I glanced back in confusion. They'd come back to *follow* me, not save me.

Kip shot me a strange look through the greasy strands of black hair that had fallen across his face before turning to rifle through my bags in the back seat, keeping the gun in one hand. "Once again, you don't disappoint."

Cassa's eyes widened at the sight of food. "Maybe you were onto something after all, love," she said to Kip.

They tore into the sandwiches. Cassa stuffed half the first one into her mouth. Kip did the same a moment later. The chips came next. She crunched them loudly. Through the rear view mirror, I watched her wipe her hands on the seat, leaving streaks of grease dotted with crumbs.

A light rain splattered against the windshield, and the wipers began their rhythmic response. Kip, Isaiah, and I were silent, and Cassa had little to say of interest. She mostly commented, between gulps of food, about the plight of the people we passed. "Toast. Toast. Space debris, look at her." I wrestled thoughts of Meghan to the back of my mind. It was probably the only chance I'd get to plan my next move.

I had a few things in my favor, in spite of the gun at my back. Namely, Kip and Cassa didn't know about the starpass. I had no idea how they planned to find the Remnant, if it even existed, and without a starpass, they couldn't hope to board an OPT. The launch sites were, at this point, literally the most secure places on Earth. Also, Kip and Cassa were likely to underestimate Isaiah, which would be a mistake.

The thought gave me pause. Isaiah didn't have a pass, either. When it came right down to it, as it inevitably would, was I prepared to give him mine?

I thought not, and shuddered. That I could even consider leaving him behind made me sick.

What kind of person had Meghan tried to save?

Another question prickled me: where had my mother gotten an extra starpass? Surely she'd never steal one. To do so would deprive her victim of their very life, an action my mother seemed incapable of. I mean, she was a doctor. She was all about saving people. But she was a mother first, and she still seemed to love me.

It was possible that she'd taken the pass from a deceased patient. In such cases, though, the next of kin or the government would likely want the pass returned to them. Maybe someone had died, and Mom didn't report it. Whatever the case, I was grateful.

The car had a full charge, so we breezed around Boston and headed up the coast. I was lost in thought, and still without a plan, when Isaiah's mellow voice broke my reverie.

"If you were stuck here, would you rather know, or not know?" he asked.

I glanced at him. "About the Pinball?"

"Yeah."

"You *are* stuck here," said Cassa.

I ignored her. "Like, does the knowing make it worse?" I thought about it for a moment. "It probably depends on the person. I'd definitely want to know."

"Not me," said Kip. "Life is uncertain anyway."

"So you never made any mistakes?" I asked. "Nothing you'd have done differently, if you knew it was your last day?"

Kip was quieter. "There may be a few things I'd have done differently. But I'm not sure knowing would have changed anything. Not for me."

"What difference does it make?" Cassa sounded irritated. Again.

Kip turned to look out the window. "Oh, nothing, I guess."

"Just, being able to plan," I said.

"Planning to die. Sounds awesome," she said.

"No, planning how to *live*."

"Better get to it, then. What time is it? Two? So you've got ten hours till the gate closes."

Isaiah ignored her. "I wouldn't want to know the day. We all got to go sometime. Pinball or no, it's coming."

"There's a lot of clarity that comes from knowing it's today, though," I said.

He turned to me. For a moment, I imagined he could see through those dark glasses, straight inside me. Maybe he could. "Are you seeing things more clearly, Charlotte?"

It was weird when he called me that. Put me in a different frame of mind, somehow. "Maybe. Nothing I like, anyway."

He smiled. "I like *you* well enough."

It was strange to laugh. "I like you too, Isaiah. Nothing I like about myself, I mean."

Kip was staring out the window and had nothing to say about that, to my surprise. Isaiah continued. "You have a long way to go, then. What about you, Cassa?"

40

"What about me?"

"Would you want to know?"

"Doubt it. I *have* clarity. People suck, and everyone who pretends otherwise gets rewarded. It's bollocks. We're all on our own. Death doesn't change anything."

"Then why did Kip go back for Charlotte, I wonder?" Isaiah said.

"Because Char..." she paused. "Because Char has better tricks."

"That must be it," he said softly. He took his hand away from mine, finally, and I pressed mine into my leg, because it was still slightly warmer than the rest of me. Isaiah straightened in his seat. "We passed Boston yet?" he asked.

"Why?" Cassa said. "The OPT's in Maine."

"No reason. Just like to feel oriented." His fingers slipped underneath the dash, and I mimicked his posture, sitting straight, facing forward. Was he trying to find the glove compartment? I didn't look at him again, to keep him from drawing Cassa's attention. She was Kip's mirror: gazing out the opposite window, a strange expression on her face.

"Maybe an hour back," I said. "We went around."

"I'd have been happy to let you out, Mole," said Cassa. "I still am. Not that you'd have found where you're going."

"No need, Cassa. I'm going with Charlotte, here, for a little while."

"I'm sure you'll be very happy orbiting the sun together. Tell me, do bodies decay in a vacuum?"

Isaiah smiled, and his fingers continued to work. "I reckon they might."

The question about Boston had thrown me off. Isaiah grew up there. Other than juvy, it was the only home he'd ever known, but I didn't see why he'd ask about it.

Unless his family had lost the lottery.

It was strange to think about. I'd taken for granted that I'd have had a spot on an OPT, if my record were clean. But then, my father had major influence over the lottery. Everyone else had nothing but hope. If they'd known there were people who could tamper with the results, they wouldn't even have had that.

I wanted to ask Isaiah about whether he'd had news from home, but it felt wrong to talk about something so personal in front of Kip and Cassa. His fingers were still under the dash, and he was unusually chatty, so I decided to follow his lead. "Do you think it's like they say, up there?"

At my question, he paused for an instant before continuing whatever it was he was up to. He opened his mouth to reply, but Cassa was quicker.

"Oh, you mean will everyone have a fresh start and the same stuff as everyone else? And we'll all be equals? Of *course* we will. And we'll be attended by unicorns and fairies."

I snorted at that. "How long has civilization been around? Six thousand years, give or take? Ten? Our species gets a clean slate, plus all that experience. Humanity *could* finally get it right."

Kip finally spoke. "You believe that, Char?"

"She's just stupid enough," said Cassa.

I thought for another moment. I needed to keep Kip and Cassa talking. It would be easier to beat them if they let down their guard. "I don't want anyone to die. But it seems like we have a real shot at... utopia. Whatever you call it. Democracy."

"No, we don't," said Cassa. "Because it's being built by the same people who broke the current system. You bunnies don't get it. You're either weak, or you're strong. The people on the Arks will be stronger than the ones left down here, but they're still just people. Before long, it'll be every man for himself. Just like here. That's why we'll need the Remnant."

"That's still the plan?" I asked. "Find the Remnant, escape to space?"

"You got a better one? Kip says they'll recruit at the launch site." Cassa sounded less sure of that than I expected.

"Recruit?" said Isaiah. "Group like that doesn't need to do much recruiting. You join up or you die."

"I thought you didn't believe in them," said Cassa. Her voice made her sound unsteady. I pictured her trying to catch her balance, and I realized all at once that Cassa didn't believe in the Remnant any more than I did.

"I don't," Isaiah answered. "But I *sure* don't believe they're recruiting."

"Kip says—" Cassa cut herself off. "Never mind."

There was a long silence, and it finally dawned on me that Cassa wasn't trying to find the Remnant at all. She was just following Kip. Right to the end.

The sun continued its final arc across the horizon. I ran a finger over a small, circular burn on the roof of the car. I imagined Meghan scoring a real, sure-enough cigarette, then driving out of town to enjoy it. That way, her behavior wouldn't reflect badly on her son, the prison guard. Maybe she'd even gotten it from him.

Click, snap, CLICK. The car jerked to a stop, jolting me from my thoughts about Meghan. My seatbelt bit into my shoulder, forcing me back into the seat.

"What was that?" said Kip. "What's going on?"

I shrugged.

"Maybe a short?" said Isaiah. "I could check it out."

"How dumb do you think we are?" said Cassa. "Char, you go."

"To look for a *short*? I have no idea—"

"I'm going," said Kip. "Pop the hood."

Kip had barely set foot on the ground when Isaiah leaned across my lap, reaching to the other side of the steering wheel. "I'm on it," he muttered. A moment later, the trunk popped open, followed by Isaiah's door.

"Mole! Mo— *Isaiah*. Get back here," said Cassa.

He called back to her without slowing down. It was the loudest I'd ever heard his voice. "I'm just looking."

"What? You're blind."

"Can't do no harm then, right, baby?"

She waved the gun. "I will shoot you."

"Maybe he can help?" I said. "Maybe we should let—"

"Char. I can. NOT. Emphasize this enough: Shut up."

Cassa was panicking. Panic is weakness, and a great way to lose the game at the last minute, but her instincts were right: Isaiah was up to something. I was glad she hadn't seen him tinkering under the dash. She'd have shot him, cold. And it would have been the right move for her, then.

But it was too late for that now.

Her voice raised in pitch. "Mole! I will shoot her!"

Isaiah spoke calmly from behind the trunk. "Who's gonna drive the car, Cassa? You? Maybe I should try it."

Cassa realized the futility of her stance. She couldn't possibly shoot me yet. We were six hours from Saint John and the OPT, and I was the only one who could drive the car.

But she could kill Isaiah.

She shot out of the car. I fumbled with my seatbelt for an instant before following her. My view of Isaiah was blocked by the open trunk.

Kip realized what Isaiah was up to before I did. But he was all the way in the front of the car, trying to pry open the hood. And Isaiah was nearly to the trunk.

I figured it out when I saw the look on Kip's face. He bolted towards Isaiah, who had just ducked behind the open trunk. I threw open my door, slamming it into Kip's hips. It barely slowed him down, but it was all the time Isaiah needed. He emerged from behind the trunk holding the rifle.

Cassa leveled the gun at Isaiah's heart. I threw myself at her, making contact as the shot went off.

"Hoo, now," said Isaiah. I breathed out. It had missed him.

I scrambled to my feet, but Cassa was faster. Her gun squared with my face. I froze, halfway to standing, and lifted my hands. But I knew it wouldn't matter. She wore her hatred as plainly as the features of her face. In that moment, she wanted me dead more than she wanted the car to run. More than anything.

A second shot rang out, deeper and more hollow than the first, rattling back and forth between the trees on either side of the interstate.

Cassa hit the ground, face up, and didn't move. Red splotches blossomed over her shirt. Isaiah stepped out from behind the trunk. He had a steady grip on Meghan's rifle.

Kip was quick, but I had always been quicker. By the time he started moving, I had pried the gun from Cassa's fingers and pointed it at Kip.

I hazarded a shaky glance back at Isaiah. From the look of it, he was well aware that his shot had hit its mark.

My attention turned back to Kip, whose hands were raised and whose face was marked with defeat. He stepped back, knowing already that we weren't going to shoot him unless he tried to get back in the car. Neither of us spoke to the other. I guess we had already said everything there was to say.

We left him there, on the side of the interstate, with Cassa's body. Even after everything that had come between us, I knew I'd never recover the piece of my soul that stayed with them.

It was a long time before Isaiah spoke. "Thank you," he said. "For stopping her. And for bringing me."

"Thank you, too. You know." I gestured at the shrinking forms of Kip and Cassa in the rear view mirror, as though Isaiah could see me, or them.

"It's nothing."

His words hung in the air. We were quiet for a few more miles, and then Isaiah spoke. "Charlotte."

"Yes?"

"Maybe I do want out after all."

Isaiah leaned back in his seat. He looked content, comfortable. Too comfortable, if I'd understood him correctly.

Which I pretended not to. "Out of what?"

"This. All this."

"Meaning..."

He tilted his head up and touched the roof of the car with one long finger.

I sighed. "Meaning we're going to Boston."

He smiled. "If you'll take me."

I stared at the road, saying nothing, calculating the miles and hours in my head. After a long moment, I turned the car around.

Six

The car door slammed shut, and I blinked at the harsh white of the sidewalk in front of Isaiah's home.

He was already at the front door. He'd dealt with Cassa almost single-handedly, and he'd had no problem directing me to his house, so I couldn't figure why it struck me as bizarre to watch him find his way to the front door without me.

It wasn't his blindness. In juvy, he'd moved with an easy confidence. It was magnetic. Other people sought him out, and when they walked together, they matched their pace to his.

But he was different here, in this moment. He looked out of place. His confidence had dissipated, and only determination filled its place. He was slower, relying heavily on his cane. I watched it sweep over the path to the door, making more passes than usual. I wasn't fooled for a moment. He could have found his way without it. Then he reached forward to knock on the door, and I felt his shame, his *brokenness*, as he'd put it, and understood.

It sucks to knock on the door of your own home.

I continued to stare as a small curtain shifted to reveal a face. The curtain froze, then swished back into place. Long moments passed before the door finally cracked.

A young man stepped onto the porch and regarded Isaiah with frank distaste. I regretted leaving our weapons in the car, but Isaiah had insisted.

The man shook his head. "So they let you out."

Isaiah cleared his throat. "Something like that." He seemed younger, suddenly. He'd always been, to me, one of the oldest souls in juvy. Full of wisdom and easy laughter. But all that was gone now. He was exposed, vulnerable. Childlike.

"And you came here."

"Abel. I just want to see Mom."

"There's nothing for you here, Ise. Leave us be."

This must be Isaiah's brother. The man who'd blinded him. They stood there like statues, but I wanted to scream. "He can't leave, not now. It's the last—"

Abel looked at me. My jaw snapped shut, and I stepped back inadvertently. But his words to me were softer than I expected. "It's too late for him. You can stay, if you need a place to be. But Isaiah is not welcome here."

Isaiah let out a long breath. For the first time since I'd known him, I saw his youth. Really saw it. His cheeks and lips were full. His hands were smooth against his cane. The lines on his forehead would have disappeared if he'd relaxed his face.

When he spoke, his voice was small. "Just let me see Mom. Just tell her I'm here."

Abel's face hardened, and I lay a hand on Isaiah's arm. I knew that look, and I could guess what was coming next. The door opened a hair further, and the gun sliced into view.

Abel cocked it, so that Isaiah knew it was there, and spoke through tight lips. "Get out. Last chance, Ise." He'd stopped just short of aiming the barrel at his brother, but Isaiah couldn't have known that.

Isaiah's hands lifted in surrender, then jerked back to his side. "No."

I pulled against him, and he was obliged to step backward. "We're leaving. We're *leaving*, Isaiah."

Abel nodded at me, and I put my full weight into dragging Isaiah off the porch. "Come on. There's a step down here."

Isaiah stumbled, and for a moment, he allowed me to lead him. But halfway off the stoop, he stopped. I tugged harder, not caring that he could stumble. Everyone had a gun these days, but Abel was ready to use his. I could almost have understood him, at the time. He wanted to protect his family for as long as he could.

It was a few seconds before I realized that Isaiah wasn't moving any more, no matter how hard I tried. He might as well have been an oak tree, for all the good it did me to pull on him like that. Another moment passed, and I gave up struggling.

I looked at Abel, wide-eyed. There would be no consequences for shooting us. We'd just done the same to Cassa, after all.

I kept a hand on Isaiah's arm, so he'd know I hadn't left him, but it fell to my side when he uttered his next words.

"I found the Remnant."

Abel snorted. "You're too old for this. *I'm* too old for this."

"He did," I blurted out before thinking. "He found them."

Some small muscle twitched in Isaiah's neck, but he stayed steady. Abel looked at me, unconvinced, and I summoned every ounce of steel I had. I could not afford to flinch. "You knew he would."

"That's just some story people tell."

"They're real, Abe. It's gonna be a whole new setup up there. Let me see Mom, and I'll take you with me."

"What about Mom? You'll take her, too?"

Isaiah hesitated. "It doesn't work like that. Just you and me."

That was smart. If he'd promised to take everyone, Abel would never have believed the lie. Isaiah was back to form.

Abel glanced at me. "And the girl?"

I gave him a convincing smile. "Obviously. Why do you think I'm with him?"

His doubts were smattered across his face, but the Remnant was more than anyone could resist. The gun disappeared behind his back. His face remained tense. "I'm warning you, Ise. I'm done with your games. You play me, you'll regret it. It's not too late to make you regret it."

Isaiah's shoulders relaxed. I allowed myself a breath.

That was when the impossibility of my situation hit me. Something slippery swirled in my stomach, and I felt sick. I couldn't stay with Isaiah and his family, or I'd miss the OPT. But I couldn't leave, either, because Abel would know we were lying, and Isaiah would pay for it.

I told myself that I didn't have a choice, that it was his decision to come here. But deep down, I didn't know if I had what it took to walk away.

For now, at least, I still had time before I had to act, time to find the smart move. I could play this out. I willed the slippery thing to hold still for a little longer.

I squared my shoulders, and noticed Isaiah doing the same. "You can keep the gun out, Abe," he said. "I've gotta get something from the car."

"Like hell you do."

"Like I said. Keep the gun out if you like. That way, we understand each other."

"Maybe we don't."

But Isaiah was already halfway to the car. I shrugged at

Abel, pretending not to understand the warning in his voice, and casually placed myself between Isaiah and the gun.

Isaiah popped the trunk a moment later. As I expected, he came out with Meghan's rifle. What I didn't expect was where he aimed it.

At me.

"Step aside, Abe. I'm a fair shot, most of the time, but I'm not as sure as I used to be."

I floundered, trying to figure out the play here, and felt the slippery thing in my belly harden into stone. Surely Isaiah would never tell Abel about my starpass. Surely.

"No." The word escaped my lips before I thought it. "Isaiah. Don't do this."

"I can take one person with me, little bird. And it's not you."

I shook my head, confused. I glanced back at Abel in time to see him pull his gun again.

"I got her," he said.

"No need," said Isaiah. "Get in the car, Char. Drive away. I'm only gonna say it once."

It was the way he said my name that finally tipped me off to his plan. He had never called me Char. It was an act.

Abel spoke. "We don't have to kill you unless you get stubborn. So you better start moving."

I stole one final glance at Isaiah before I started running. He almost seemed to return my gaze. "Thanks for the ride, sweetheart."

Another phony name. It was the perfect move. He was saving both of us, in a way I never could. So it made no sense to me, in that moment, that my heart was breaking.

I shut the door and powered on the car like a robot.

It wasn't until I turned the corner, never to see him again, that I realized we never said goodbye.

Seven

I made it to Calais, Maine, in record time, not that I knew much about what constituted regular time. Maine wasn't the type of place where girls like me tended to take road trips. Every so often, I'd think about how much time I had left, before the gate closed, and the blood would pull away from the tips of my fingers, leaving them slightly blue.

Whenever I passed a town, or a deserted shopping mall, I tried to fit it in my head that in a few hours, they wouldn't exist anymore. They'd be gone. *Space debris.*

I couldn't picture it, no matter how hard I tried. There were no cars on the road, and most of the cops were up in space already, so I pretty much floored it the whole way. As soon as I got to Calais, however, traffic materialized out of nowhere, and I screeched to a stop. I was still seventy-five miles from the launch site in Saint John.

It took me a good ten minutes to realize that traffic was going nowhere. Everyone on this side of the continent wanted to be in Saint John right now, including me. A lot of people, like Meghan, had chosen to spend their remaining hours in the comfort of their home. People who had no shot at getting on board, due to age or disability. But a lot of people would try to get on the OPT at the last minute, whether or not they had a ticket. People like me. And the OPT wouldn't let them, and their cars would stay in the road, and I would never get there.

I needed a plan B. I jerked the wheel to the right and steered the car through the shoulder and toward the nearest exit ramp, which was also blocked. "Car!" I shouted, activating the system.

"Good afternoon." The reply was cold, even for a robot.

"Is there an airport nearby?"

"You are four miles from Saint Stephen Airport."

"Are there any planes there?"

"The airport is currently out of service." That made sense. Under the Treaty, every airplane on Earth was grounded all week. Hijacking and piloting an abandoned airplane was above my pay grade, so I needed another tack. "What about the harbor?"

"You are one half-mile from the harbor. An international edict prevents navigation of waterways within one hundred miles of Saint John, New Brunswick."

"Yeah, well, it's not like there's anyone left to stop me." I turned east and pressed the accelerator into the floorboard, sending the car flying over a curb and through a vacant parking lot.

"You may steer the car away from the port now."

"No chance of that." I was about four feet from a mostly empty side street, and I felt a tiny thrill of adrenaline as I pressed the accelerator harder. The electric engine snapped gently at the sudden velocity, then... clicked off. My chest slammed into my seatbelt.

"What the heck, car!"

"Your criminal intent is apparent. Car is powering down. Goodbye."

So the cars on the road weren't just stuck in traffic. They had probably powered down, too, at some point nearer the launch site. Awesome.

I slipped off my heels and shoved them into the satchel. Then I grabbed what was left of the food and a coat from the back seat and sprinted toward the water for all I was worth. I would have to try my luck with the boats.

My nylons plucked against the blacktop in the first few paces, so that by the time I reached the end of the block, they were sporting gaping holes on the soles of my feet. This was for the birds. Seriously, did these things serve any purpose at all? I paused just long enough to poke my feet through the holes and bunch the shredded ends around my ankles. That would have to do. I had a lot of tricks up my sleeve, but running in heels wasn't one of them.

I was within a few blocks of the water when the air around me seemed to change subtly. At first, I couldn't figure out what was different. I passed a man on a bench, leaning on a cane, then a group of people sitting in a circle on a big patch of grass. Someone had a guitar out, and several in the group were holding hands. I assumed they were around college age, but when I got closer, I saw that they were families. Old and young, huddled together. Small children ran in circles at the center of the cluster. No one so much as glanced at me as I sprinted by, and that was what had changed. I was no longer an outcast to be stared at, eyes narrowed. No one was judging me. I might as well have been invisible. Death had made us all equals.

I hustled past an antique store full of digital clocks, the old-fashioned kind that people used to plug into their walls or set out on a desk or a nightstand. Every clock faced the outside, so that the window was full of green and red square-shaped numbers, all reading 9:35 p.m. That's also when I realized that every light in town was on. Of course. No one was concerned about saving electricity anymore.

Next was a convenience store with a cardboard sign taped on the window: "Take what you need." Its fluorescent lights illuminated empty shelves. When the water of the harbor glinted into view, I started seeing restaurants. Every chair was occupied. I slowed my pace in spite of myself, trying to take in every aspect of the scene. The woman who caught my attention was draped over a chair, her long black gown spread out over the cheap red and brown carpet. She wore a diamond necklace and matching earrings. Also at her table were a teenage boy wearing a collared shirt and a man in shorts and flip flops.

The dining room was filled with tableaus as diverse as hers. There was a lot of wine, and a single man ran among the tables with food and bottles of liquor. He wore a smile.

A group of six sitting around a table for four waved at me, beckoning me to join them. The woman—I assumed she was the mother—slid to the side of her seat, indicating that I could share it with her. I didn't even know I had stopped running. I was just standing at the window, taking it all in.

I almost joined her. I almost sat among this family of strangers and whiled away my remaining hours of life basking in their companionship, their acceptance. Maybe I would even tell them the truth about my life: that I had failed, in every possible way, that my family could never love me, that they'd left me to die in a prison commissary. I glanced at one of the boys at their table and thought that I would at least tell them about West, but not that he hadn't come for me. I couldn't tell anyone about that.

But I wasn't one of them. I didn't belong with their family. As much as I longed to fit into a group like that, it wasn't in me. Maybe I would make it onto the OPT, and maybe I would die when the meteor struck. Maybe I would get all the way to the Ark, but not make it inside. Then I would die in space, alone. But I could never sit in a restaurant, drinking wine, and wait for fate to take me. One way or another, I was going to Saint John.

The harbor was clean and dark, and it smelled like fish and saltwater. A faint steam rose from the tips of the small waves, which were painted silver in the moonlight and dancing under the lights from the harbor. There were several larger boats and a few fishing rigs docked along a series of short piers. Glancing around, I climbed to the tallest point I could—a set of concrete steps leading to an American flag—and began to scan the gently bobbing boats. Most would have government-issue GPS systems and wouldn't run. After checking the first few rows, I started to panic, just a little.

Then I saw it. It was about the size of a ski boat and mostly white, with plenty of peeling paint. The word "Bandito" scrolled across the bow in elegant script. It had to be at least twenty-five years old, before they started installing GPS on everything that moved. It was perfect.

It was also occupied. A man stood along the pier, pulling a length of rope hand over fist. Despite the slight chill in the summer air, he was stripped to the waist, and his skin appeared tanned in the half-light.

He turned to me as soon as the dock bobbled with my weight, and I raised my eyebrows.

"You're Trin Lector." I'd seen all his movies. His latest, about a group of renegade astronauts sent to uncover a plot to destroy the International Space Station, had been screened in the detention center right after the news about the meteor broke. It had broken every box office record ever, and it hadn't even been that good, at least in my opinion. Not like his earlier stuff, anyway. But people flocked to anything involving spaceships these days.

The movie industry imploded after that, like everything else, but the demand for movies was higher than ever. No one cared about money. Executives quit. Studios collapsed. But the actors kept acting, and the writers kept writing. They said they were doing it for the fans, but I knew better. Immortality had never been more appealing, more urgent.

The most famous movie star in the world snorted at me. "No autographs."

So he was a jerk. A jerk with a boat, though, so I couldn't respond in kind. "No. I mean, sure. I am a fan, though."

"Great."

A cigarette dangled from his lips, and for an instant, I just stared. I hadn't seen a real, lit cigarette since right after my first stint in detention, when Kip had given me one as a welcome home present. This guy must have saved up a pretty big supply when they went off the market fifteen years ago. That, or he'd only saved the one.

"Get going. I'm not taking any passengers." His tone was less strained than before. He was used to being stared at.

"Just a couple hours. I need to get to—"

"Saint John. Yeah. You're the first to ask." The sarcasm brought the edge back to his voice. He turned to the rope.

"You can just drop me off and keep going wherever you're going."

"Fine idea. I don't plan on getting shot, even if it's all the same now. I'm going out to the middle of the ocean to meet the Pinball head on."

"They're guarding the harbor there?"

He sighed and made a show of stopping his work to face me. "They're guarding *everything*. Can you blame them?" His forehead relaxed slightly as he took another drag. I watched, fascinated, as the tip of the cigarette glowed bright orange, then white, as he sucked in. "Your best bet is to turn back and find a group to join. Make some friends." He stumbled back a little, and I saw that he had been drinking.

"I don't need friends. I need a ride to Saint John."

He grunted. "Wouldn't do you any good anyway. You gotta have a starpass to set foot in town, much less get to the gate. Only cops left on earth are the ones guarding the transport cities."

"I have a starpass."

"And I got a rocket right here in my pocket." It was a line from the movie about the astronauts. I suppressed the urge to roll my eyes, and he slung the rope into the boat, swaying more than the action required.

"I'm serious. Look." I dug into my shirt and pried the pass from my skin. I held it up and walked toward him, yanking Band-Aids off its corners and flicking them into the water along the way.

"Let me see that."

I pulled my arm back. "Let me on the boat."

He threw me a look I couldn't read, then suddenly shrugged. "Worth a shot. All aboard."

My satchel and food bag were on the floor of the boat in the next second, and I followed not a moment later. "Thank you. Thank you so much," I said, straightening. "You have no idea—"

"Alright, alright." Trin clambered into the front of the boat as I took my seat next to the inboard motor. "Let's see the pass."

"Here." I held it toward his face.

He made a grab for it, but he was good and drunk, and I jerked it back with room to spare. "I'll hang on to it."

"Fine, fine," he muttered into the dashboard. The engine sputtered to life, and I realized the boat ran on gasoline. This was old school. We went fast, much faster than I expected. The harbor shrank into the distance, and the light from the boat showed grass on both sides of the waterway. I was glad I'd brought the shapeless coat from the back seat of Meghan's car. I slid it over my shoulders, careful to maintain an iron grip on the starpass. I wished I hadn't tossed away the Band-Aids. Hands were not the most reliable way to keep up with stuff.

When the boat skimmed past the last mounds of earth and into the open water, I allowed myself to smile. As I expected, Trin swerved us to the left, and we swept north up the coast of Maine.

My moment of relief came crashing down an instant later when the engine died. I squinted at the actor, who was barely visible in the light from the dashboard. I couldn't see his left hand, but his right slipped something small and metal into the pocket of his shorts. The boat key.

When he turned around, I imagined the gun in his hand before I saw it.

"Woah. Sit back down," he said. "That's right. Now just hand over that pass."

"You have got to be kidding me. There's no way they'll let you on the transport. They're gonna know you're over forty."

"We'll see about that," he said, in a tone that implied that he usually got what he wanted. "Give it here. Your bags, too." Up close, his hands were enormous. His fingers were thicker than the barrel of the gun. They stretched toward my face like wooden stumps.

I drew a ragged breath and pretended to fumble for the pass. "Please don't do this." My breath came a little harder, and shorter.

He was unmoved. "Now."

"Okay. Okay, I'm just—here." I let my voice shake and held the pass toward him. His red-rimmed eyes were totally focused on that shiny blue card. When those wooden fingers were inches away, I dropped the pass and yanked them, using his weight to swing myself up to a standing position.

He fell forward, and I shoved my body against the side of the boat. The gun went off, and my heart squeezed. Did the bullet hit the motor behind me?

His right elbow slammed into my face with unexpected force, and my field of vision swung upward, toward the stars. It occurred to me, too late, that he'd probably had combat training for half the movies he'd starred in. I found myself leaning backward over the side of the boat, jerking my head away from the choppy surface of the water.

I grabbed the back of his neck just as he cocked the gun a second time, a fact I barely registered before my mouth connected to his skin. I bit down, suppressing the urge to gag. He crumpled, but only for an instant.

It was all I needed. I hit him in the side of the head as hard as I could, then reached for his pistol arm. Using every ounce of strength I possessed, I flung him into the side of the boat.

He tottered for a sickening moment, and I ducked and reached for his ankles. Above me, the gun went off a second time. I pulled his legs up while simultaneously shoving my head into his sternum, and Trin Lector went over the side of the boat.

With the boat key still in his pocket.

I figured I had less than a minute before he got back on board, gun in hand. Although his boat was old school, the gun was a more recent design. It would fire despite being wet.

Luckily for me, I didn't need that much time. I yanked the cover off the keyswitch and grappled for the wires in the darkness. I threw the switch for the dash lights and studied the wad of wires in my hand. Then I reached for a razor blade.

Blast.

My razor blades. I'd left them in Meghan's bathroom. *Not good, Char. Not good.*

I forced myself to block out the sound of the splashing nearing the back of the boat and threw down the lid of the glove compartment, frantically tossing its contents onto the seat. Surely he kept a knife in here somewhere.

A glint of red the size of my thumb caught my eye. A pocketknife. Brilliant.

Within seconds I had stripped every wire I had uncovered. I had never hotwired a boat before, but the rules were always the same when there was no computer involved. Find the positive, connect it to the negative, and touch that to the starter wire. Problem was, before the government standardized this stuff, every manufacturer used different colors for the wires.

My hands did not shake even as the boat pitched backward very slightly, signaling that Trin had reached the back of the boat and was hoisting himself up. I tried combo after combo, steady as a cat. It did not pay to have shaky hands when the game was playing out.

"Hold it right there."

I'll never know why he didn't just shoot first. Maybe he had lost the key in the water, and didn't know how to hotwire the boat without me. Or maybe there was some shred of him that couldn't shoot another person in cold blood, even drunk. Even when the stakes were as high as they were that night.

I tried not to wonder which it was.

But he didn't shoot. Instead, he said, "Hold it right there," like we were in a movie, and that was all the time I needed. The motor growled to life, and I pressed the throttle into first position. An instant later, the engine compressed, and it was all over.

I slammed the throttle fully open. The boat jerked forward, and the sound of his splash was drowned in the roar of the motor.

I don't know if he caught in the blades or hit the water clean. I did not look behind me.

Eight

I stopped only once, to retrieve the pass from the floor of the boat, and only after I was at least a mile away. As I slid it into my nylons, next to my thigh, I wondered what Meghan would have thought of my leaving Trin in the water and decided not to dwell on that. He'd planned to kill me, and I had done the only thing I could. Hopefully Meghan would have understood that.

The night was beautiful, and despite its age, the *Bandito* had a strong light on its prow. I hugged the coast and kept a constant speed, so that I knew how far I had traveled. After sixty miles, I slowed at each cluster of lights along the shoreline, but I needn't have worried. Saint John was unmistakable.

The Coast Guard surrounded the harbor, holding the last fifty or so feet of water open. Each official-looking boat had a floodlight and a loudspeaker, and the same message played over and over. "Civilian watercraft must maintain a distance of one hundred miles. Only citizens in possession of OPT passes will be allowed in the harbor. For the safety of law-abiding citizens, those violating orders will be shot. Anyone attempting to board a military vessel will be shot."

A mass of boats formed a halo around the crescent of Guard boats, leaving no more than a few feet of distance between the civilians and the military. My hands were tight on the steering wheel. The situation was tense, and it would only get worse in the remaining twenty-five minutes before midnight, before we were all locked out forever.

I allowed myself ten seconds to scan the scene before guiding the *Bandito* into the only gap at the back of the crowd, but once I had wedged in, there was no way to get closer. The boats were packed too tightly. I pushed my hair out of my face, aware that my expression probably mirrored those around me: fear and desperation.

When the boat next to me jostled against mine, I shouldered my satchel and bag of food out of instinct. They were too vulnerable on the floor. Anyone could just jump right into my boat. Not that they would want to. I was probably the farthest person from the harbor. Another moment passed, and the Pinball was that much closer to us all. Twenty-three minutes before the gates closed. I scanned the scene before me, ignoring the dread rising up in my chest. *Come on, Char.* What was the move here?

Wait. Anyone could jump into my boat.

That was the move.

I pressed my bags into my side and scrambled into the front of the boat. The woman in the next boat up saw me coming and nudged her companion, her face tight.

"Oh, no you don't," the man called out. He stood, intending to block my way, but he was too slow. My feet touched their boat four times, and each step brought me closer to the prow. And then I was gone.

The next boat was much the same, as was the next. By the time I clambered onto my fourth, a yacht, I had commanded the attention of several people in the surrounding vessels. We were well lit by the Coast Guard's floodlights. I caught the eye of a man of about thirty in the boat next to the yacht. His look of despair changed to hope in that instant. He gripped the rail on the front of his own boat, mirroring my movements, and jumped heavily into the craft in front of him.

I took a split second to stand up and assess the situation in front of me. At least ten more rows of boats stood between me and the Coast Guard. To my left and my right, people were abandoning their vessels and sweeping forward into the boats in front of them. Soon, too soon, this would get ugly. When the mob reached the Coast Guard, they would open fire, rather than allow themselves to be boarded. I had to stay ahead of the crowd, but there was no room for a misstep. If I fell into the water, or was pushed in, I would be crushed between the jostling boats or held underwater beneath them.

Voices filled the air around me, with protests increasing in volume, but those of us who climbed forward fastest were silent. Somewhere near me, a gun went off. The sound sent a jolt through my entire body. The message from the loud-speakers continued in the background, uninterrupted, closer and louder with each boat I overtook.

When at last I had reached the final boat, everything changed again. The announcement from the Coast Guard stopped, and I squinted into their floodlights. Each Guard boat was a blazing light. The Guards themselves were mere shadows in the darkness behind the lights.

We were close enough that I could count the number of Guards in each boat, even though I couldn't see their faces. Something jostled me from behind, and I realized that I was standing on the front line of a huge crowd of people.

To my left and right, faces of all ages and ethnicities glowed in the spotlights. We stood precariously, knowing that to fall into the water would mean certain death.

There are too many of us. It was only a matter of time until the Coast Guard decided that we were enough of a threat to take action. And we were hopelessly outgunned. My breath shortened.

It occurred to me that my position, including my grip on the bitt at the prow, was prime real estate. I clamped down harder, resisting the urge to cry out when someone's heel found my knuckles. The crowd bore forward, and the crashes of people hitting the water were all around me, along with their screams. We were so well illuminated by the Coast Guard's lights that each bobbing, drowning head was impossible to miss.

A hand clamped onto my arm, and I shifted my weight, preparing to elbow its owner in the eye socket. But when I turned to look at my target, I stopped.

A young boy crouched next to me. His eyes were as dark as West's, and my free hand wrapped around his wrist instead, surprising me. We were both as low to the boat as possible, so that we'd be harder to knock overboard, but that didn't discourage people from trying. A moment later, a shin drove into the boy's back, and he scrambled only for an instant before falling forward.

My heart squeezed, and the full horror of the situation hit me all at once.

We are all going to die.

There is no way to save any of us.

There was no point in even trying.

But my body ignored this logic, and my terror only fueled my actions. My grip on his wrist became like iron, and I yanked upward as hard as I could. He hadn't lost his hold on me, either, and together, we pulled him back to the relative safety of the deck.

I realized that our eyes hadn't left each other, and blinked.

"Thanks," he said.

I managed to choke out a response. "Yeah. No problem."

Then we heard the sound of motors shifting gear, and the floodlights began to move. For an instant, everyone froze.

The Coast Guard were leaving.

When their lights moved, I got my first view of the harbor, or what remained of it. Instead of docks, an enormous concrete wall rose up from the bay, with a single opening at water level. As I watched, the closest of the Guard boats slipped through the gap.

I had to get onto a Guard boat. It was the only way to get through the barrier in the harbor. Before this thought had fully formed in my mind, the slick surface beneath me lurched forward. I pitched backward and slammed onto the deck. My arms and legs grappled for purchase as the boat increased its speed. Just as I was about to slide into the water, my hip rammed into the bitt. I clawed at it with both hands, trying to get a solid grip. My bags shot overboard, but their straps were wrapped around my wrist, so that their weight yanked against my hold on the bitt. Beside me, the boy was doing the same.

A few people hit the water, and I willed myself not to look. Other boats had engaged their motors, too. Anyone in the water was likely to be run over. It was a bad time to lose balance.

I steadied myself with difficulty, then spared a moment of appreciation for the captain. He must have figured out a way around the GPS shutdown, but had the foresight to wait until the Guard boats moved first, so that he wouldn't be fired on.

He also probably wanted to get rid of us before he got to the nearest Guard boat. I couldn't blame him there. He was headed toward the tiny gap between the two Guard boats directly in front of us. Behind us, the swarm of boat-hoppers began to shout at the retreating boats, but the government-controlled GPS system had rendered all but a few of them immobile.

The man driving the boat had come prepared, and he had been on the front line, so he'd been parked there awhile—long enough to figure out his next move. I had no intention of finding out what that was.

I turned to the boy. "We have to jump."

He nodded, wide-eyed.

"Get ready," I shouted.

When we were within ten feet of the Coast Guard boat, I gathered my legs under me and perched on the front of the boat. One arm maintained my death-grip on the bitt, and the other squeezed my bags against my ribcage.

When we were four feet from the Guard boat, I jumped.

I hit the prow of the Guard boat so hard I had to wonder if I'd broken a rib. When my bags swung into my side an instant later, I decided it was a distinct possibility. I grabbed onto the chrome railing and swung myself over.

The world exploded into red and orange as I landed on the floor of the boat. I had barely a second to register that the boy had made it, too—and more gracefully than I. There was a deafening noise, like a crash, and we scrambled to our feet. The boat I had just jumped from was on fire. At least, what was left of it. A magnificent bonfire rose up from the waves, its heat strong enough to curl my hair.

Had the Coast Guard just torpedoed an unarmed civilian boat? I had to remind myself to breathe.

I looked over my shoulder, as though my new shipmates would answer the question for me. I could not feign surprise at the young man who pointed a gun at my chest, since I had not expected a warm reception. But the shock of the explosion was evident on my face.

"That. He just…"

I must have been doing a killer damsel-in-distress, because he lowered his gun almost immediately. "I'll have to ask you to keep your hands where I can see them, ma'am." His eyes darted from me to the remains of the boat, and back to me. The blaze illuminated the sweat on his face.

Near us, another Guard was escorting the boy away from us. The Guard with the gun saw my panic. "He'll be checked over there. For safety."

"I have a starpass! I couldn't get to the OPT. Everything was blocked." Against my will, I glanced back at the burning boat behind us.

"It's for everyone's safety." He spoke a little too quickly, and his words spilled into each other. "We anticipated someone might bypass the GPS shutdown. We can't afford to be mobbed, and it's too late to arrest anyone. Everyone in our ships has to get through the gate before it closes."

My tongue was frozen in my mouth.

"Really, it's for the best. I'm sure they didn't feel any pain."

The Guard was referring to the torpedo, but his words echoed the line they'd been repeating on the broadcasts about the meteor, over and over: "It will be quick. Citizens remaining on Earth won't feel any pain."

He continued. "Look. If you really do have valid passes, I'll take you to the gate myself."

"Thanks. I'm Magda." I let my voice shake a little. I'd already gathered that helpless was a good look for me when dealing with this guy.

He looked at me for a moment, jaw clenched. "Eren. Let's see that starpass, please."

I slid my hand into the waistband of my skirt, shoving my arm into my hose all the way to the elbow. When Eren averted his glance, I remembered to look embarrassed. The kind of girl who wears skirt suits probably doesn't get searched by men in uniform all that often.

"It's just—everyone wanted to steal it."

"I can imagine."

"Here."

He leaned forward to take the pass, his face illuminated by the blaze behind me. Despite his apparent willingness to help me, there was a hardness in his eyes, as though he didn't believe the pass would be valid. I thought about the dead man in the boat I'd jumped from and shivered.

What would happen to the boy?

The scanner on his belt glowed green almost instantly, and I let out a silent breath of relief. Until that moment, I hadn't let myself wonder whether the pass was legit. A valid pass was more valuable than all the money in the world, which wasn't saying much. How had my parents gotten their hands on an extra one?

Eren stared at his screen for several minutes, long enough for me to notice a twitch in the side of his jaw. After what seemed like forever, he drew a deep breath and turned back to me, his expression unreadable. "Your pass is good. You can come with me. Look, I really am sorry about the boat. But you should have made your plans to be here a lot sooner."

"I—I couldn't leave my family."

He nodded. "You're here now. I'll see you make it to the gate. Stay here." He handed the pass back to me. "We'll be there in a minute."

The boat passed through the gap in the barrier as he turned from me. Rows of black transport vehicles, the kind with benches full of soldiers, awaited us at the dock. Eren guided me onto the nearest one, which was already half-full of Coast Guard personnel. To my enormous relief, another guard appeared behind us, escorting the boy from the boat.

The guards exchanged a look with each other, but neither spoke. We settled onto the bench in the transport vehicle, squeezing all the way over to make as much room as possible for those still to come.

I ignored the questioning stares of those around us out of habit, but Eren the Guard was visibly uncomfortable. "Valid starpass," he explained. "Couldn't leave her on the water."

The guard I was sitting next to gave me a quick nod as the vehicle lurched into motion. "Keep a good grip on the pass. You never know what this kind of riffraff will try to pull off. Stay close."

I decided not to point out that the "riffraff" were nothing but ordinary citizens driven to desperation because their government had left them to die. Didn't seem like the kind of thing to start an argument over, at this point. All the same, my knuckles were white around the sharp metal of the pass.

We were at the OPT gate within minutes. The line at the gate was guarded by a double row of soldiers. I took a deep breath, but instantly regretted it. The thin night air was laced with the scent of blood.

No, not just blood. Death.

In addition to the gauntlet of armed soldiers, the gate was guarded by two towers, one on either side. Sniper rifles protruded from secure locations high overhead.

All around us, people were clamoring for admission, undeterred by the bodies of the fallen strewn around them. Decorated war veterans, rendered disabled in service to their country, were forcibly shoved back into the crowd. Mothers and fathers attempted to press babies into the arms of those in line. I glanced at one such child. He was covered in jewelry, presumably a bribe for whoever took him on board. My arms reached for the infant instinctively, but the nearest guard knocked the woman back into mass of people, and she fell with a shriek. The guard next to him pushed me forward into the line, and I turned to look at his face.

Like most of the soldiers guarding the line, he wore a mask. It was the only thing about him I could understand. I wouldn't want to show my face to those who were about to die, either.

Numb, I shuffled after Eren, trying desperately to ignore the strange feeling of gratefulness mixed with guilt that weighed my every step. If the soldiers weren't here, I would have no chance of getting to the front of the line. The thought made me sick.

Eren kept his gun on display.

The line moved quickly. If your starpass was valid, you were in. If it was forged, they dipped your hand in a barrel of dark ink and marched you out of the line at gunpoint. The area was well lit, and I saw more than a few black-stained hands in the crowd around the line.

I had almost reached the front of the line when a voice cut through my consciousness.

"Oi! That's a real pass! You can't—stop!—you can't do this to me!"

Kip. Kip was here.

There was a gentle splash as his hand was pushed into the barrel of ink. "Stay back or you'll be shot. Anyone with ink on their hands is liable for fraudulent misuse of Transport resources and may be shot on sight."

The soldier at the front of the line grabbed Kip by the shoulder of his sleeve and shoved him several feet back. "Get moving, kid."

As he turned, he saw me. His recognition rooted me to my spot, and a thousand possibilities flashed through my mind. Would he blow my cover? I didn't think so. It wasn't like Kip to snitch, and he would never get in the way of a job, even one he wasn't part of. But he might still be angry that I rolled on him, or that I had left the group. And him.

I lifted my eyebrows in a silent plea, and the corners of his mouth lifted almost imperceptibly. I didn't see what was so amusing.

He began softly. In the harsh light, one hand glowed naked and pink, and the other was velvety black. "One thing I'll say for myself. I never underestimated you."

He could have been speaking to the crowd, or the soldiers, except that his glance came back to me. Eren looked at me, and I forced myself to shrug.

Worry makes you look suspicious.

But Kip wasn't planning to give me away. He made a sweeping gesture toward the entire line and began to shout. "Enjoy your life out there among the stars. All I ask is that you remember me. Remember that I knew you for what you were, and I never tried to change you."

All around me, people carefully ignored him, facing forward. The gatekeeper waved, and the soldier reappeared. "That's enough, Shakespeare." The guard shoved Kip again, and this time, he kept contact until they were both several feet away from the gate. I stared after them. Kip was smaller than I realized. "Now stay away." The guard gave Kip's shoulder a final shove.

Kip had never been one for following orders, and he literally had nothing left to lose. So it wasn't hard to predict what would happen next.

He took three or four steps away from the door, then turned back sharply. In seconds, his shoulder made contact with the soldier's ribcage. I had seen that move take out guards twice Kip's size. It was all about where you aimed your collarbone.

He got much farther than I expected. That was the strange part: the stretched-out silence while he sprinted toward the gate. He was ten steps away, then five. A lifetime played out in those moments, but the shots came soon enough. There was a pop of compressed air exploding, and Kip—my Kip—crumpled onto the pavement.

I made a sound like a hiccup, then held my breath.

Eren looked back at me. A confused look played across his face, but his voice remained authoritative. "I'm sorry you had to see that."

My chest spasmed, and I breathed again, but without the tears I expected. A moment passed, and I realized all at once that I didn't have to fight to keep from crying. I had no tears for Kip. What was wrong with me?

Eren put a tentative arm around my shoulder. "This will all be over soon. Try not to think about it. Guns are forbidden on board the Arks," he said, quoting directly from the Treaty of Phoenix. "Humanity will work together toward the common goal of survival." As if to make his point, he surrendered his firearm to the gatekeeper's assistant. He cleared his throat. "It really is all for the best, Magda."

I gritted my teeth and stepped forward to the front of the line.

Nine

The last war had been coming for years. Worldwide energy crises didn't tend to resolve themselves. But this time, the scale of destruction was unprecedented.

No one really knew who lit the first bomb. Everything happened so fast that the governments hardly had to explain themselves. America insisted it came from those still loyal to what used to be North Korea. Several Asian governments claimed that it came from the North American territories on their continent. Everyone suspected the Saudis, since they controlled everything in the Middle East. Only two things were immediately clear: most countries on Earth had nuclear capabilities, and no one in charge was afraid to use them.

World War III was underway.

At the height of the conflict, "mutually assured destruction" was the main phrase on everyone's lips. It was abruptly displaced when we found a new threat to argue about: Afro-Australian scientists claimed to have discovered a new meteor in our galaxy. Earth's path of orbit, combined with its gravitational pull, placed our odds of impact around eighty-five percent.

Afro-Australia's claims were verified by South America's government-owned scientists, and soon enough, Asia had recruited Afro-Australia into peace talks. North and South America allied, followed by Europe.

As months passed, it became clear that the meteor had the capacity to end life on Earth. When the date of destruction was definitively calculated to be ten years in the future, the world's governments pursued peace in earnest, allying into five powerful groups. The Treaty of Phoenix took another year to hammer out, and then *bam*—we were all agreed.

No more nuclear war. No more fighting at all, actually. From now on, we'd build spaceships together.

We built five massive bioships, one for each alliance, called Arks, to be accessed by ten OPTs each. The Arks were built in space, since there wasn't enough fuel on Earth to launch them off the planet.

Each Ark would hold a hundred thousand people. Half an Ark's population was chosen by its government. The other half was by worldwide lottery, so that on any given Ark, half its passengers were foreign. Those who drafted the rules were trying to avoid ethnicity-based conflict among the five Arks, which, at the moment, were floating in the darkness of space, awaiting the arrival of the final OPTs from our doomed planet.

Weapons were outlawed, as everyone agreed that in space, our resources would be better spent colonizing Eirenea, a planetoid in the Kuiper Belt. The terms of the Treaty were carried out in all haste. Bureaucracy was a relic of the past, when we had time to quibble about things like fairness and democracy.

And now, Earth's final day had arrived.

The boy and the other guard reached the front of the line next to me while Eren's starpass was being scanned. This was the moment. The boy would either make it through the gate, or be sent away to his death. His gaze locked on mine for an instant, but it was long enough. His expression told me that he didn't have a pass.

"Passes," the gatekeeper barked from behind her mask. Like the boy, I stopped breathing. But then the guard spoke.

"I'm executing an elective transfer under Clause Sixteen of the Treaty. The transferee is younger than the pass holder and of sound mind and body," he said.

On my side of the line, the scanner glowed green as the gatekeeper waved it over the pass. I barely registered this, since my attention was glued to the other side. The other gatekeeper took a moment to stare at the guard and the boy. "You understand this is irrevocable?"

The guard squared his shoulders. "I do."

"Once he goes through the gate, you will leave and not return."

Around them, the crowd was still, and the voice of the guard carried. "Ma'am, I just torpedoed a civilian watercraft. I've made enough decisions I can't live with. This is the one decision I can."

Speechless, the boy looked up at the guard while the pass was scanned. As soon as the light turned green, the guard disappeared into the crowd, and the boy was shoved forward through the gate. It wasn't until he'd taken several steps that he found his tongue. He turned, too late, to scream into the crowd.

"Wait! Thank you! Tell him thank you!"

I distanced myself from Eren as soon as I was through the gate. I didn't know whether my starpass had been assigned to a specific person, and whether I would need to start calling myself by that person's name, and I didn't want him around to ask questions. I prayed that no one would ask to see my ID, since Magda Notting's had been expired for several years.

The hallway for non-military passengers was crisp and white, with several doors on one side. I concentrated on the sound of my footsteps in an effort to block out the distant screaming from the mob.

After several yards, I was ushered into one of the side rooms by a woman in an unmarked uniform the color of my pass. "This way, please."

I felt a thrill in spite of myself. I was bound for a new world, with new loyalties. No one had a criminal record, so everyone would be on equal footing. Where I was going, they might not even have prisons, much less a military.

The room was small, bright, and empty except for a black plastic bin.

"Your clothes and possessions in the bin. Anything that does not fit into the bin must be discarded, just here." She indicated a flap on the wall. "The sanitizing will begin when you insert your pass into this slot and will proceed as described in your pre-boarding materials." She waved at a place on the wall, and I noticed a bronze showerhead above it. "The screening will take place directly after. You will remain standing on the mat throughout both processes. When the bell rings, you may dress. When the door opens on the far side, please proceed forward for further instructions."

I released a slow breath. That sounded easy enough.

But she wasn't finished. "If the door opens in this direction, you will proceed out the way you came."

Wait, what? I stared at her. "You mean—"

"Citizens with communicable diseases will not be allowed on board the Transport, except those given passage as test subjects for the science and medical divisions. There will be no further access if you fail to pass the screening. Good luck."

She stepped backward, and the door clanged shut between us.

I stared after her for a moment, then stripped off my clothes. I put everything I was wearing and everything I carried, except for the starpass, into the bin and popped the lid closed. Then I took a deep breath and slid the dark blue metal card into the slot.

The now-familiar robotic female voice thrummed through an unseen speaker. "Shower initializing. Remember to close your eyes and mouth. Primary wash in three... two... one."

A sharp jet of warm liquid shot out from the showerhead, which began to circle the walls over my head. It looked and felt like water, but the smell was odd, like a mix of ginger and formaldehyde. I hated it. After it made one complete round, it whirred down the wall and sprayed up and down in a second circle at the height of my waist.

"Secondary wash in three... two... one."

This round may have been water, but it smelled like grapefruits. It was hot, and I felt it drive the first liquid off my skin and hair and down my back. I touched my hand to my hair and was surprised to find it completely dry.

"Tertiary wash in three... two... one."

This round was not liquid at all. It was some kind of ultraviolet light. I closed my eyes a little harder, and the hot light swept my body in the same pattern as the first two sprays. Just as the light began to burn, the voice sounded again.

"Sanitation complete. Beginning passenger scan."

There was a beep, then a bell.

"Passenger scan complete. No diseases detected. Welcome to the Off-Planet Transport, North American Ark division."

I blinked. Was that it? And was it just me, or had the disembodied voice become much friendlier since declaring me clean?

I yanked my card from the slot, then tore open the bin and rifled through my satchel for the other outfit I had packed: black shirt, black pants, black boots. I glanced at my hands as I pulled on the pants, and stopped short. My skin was glowing. Literally. A soft, pale blue light emanated from every inch of my body and reflected against the white of the walls around me.

That was new. But I didn't have time to dwell on it.

Into the satchel went the blue skirt suit. After a moment's hesitation, I flung the used nylons through the trash flap. If I really were going to a better place, I didn't want to reintroduce humanity to the concept of pantyhose.

A few minutes after I dressed, the wall in front of me slid into itself, and I stepped forward onto the loading dock. All around me, people shared the same expression: total awe. And it wasn't hard to see why. The OPT was before us.

It was *huge*. At least as big as a stadium. I supposed that made sense. If every Ark had ten transports, then each transport had to hold ten thousand passengers, plus crew. From what I could see, it consisted of a massive central unit surrounded by hallways suspended several stories in the air. The hallways resembled wings and radiated directly outward from the core. Four such wings were visible from where I stood, gazing up. Ten or twelve feet above me was a thin platform serviced by a series of lifts. Passengers on the platform were loading onto the lifts, which carried them to the wings.

A man wearing the same unmarked blue uniform was weaving through the crowd of gently glowing passengers. "Please ascend to the platforms in an orderly fashion," he called out.

"How?" someone asked.

"The ladders," came the reply. He gestured toward a row of thin metal rungs that led to the platform.

I shuffled into the line forming at the bottom of the nearest ladder. I was halfway through it before I realized that if you didn't have both arms and legs in good working order, you weren't getting on the platform. And if you couldn't reach the platform, you weren't going to make it to the Transport.

Not that anyone around me had an issue with that. I was surrounded by the youngest, healthiest group of people I had ever seen. Except for the part where they radiated blue, everyone was clean-cut, too, as though they were fresh out of a family photo session.

My thoughts were broken by the same blue-uniformed man. His voice had that practiced, pleasant tone calculated to position him as the voice of reason to everyone else within earshot. "Sir. Please make your way to a ladder. We're on a schedule." A couple heads turned.

There was no response.

"Sir. I'll have to ask you to find a line. As stated in your pre-boarding materials, counselors will be available once we're on board the Ark, but hesitation at the launch site is discouraged."

Again, there was no response. Several more people turned to watch the scene unfold. I couldn't afford to stand out, so I ignored it.

The uniformed man cleared his throat. "If you're having second thoughts—"

The "Sir" in question finally spoke. "I am not. I will board in due time. I'm waiting for someone."

My chest squeezed so suddenly that I felt faint. There was only one man in the world who could silence an armed guard so cleanly.

My mouth flapped open as I turned. "Dad."

"Charlotte." In three efficient strides, he stood beside me in line. I reached out to hug him, and his arm stretched around my shoulders. I felt warmer than I had all day.

He had been waiting for me. I smiled up at him. He met my eye, then guided me forward in line.

"I can't believe it," I said.

He didn't respond. Instead, he squeezed my shoulder again. I beamed.

"Where's Mom? And West?"

My father cleared his throat. "Your brother has already boarded."

"Oh, right." They'd probably gotten here hours ago, but Dad had insisted on waiting for me at the bottom of the ladders so that we could all sit together. It was the reunion I'd dreamed about for years. We finally had a fresh start.

"Thanks for waiting for me, Dad. It... it means a lot."

"Your mother insisted."

I paused. Of course, he'd still have reservations about me. It had been a long time since I'd done anything worthy of his approval. He couldn't have known—truly known—that I had changed. But now, I had the rest of our lives to show him. I sighed happily.

The line was surprisingly fast, considering it depended on people scaling a totally vertical ladder, and by the time I found my tongue again, I was nearly at the front.

"I want you to know that I'm different. I won't screw this up." My words were urgent, but stilted. I told myself that it didn't matter. We'd be together, and he'd see. He'd understand, eventually, and we would be a family again.

He looked pained, but that was to be expected, too. He waved me in front of him, and I gripped the ladder. When I was about four feet in the air, I turned back. "Look, Dad. I know what it must have cost you to find an extra starpass, and I'll never take it for granted. I won't—"

"No. You don't."

His tone extinguished my grin. "I don't... what?"

"You don't know what it cost. There is no such thing as an *extra* OPT pass, Char."

He'd never, ever called me that before, and it stung. I looked at him, *really* looked, for the first time. When I took in his face, something sharp lodged itself in my heart, and I felt the world slipping away. The man in the blue uniform told me to keep climbing, but he was a billion miles away, in a different world.

A world where my mother had boarded the OPT.

My mouth opened, then shut. "Mom," I whispered. "Where is Mom." It was a statement, not a question. It was a dare. He had to contradict me, to tell me that she hadn't given me her starpass. Then I saw that he hadn't mounted the ladder after me. Instead, the way down was blocked by the next person in line.

"She didn't tell me until I had gotten through the line. I had to tell her goodbye across a line of assault rifles. She made me promise to go with West. And I went." He made a sound like a cough, and became smaller than I'd ever seen him before. "I *went*."

To my horror, he began to back away.

"Dad, wait."

"For years, I never let myself think of you, except as a little girl. And you were. My little Charlotte." He laughed, a tight laugh, choked by grief and anger. "I'm sorry, Char... Charlotte. I can't know you anymore." He turned abruptly and sprinted into the crowd.

The guard swung into my field of vision. "Miss, you must climb. You're delaying the boarding pro—"

"Wait! Dad—" A pair of hands shoved me another rung up on the ladder, and I looked down in surprise. When I looked back up, redoubling my grip on the rung, I couldn't find him. "Let me down! Move off!" But the person behind me refused to leave the ladder. Even inside the launch site, the fear of death lingered over the crowd, just below the surface.

So I jumped. It wasn't far to the ground—maybe six feet or so—but the impact was meteoric. My knees connected to the asphalt, and a sharp groan pressed out from my lungs. I stood and breathed, then began to scream.

"DAD! DAAD!" Over and over, like a sheep stuck in a fence. Around me, the crowd froze.

I know he heard me. But I never found him again, and he never came back.

Ten

"I must ask you to stand." The blue-clad guard wrenched my upper arm, and I winced. Somehow, I also stopped screaming.

"Please start climbing, miss," he said. "The line is empty."

No way. There was no way I could board the OPT, now that I knew my mother was out there. I glanced up the ladder. The last person was about halfway up. "I can't," I said firmly. "I have to go back. Could you show me how to get back to the gate?"

We locked eyes, and a flicker of understanding passed across his face. "Come with me," he said.

There was nothing for me up there, anyway. My own father didn't want to know me anymore. But I still had a few hours before the meteor hit. I would find my mother. I would tell her, once and for all, that I loved her. I'd find someone in the crowd to give the pass to. Someone worthy of living. The woman with the baby.

I turned in the direction the guard had indicated and lifted my chin. I would tell my mom that we had saved two lives.

I never saw the needle, but I felt it a moment later. There was a sharp pinch at my back, just below my shoulder blade. My legs buckled, and I tried looking back at the guard, but my neck was suddenly unable to support my head, and the concrete swung up to meet my face.

I landed roughly against a rock-solid forearm, and the ground pulled away before I hit it. "I'm sorry, miss. Boarding is compulsory for everyone who clears the screening."

The guard swung me around before lifting me like a doll, and my head lolled backward. "No pain, no effect on the mind. It wears off fast." He seemed like he was trying to sell me on whatever he'd done to me, but there was a note of disappointment there, too, like he wouldn't have minded causing pain.

Either way, he was right. My legs twitched a moment later, and I lifted my head just as we passed through a metal doorway marked "OPT Personnel ONLY." A moment later, I began to struggle.

And then I stopped. The guard was easily twice my size, but he was ten times as strong, and the effects of the drug were steadily increasing. I felt detached from reality, like I was trying to view my surroundings through a suffocating film of smoke and plastic. Wherever he was taking me, I couldn't do anything about it until we got there.

I didn't have long to wait. He stepped onto a thin metal platform and hit a button with his knee. We pressed upward, toward the loading platform, and arrived well ahead of the people still climbing the ladder.

Up close, I understood that the core of the Transport was the rocket, and the wings contained the rows of passenger seats, twenty rows per wing, stacked theatre-style and all facing the same direction. There were ten wings sticking out of the core like the spokes of a wagon wheel.

Still holding me in his arms, the guard stalked onto the nearest wing and deposited me into a shiny black leather seat with a horn sticking up in the middle. He slipped my bag off my shoulder—I'd forgotten it was even there—and dumped it into a plastic bin underneath me. Then he pulled the restraint over my shoulders. It was heavy, and it attached to the horn between my legs. When the lock clicked into place, I was completely trapped, but the drug he'd given me stopped me from caring. He barely had time to mutter an insincere "Have a nice flight" before disappearing.

It occurred to me that you wouldn't have to be much larger than I was before you no longer fit in the seat. But again, that didn't seem to be an issue for any of my fellow passengers, who hopped into their chairs as though they'd been doing this all their lives.

The seats were right up against each other, but the restraints were such that no one could touch anyone else. Some of the passengers were making small talk, but my tongue seemed thick in my mouth, and I didn't try to chat. The back wall of the wing was a black panel, but in front of me was a wall of thick, clear plastic. I couldn't see the crowd below me, but I looked out into the darkness and imagined that, from this height, I'd have a view of several miles.

The robotic female voice sounded again. "The time is two a.m. Takeoff will begin in four hours. Passengers are encouraged to rest quietly."

They wanted us to sleep? Really? I was about to blast into outer space, and, oh, right, the world was ending, but sure. A catnap could happen.

I was only dimly aware of the passage of time, and only because the announcement seemed to ring out more and more frequently. If I'd been able to panic, I would have. But instead, I floated through my final moments on Earth in a sticky, blurry haze.

At five fifty, I felt a surge of panic, as though I were a prisoner in someone else's body. I squeezed my hands into fists, then released them, over and over. My skin felt tingly, and I wondered whether it was from the UV light-bath, or if there was something seriously wrong with me. And was it my imagination, or was it hard to breathe?

Just as I calmed down enough to breathe without conscious effort, my seat swung out without warning, so that my legs came into view in front of the window, and I was lying on my back. My nerves returned, forcing me to start from scratch.

I wasn't alone. Somewhere nearby, a group of kids cried out together, and a man chanted a prayer under his breath. On the far end of the wing, someone sang a soft hymn.

The rumbling began with the earliest rays of Earth's final sunrise.

It started in a place deep below us, and swelled up to the wings. My seat began to vibrate violently, but it felt like the rumbling was inside my chest, as though I might come apart from the inside.

I had no control over anything, not even my own body. My terror forced its way through the druggy fog and into my brain, and I willed myself not to pass out.

Then came the pressure. Slowly, ounce by ounce, my body was being compressed into the seat behind me. The noise was overwhelming. We were taking off.

The force that pushed me down continued for an eternity.

And then, more quickly than it had begun, it stopped. There was still a pull, but it gradually shifted us toward the window, instead of back into our seats.

The terrible rumbling was replaced by a slow, swinging sensation. We had broken through the atmosphere. We were in space. A cheer broke out among the passengers, but I did not join in. Our seats shifted back to their original positions, so that I had a clear view of the window, and Earth.

"It's the orbit," said the woman next to me.

"Sorry?"

"One last view of the whole thing, to gain momentum. Then we slingshot into space." She seemed to be speaking more for her own benefit than mine. Her eyes never left the window.

"Out of the frying pan," I mumbled, and she gave me a strange look before turning pointedly away.

Conversation broke out around us, this time in earnest. I got the feeling that, having come through the takeoff together, people felt bonded to each other.

I wasn't much for bonding, so I kept my mouth shut.

Things continued like that for a few more hours, until the drugs and adrenaline began to burn off, and I felt the first tugs of sleep behind my eyes. Still, I could not rest. The Pinball would strike any minute now, and I would not waste a moment of my last chance to gaze at Earth. From this distance, the world was a tiny, helpless thing, like a child's toy.

The meteor struck at ten, as predicted.

It was a bright light against the small planet. At the moment of impact, time stopped. We leaned forward into our restraints, taking in a view we could not yet process. The Pinball struck Africa directly. The mighty continent split apart, creating instant shockwaves that coursed over the surface of the Earth. Australia was underwater within moments, along with all of Western Europe. Near the poles, the remaining clouds ripped apart, then evaporated as the atmosphere shattered.

Earth no longer existed.

Instead, for a brief window, there were only pieces of the Earth That Was. Without centralized gravity, the moon would be free of its orbit and would now circle the sun alone, accompanied by the shards of the broken planet.

My mother no longer existed, either. This thought was as catastrophic as any other. Maybe worse.

The rumbling that shook my body was not the result of the transport's rockets. As gravity decentralized, we were flung into deep space, out of view of our home planet forever. For a length of time, I was conscious of nothing. At some point, I began to hear the screams of those around me, and my thoughts returned.

The wing was filled with the cries of the insensible. The screaming filled the cabin, and my head, until I pressed my hands to my ears. What I heard was not grief. It was not sorrow. The enormity of what had happened blacked out the senses. We were like animals.

Then there was a sharp hissing noise. For an instant, I wondered whether the wing had sprung a leak, and we were all going to die in space, along with the rest of our species. But then I tasted a sudden sweetness in the air, and I knew that we were being gassed. And I realized that I longed for sleep, or death, and that my wish had been granted as soon as it formed in my mind.

I don't know how long I slept. When I awoke, we had already docked with the Ark. I was numb. I stood; I took my things; I exited the wing. I did not wonder at the existence of gravity because that would require me to deal with reality: I was in space. I would never return to Earth.

There was no Earth. The reality hit me again and again, but never seemed to solidify in my mind. It slipped past me and all around me, unseeable, haunting my periphery, seeking out soft, unprotected places to land its blows.

Meanwhile, here, over two hundred thousand miles away, our OPT had found the Ark. We were being herded down the core of the transport and toward a massive airlock at its center, where we waited for the Ark to clear us for entry, but I could only gasp for air and grope for a wall. Uniformed officials exchanged a knowing look, and someone came to press me forward, toward the Ark's entrance.

I was given a shot in my arm and a cup of water; I accepted both without question. The faintest of warnings rang in the back of my mind, but I was too numb to heed it.

Instead, I watched as the doors of the airlock sucked apart. I worked my jaw open and closed until my ears were pressurized.

The alarm in my mind rang again when we crowded through the lock. It was a silent bell, ringing only for me. It was the part of me that knew when I was in danger, that kept me on my game when I needed it the most. And it was definitely ringing now.

The lush robotic voice floated out over the loudspeaker. "Welcome to the North American Ark. Citizens are encouraged to form an orderly line to pass through the final phase of immigration. An officer of the Ark will escort you to your new home shortly." After a pause, the message began again. "Welcome to the North—"

That's when I noticed the row of blue-clad officers spread out along the wall in front of us. We must have looked confused, because they wore identical looks of patient contentment. "Let's get started with you!" A particularly cheerful woman stepped away from the wall and touched my arm. "I'll just scan your pass, and that will tell us what level and which room you'll be living in. Then we'll be on our way!" I was still formulating a response when she held up her screen, as if to show it to me, then swung it down to wave it over my pass, which was still in my hand.

Immediately, my mother's face appeared on the screen. My hair, my nose. My mouth, when I wasn't smirking.

West's eyes.

The officer's smile widened. "Dr. Turner. Welcome on board. We're so honored to have you."

Hearing my mother's name was like expecting that first gasp of air when you've been underwater, but instead, you breathe too soon, before you've surfaced. My lungs burned.

The attendant didn't notice. "Let's see. There's a note here that your husband and son have already checked into your new apartment. I'm afraid they couldn't wait for you. We're supposed to clear everyone out of the docking bay as soon as possible. This way."

I attempted to return her smile, but my mouth was frozen. I couldn't take my eyes off the image of my mother on the screen, and when I did, I looked around for her, stupidly. Breath, pain. Some remote part of my mind was working out whether it was worse to float through space, gasping for air, or to drown.

"Now, I just need to check your vitals." She slid a monitor ring over my finger and turned back to the screen. "Well! You're as strong as an ox! You have the health energy of a woman half your age."

As she said this, her smile faltered, and the alarm in my head grew to a full-blown siren. I ignored it. It couldn't fix the pain in my lungs. Surely it would be easier to drown. Water is more peaceful than nothingness.

"May I have the ring back, Dr. Turner?"

I slipped it off my finger and held it out to her, but she was easily one step ahead of me. The cuff clasped over my wrist before I knew what was happening. Two more officers appeared at my side and ushered me out of the receiving room. I should have tried to get away. I should have made some kind of scene, or yanked a weapon off the slow-looking one before he got the cuff on my other wrist. I should have used my head.

But all I could think about was my mother's face on the screen, and whether she had tried to breathe after the meteor struck.

Eleven

I am in a holding room, sitting on an iron folding chair. The walls are darker gray than the usual steel blue of juvy, and my lawyer asks me to stop looking at them, to look at her. My parents are on their way, she says, and we have a lot to do before the end of the visit.

"For example, we need to go over a viable defense strategy." I get the impression that she uses words like "viable" to impress me, so that I'll do what she wants.

I look at her. "You don't understand. I really didn't do it."

She bites her lip, an exaggerated gesture reserved for people like me, half her age, none of her potential. She's the best that money can buy, so I really should be grateful that she's here. Kip and Cassa could never afford an attorney like this.

"Charlotte, we'll get so much further if you just tell me what really happened. You're not the one they want. It's this James Kingston, the ringleader. Or those other two. The other kids you work with."

"We'll get farther if you believe me. I don't work for Jimmy anymore."

"Further."

"What?"

"It's fur-ther," *she pronounces carefully. I raise an eyebrow; she returns my gaze in silence. Like I'm really going to talk about grammar right now.*

I continue to stare, nonplussed, and eventually she looks down at her legal pad with a world-weary sigh.

I decide to start over. "Ms. Liston, I left him. I swear."

"You had six calls from Kip Carston the day before the robbery."

"That's... that's not related."

"Then what was he calling you about?"

"He never mentioned a job. We were just talking. Really."

She leans forward. "If you don't plead out of this, you'll be ineligible for the Ark. You realize that. This is your third offense, and the victim isn't going to make it through the trial. You'll go away until you're twenty-one, at least, and the meteor hits in one year. You'll miss the final lottery. It's the end of the line, Charlotte."

"I'll tell them everything I know about Kingston, but I can't plead out. Not this time."

"Why not?"

I know better than to explain myself to people like her. People who only hear the worst. No matter what you say, they think you're lying. And everything in your head, everything that you want to believe about yourself, feels thin, dirty.

But she has a point. I really have to beat this one. So I try to explain. "I made a promise. After the last job. When I got out, I swore I'd leave Kingston. This is literally my last chance to prove myself. That's why I can't plead guilty."

"You made a promise to your parents? They'll understand."

"Not to my parents. To someone else."

"To Kip Carston?! Charlotte, he's a thief."

95

Kip is the fur-thest *thing from my mind just now. I roll my eyes, even though that never helps in these situations.* "So I've heard."

My lawyer removes her glasses and fake-massages the bridge of her nose, another move reserved for people like me, who are beneath her. But I can't change my mind on this one, and she won't help me unless I do, so there's nothing else to talk about. I go back to staring at the walls.

We're still sitting like that when my parents show up. Mom hasn't been crying this time, which is unsettling, and my dad looks at me like I'm a stranger, which is something I've gotten used to by now.

I stand, but Mom doesn't try to hug me. Her arms are crossed, even though I've just been through the scariest night of my life, and I haven't seen her since yesterday morning. "I didn't do it."

She shakes her head. She expected that. Now she's backing away. "Charlotte, sweetheart."

"Don't start with that, Cecelia. She's got to see reason. Sit down, Charlotte." My father is all business. He looks at me, right in the eyes. "Now. Tell Ms. Liston what happened, so that we can figure a way to get you out of this within the year."

"Dad, I did. I was walking back, and someone grabbed me, and that's how I got this bruise!" I try to show him my neck and shoulder, but he looks away when I pull my collar back. "They... did something to me, and I blacked out. When they let me go, I was in the house, and there was blood, and the police were at the door."

"There was no evidence of drugs in your system, Charlotte." Ms. Liston has adopted the tone of a caring grandmother. This is behavior reserved for people she wants to impress, like my dad. Everyone's at their best around Senator Turner.

"*The police will say you got that from the victim, during the struggle.*" Her voice lilts upward when she says "police," as though she really means "everyone."

"*I'm not lying.*" I will not cry. I will not cry. But my voice still shakes a little. "*You said I could start over! You said you could forgive me. So why won't you believe me?*"

"*That's enough theatrics, Charlotte.*" Dad looks away again. He doesn't hear what I'm saying unless I say what he wants to hear.

I make my voice calm and low. "*I'm not lying.*"

My dad grabs my arm. "*At this point, that doesn't even matter. I know people who will work the lottery, but even I can't help if you're in here.*" He waves at the holding room. "*The only thing that matters is that we get you a deal where you're not locked up next year.*"

My mother is suddenly hysterical. "*Charlotte, please! Please, just do this.*"

"*Mom—*"

"*For Pete's sake, Charlotte. You're killing your mother. Is that what you want?*"

Mom clasps her hands in front of her chest. "*Just make it through this, and we can start over again when we get to the Ark, as a family. Everything will be different there. I promise.*"

There is a long pause. The three of them surround my chair, looming over me. They are the only people on Earth who care enough to be here, even if one of them is getting paid for it. This is my last chance.

"*Okay. I'll take the deal.*"

But West will never forgive me.

There was no way to have known, then, that the judge would not respond to a plea deal. That he was sick and tired of seeing the same kids, year after year. We couldn't have known that he hated the thought of a girl like me making it off the planet while decent people stayed behind to die. It wasn't a fair trade at all.

I hated him because I understood him.

I hated him because he was right.

Twelve

A holding room is a holding room, whether you're caught shoplifting at a pawn shop or hanging out at the precinct after breaking into the nicest house on the block. Or on a massive bioship thousands of miles from the shattered remains of your home planet, as the case may be. It's usually a desk, a chair, and a screen. If you've seen one, you've seen them all. So once the officers had dropped me off, I was in familiar territory. The door slammed shut, and my mind did a kind of reboot, so that I was more like my normal self. I could think, could function.

I could get out of this.

They never came in right away; they liked to let the tension build first. It was meant to be stressful, and it probably was, for a first-timer. But for me, it was kinda calming. I'd have a few minutes to get my act together while they informed their supervisor what a bad girl I'd been.

The first step was to put thoughts of my mother out of my mind. There was a terrible, low pull deep in my chest, but I told myself I'd have to deal with that later. After her sacrifice, I couldn't let myself get locked up in the first ten minutes. I had to focus.

I caught snippets of the conversation outside the door. The woman who'd pinched me was taking a good bit of heat off her superior, despite the fact that she had nothing to do with my presence on the ship. Her responses were a lot softer than his shouting, but she didn't seem to be getting much in anyway. Soon, the only voice I could hear was his. "What do you mean she's not... *I'm* not telling the CO that we're short one medic... Well, she's married to the blasted...; how do *you* think he's going to take the news that his wife...?"

Ugh. He was not going to like me at all.

Hopefully, he wouldn't have to deal with me for long. Most officers make one or two mistakes during each arrest. The trick is to figure out what those mistakes will be before the officer does. For example, I already knew that Mr. Charming outside wasn't going to come in here totally clear-headed. That was mistake number one. I also knew he was too worked up to leave me for someone else to deal with. So what I really needed was something to throw him off-balance and keep him that way until I could disappear.

Mistake number two was in the drawer of the desk, where someone had left a screen stem, the kind they give school children when they're learning how to write letters on their screens. I never saw the point of learning to write by hand, even though my parents had insisted. But sure, all those lessons would come in handy if I were ever marooned on a desert island and had to scratch out a poem in the sand, or something.

But I could totally use a stem. First of all, they're pliable enough that you can sharpen the tips, if you use enough force. And second of all, they're easy to conceal. I had worked my cuffed hands from behind me to in front of me almost before they'd closed the door behind them. The desk was bolted to the ground, so I stuck the end of the stem under one of the feet of my chair, and sat down. Hard. Then I stood back up and sat back down on it again. I twisted the stem a little and repeated the process. Soon, I had myself a weapon.

Ideally, I'd have liked to sharpen the stem to the thickness of a paperclip. Then I could have dealt with the handcuffs. But realistically, there wasn't time. Mr. Charming would want to get in here while his anger was hot. And sadly, a ship like this wouldn't have any paper, much less actual paperclips, so I'd have to deal with the handcuffs another time.

I felt a little weird thinking about paper. It reminded me that I'd never see a tree again.

I had perfected my next trick four years earlier, at the tender age of thirteen. As far as I could see, adults thought there were only two kinds of kids in the world: good ones and bad ones. Bad ones were like animals. They were a drain on the good people of society, and they could never be reformed, because they didn't feel remorse. You could lock them away and toss out the key, and you've basically done the world a favor. Good ones were like... the opposite, I guess. The main thing was to look remorseful, like you'd really learned your lesson. I closed my eyes and pulled my face down as far as I could, letting some of my hair fall over my cheek. Soon, the tears came. When the door opened, I was ready.

He announced his presence by tossing his screen onto the table. It clattered, and I let myself appear startled. This was not a good first sign. Officers who treated the stuff in the room roughly were not likely to show a lot of sympathy for me, either. I slid the sharpened screen stem up my sleeve.

"Why don't we start with your name. I know it's not *Doctor* Cecelia Turner," he spat.

"Mag—"

"And I know it isn't Magda Notting, either, since this expired some time ago." He flipped Magda's license onto the table next to the screen. I raised my head long enough to look at them both, and immediately regretted it. The screen was still open to the picture of Mom.

He barely flinched when he saw my tears.

So much for that.

"I want you to take a good look at this photo. Because I'm not sure I'll get the chance to make this clear to you during the trial." He shoved the screen into my chest, right up under my chin. "This is the face of the person you killed. Her name was Cecelia Turner."

Just like that, my tears weren't an act. I couldn't afford to lose control again. I forced myself to keep breathing while he pressed on. "When you took this woman's pass, you took her life. You took someone's wife. Someone's mother. Someone's doctor. So you think about that when they're putting you down."

I looked up in surprise.

He smirked. "Yeah, we got the death penalty up here, but there's only one crime we give it for, and that's stealing someone else's spot. A life for a life. You go before the Tribune next week. And it doesn't matter you're a minor. There's no one over forty on the whole ship. You're practically middle-aged, here. I got nothing else to say to you."

I had to keep him in the room.

He reached for the screen with one arm, but partially turned toward the door at the same time. That was my chance. I wouldn't get another. I raised my arms, which were still cuffed together, and smashed an elbow into the screen. A web of broken glass emanated from the point of impact.

He gave an ugly laugh. "You stupid girl. You've got to be kidding me."

He yanked the screen away, drew it back, and slammed it across my face.

I had not seen that coming. There was a beat, then the pain spread through my cheek and jaw. I kept my eyes down and tried not to react. He seemed like the type who would keep going until he got a reaction, and that was what I needed.

"You know how much these cost to replace up here? It's not like we've got some kind of factory!"

He raised the screen again, but this time, I was ready. I slipped the stem out from my sleeve and into my waiting fist. From there, it was only a moment before I had it lodged in his thigh. I gave it a hard twist, for good measure, though that part probably wasn't necessary.

He let out a roar, but I was already on my feet and at the door before he crouched to kneel on his good leg, cradling the protruding stem in both his hands.

By the time he'd formulated some kind of ridiculous command, which I'm assuming went something like "Get back here," I was halfway down the hallway.

And that was the last I saw of Mr. Charming.

The hallway was narrow, but well lit. I couldn't afford to stay here, what with the handcuffs and all. Those tended to stand out. Normally, they wouldn't have presented much of a challenge, but I didn't have my tools with me.

I shouldered through a door at the end of the hallway at full speed and found myself in a stairwell. I figured my best bet was to find another level. If this floor was dedicated to passenger processing, then I'd be less suspicious on a different one. And if the OPT docked with an airlock on this level, then I was probably either near the top or the bottom of the Ark.

That was assuming you could have a "top" and a "bottom" in space, where there wasn't even an up or a down. The thought disoriented me, but I pushed it from my mind and forced my legs to carry me down the first flight of steps.

The other thing that bothered me was the feeling that my body weighed more than it should. The sensation was slight, at first, but the more I ran, the more I felt it. My legs were drawn to the ground. My head was heavy on my neck. Within a few minutes, I had to fight the urge to lie down flat. I shouldered through a door at the end of the hallway at full speed.

Soon, my entire body was on fire. Seriously, it's not like I ran track or anything, so I expected to be out of breath, but this *hurt*. There was no time to stop. I threw myself onto the next platform down. And then the next, and the next.

I made it fewer than ten flights before I flat-out had to stop moving. My limbs threatened mutiny, and my lungs were in danger of bursting. I allowed myself to sit for a few minutes, doing nothing more taxing than breathing in and out.

Until I heard a door slide shut a few floors below. I shot up silently, all thoughts of a mid-chase nap vanished from my mind. Should I keep going? Or should I try one of the doors?

Doors made noise. Stairs it was. I took the next few flights as though propelled by invisible wings. I always loved the getaway. The adrenaline, the raw battle of speed and wits. But now that my pursuers had mentioned a trial and execution in my near future, the thrill was different. Sharper. Definitely less fun.

Not long after that, I lost count of what level I'd made it to. All the doors were unmarked, so I just kept descending. I slowed my pace a little and didn't get out of breath again.

After awhile, I had no idea how long I'd been climbing, but I was positive that I weighed more. At some point, the doors went from white to blue. The staircase was wider and much taller, with every blue level clocking in at about twice the height of the white ones. At last, I reached the lowest level. I felt my head pushing down on my spine as I stepped through the final door, and smiled.

I was in a cargo hold.

Dark bins rose up all around me. I was surrounded by Earth's final exports. I'd seen places like this before, when Kip, Cassa, and I did jobs at warehouses full of crates being imported from some place or another. I wandered through the aisles until distant voices stopped me in my tracks. When they got louder, and closer, I sprinted heavily to the far wall and got to work on the seal of the last crate I could find.

The bin was locked with a newer model seal, but its mechanism was patterned after ones I'd encountered before. If I'd had my gear, it would have been cake. As it was, I needed a little more time. A moment later, I heard footsteps, and the familiar thrill of the game quickened my fingers. Other than the getaway, this was always my favorite part of a job. The seal yielded well before the steps got too close.

I closed the door behind me soft as a whisper and stood on the other side until the steps died away. The crates had been designed for people to walk in and inspect the goods. This was ideal; it meant there'd be a light somewhere, and probably a vent. Assuming the cargo hold remained pressurized from space, it would make a fair hideout, for the time being.

I ran my hand along the doorframe and located the lightpad about halfway up. I tapped it twice, and my hideout was illuminated. My breath caught in my throat.

The bin was lined to the teeth with row after row of shiny black assault weapons. The kind you use in the military.

The kind of military that wasn't supposed to exist anymore.

I stepped away from the door and touched the nearest gun, barely resting my fingers on the barrel, and let out a low whistle. There was enough here to arm a hundred soldiers.

The kind of soldiers that weren't supposed to exist anymore.

Apparently not everyone had bought into the brave new ideals for society under the Treaty of Phoenix, because whoever owned this crate meant business.

Suddenly, it was all too much.

Earth was gone. Everything I'd ever known no longer existed. West and my father wanted nothing to do with me, and I was wanted for my mother's murder. A sharp coldness sliced through my chest. I was frozen for a second, then gasping for air. My mother. She'd given me her pass. After I'd given her a lifetime of sleepless nights and the kind of heartache that makes a person stop smiling at the dinner table.

I sank to the ground in front of the door and closed my eyes. A moment later, I sat back up and tapped off the light. I couldn't afford to waste it, or to give away my position.

I was cold, sore, and unbelievably hungry, but for some reason, I didn't move. I just stared into the darkness, vaguely aware that time was passing.

Years ago, on my first night in lockup, I had cried and cried. The next day, I told myself that I could no longer think the Thought that had made me so weak. I had made my choices, and I could no longer give it purchase in my mind. But now, the Thought crept back in, stronger than ever, until it would not be denied: *I want my mom.*

And I thought that maybe I'd been wrong, years before, when I decided that things were better for her when I was in juvy. Maybe she'd missed me.

I missed her.

After what must have been hours, I moved to brush the hair out of my face. I had forgotten about the handcuffs, and they jerked into my wrist and scraped across the bruise on my cheek. The pain helped bring me back to myself.

I tapped the light on, and the guns glinted into view once again. I could hear no noises outside the bin, so I relaxed a little and tried to collect my thoughts.

Someone was planning to raise an army. Or already had.

Armies meant a lot of things. Power, control. Worst of all, war.

Under the Treaty of Phoenix, weapons were banned. Even officers of the peace could carry nothing stronger than a stunner. There was never supposed to be war again. With only half a million survivors, humanity couldn't afford to keep killing its own. We were supposed to terraform and colonize a new planet, and we needed to get there intact.

I needed to leave here. I needed food. I shoved my fist into the seal.

Nothing happened.

Great. The lock mechanism was on the outside, of course. You wouldn't smuggle a cache of illegal arms onto a space ship, then leave it lying around unprotected, so I couldn't say I was surprised.

The walls were lined with assault rifles. I didn't recognize the weapons that filled the center aisles. They were some kind of aerodynamic rockets about the length of my arm, but there was nothing resembling a launcher anywhere in sight. The middle of the bin held an enormous black box labeled

"North America/Sector 7/Cargo Level/Bin 54/Produce." I smirked. Like this was really full of apples. Or spinach. I tried as hard as I could to wedge the lid off, but it was too heavy. It was likely just another bunch of weapons, anyway.

What I really needed was a weapon I could conceal, like a sidearm. Obviously, I couldn't run around with a rifle that wasn't even supposed to exist. Surely whoever was running this operation hadn't planned to put the soldiers within rifle's range of their targets, and not equip them with handguns for when the targets got closer. I kept searching.

I trotted up one aisle and down the other, until I got to the next-to-last row.

"Bingo," I said out loud.

The last row was full of handguns. They were slightly different than the ones I was used to seeing. I guessed military-grade weapons were slightly different from street weapons, but they'd have a fair bit in common. I lifted the nearest one from its hanger pins and turned it over in my hand. Its clip was already in place.

I tapped the lights off inside the bin again, so that once I blasted the seal off the door I wouldn't be smack in the middle of the only lit area of a dark cargo hold and surrounded by contraband. I cocked the gun easily and used my other hand to guide the barrel to the locked seal, but something made me pause before pulling the trigger.

I had done it. I had made it out of prison and all the way to the OPT. Heck, I'd made it to the Ark, and if I kept it up, I could maybe, just maybe, live long enough to land on Eirenea. There was no reason to believe I couldn't. And assuming I could make my way to the residential quarters and find some way to blend in, no one here would ever know about my past. I was standing at the edge of a new life.

Except, nothing was new. I was born into a world wracked by bloodshed, and even after everyone else had made nice, I'd been in jail, where we'd had our own brand of war to wage. So you couldn't blame me if I had a low tolerance for helplessness, a condition that, in my experience, tended to present itself primarily to idiots who hadn't thought they'd need a weapon.

I tested the waistband of my pants. The steel of the gun was cold against my stomach, but the sensation didn't last. It warmed to my body soon enough.

I pulled the gun out again, weighing it. If I made it through this, I owed my life to my mother, twice over, and to Meghan, and even Isaiah. And they were all dead.

Suddenly, the gun felt heavy in my hand.

I looked around blindly. Though I couldn't see them, I was surrounded by instruments of death. In my new life, there was a war coming. In all our lives: our rebirth as a species would be marked with conflict. I would have to pick a side. I had always thought the world was full of those who were weak, and those who avoided weakness by any means possible. The ones who came out on top, and the suckers who never knew what hit them.

But maybe there was another possibility, one I hadn't considered before. Maybe I could be strong without hurting anyone else. I took a step back, keeping the gun aimed at the same spot, and pulled the trigger.

The bullet exploded from the gun. I was more prepared for the kick than the sound, which echoed through the enclosed space of the bin. I winced, then frowned. The seal remained intact.

I leaned in closer and fiddled with the mechanism. I must have missed my mark, probably because of the handcuffs. I engaged the safety and flipped the gun around, unwilling to risk the attention another gunshot could draw, then brought the butt down on the seal. It took a few blows, but the lock slowly gave way.

I laid the gun underneath the row of rifles and slipped out into the darkness.

Thirteen

The hallway ahead of me was about the last thing I expected. Gone were the steel-gray walls, the perfunctory stretch of dark carpet underfoot. This corridor was decorated with cloth wallpaper, like some sort of stateroom. Delicate chandeliers hung from the ceiling at regular intervals, and a thick, intricately patterned rug stretched as far as I could see.

I'd climbed enough stairs to know that gravity was much less oppressive on this level, which seemed to add to its opulence. I spared another moment to take it all in, then pressed forward. My first order of business was to find food.

The door to the stairwell locked shut behind me, but several of the doors on this level were open. I walked as casually as I could manage with my hands cuffed in front of me. At least if you saw me from behind, you wouldn't know anything was off.

About halfway down the length of the hallway, I found a sort of commissary. No one was there, and I wondered whether they were on break, or if this part of the Ark hadn't begun operations yet. Maybe they planned to staff it with people who'd come in on the final OPTs.

Either way, someone had already taken the time to stock it with food, so I helped myself. There was a row of chips, and I tore into the first bag I came to, happily munching away while I looked for more food. I had just spotted a loaf of sliced bread and a basket of red and green apples when a small voice stopped me cold.

"Woah. How many ration cards does your pass hold? Better be at least four."

I whirled around to see a young girl in a blue uniform with a matching apron. She couldn't have been more than twelve years old. I managed a smile.

"Sorry. I was just about to—" I broke off and cringed as she noticed my handcuffs. Her narrow eyes widened.

"You, you're the—" she said. Her glance darted toward the counter.

This was where the gun would have come in handy. Wave it around, and people usually did what you said. Instead, I'd have to use my winning personality to keep her from pressing whatever alarm button she was inching toward. I held my cuffed hands up, as if to say that I wasn't trying to hide anything from her. "Wait! Please. Don't do that."

The girl looked from me to the counter one last time, then broke into a sprint. Great.

The alarm went off about the time I reached the hallway, sans chips. It occurred to me that if everyone believed that no guns existed anymore, criminals were going to have a harder go of things.

I rounded the first turn, heading away from the stairwell. By now, it would be swarming with officers. If I could get to the far side of this level, I could maybe find another staircase and get sufficiently lost again. Sure enough, a big sliding panel at the end of the hallway came into view when I'd gone about fifty more feet. That had to lead to a staircase. It was still at least two hundred feet away.

Several doors hissed shut as I hustled past, but a few people left their doors open. I shot a quick look through each open door, and the rooms I saw were all the same. Dark carpets, nice desks, bookshelves. People in black uniforms, which I hadn't seen before. I guess not everyone on the Ark wore blue, after all. Some even ducked out of their offices to get a good look, and at least two popped open com pads and started barking out my description and location to whoever was on the other end of the line.

I had nearly reached the sliding panel when it hit me.

No one was chasing me. Their faces were calm, if curious. Everyone already knew what I had just figured out: there was no way I was getting out of this one. I slapped the button next to the sliding panel as hard as I could, but the door didn't budge. Of course. It was locked. I had nowhere to go.

One by one, the faces in the hall disappeared behind office doors, which slid shut and softly clicked into place. I pressed the button again and again, but it was no use. I was a rat at the end of a maze.

A voice came over the loudspeaker, male this time. "Stay where you are. You are under arrest. Citizens, remain behind locked doors. You are not in danger. The suspect will be apprehended shortly."

My breath came harder. There was no way they'd let me escape again.

The cops swarmed in from the turn in the hallway. They were dressed in blue, and they carried long black weapons. I was surprised they'd bring their guns out into the open, but then the tip of one of the weapons buzzed, and a white bolt of electricity leapt out. It was a stunner, not a gun. And it was going to hurt.

I backed into the wall nearest me and slid to the ground, forcing myself to keep breathing. They were a hundred yards away, then fifty. I raised my hands to show I wasn't going to resist, but the look in their eyes told me it wouldn't make any difference.

"Don't move," said the nearest one. He was totally composed, almost relaxed. The tip of the stunner let out another crack, and I pressed my lips together to keep from screaming.

At that moment, a sucking *swish* sounded behind me, followed by a deep voice in mid-conversation. "—tell *me* what needs to happen. I'm going to personally oversee—" The owner of the voice strode through the huge door panel at my side, stopping short when he saw the small army of cops who were trying to arrest me. He, too, was dressed in an all-black uniform. His face was unforgettable: steel blue eyes and immaculately clean-shaven skin, framed by a shock of silver hair. He was easily fifty or sixty years old—well over the forty-year age limit for passage on the Ark.

But all I could think about was the panel. It was open, and the only thing between me and the next hallway was the man in black.

In the split second it took for his eyes to move from the cops to the ground at his feet where I sat, I rolled past him and into the next hallway. I was running before I even stood up.

Behind me, he barked out orders: all the usual "Get her"s and "Move it"s that you'd expect. I knew better than to look back. I was small but fast, and this new hallway had myriad turns and corners. It was also much darker, lit only by chandeliers every five or ten yards. Each twist of the corridor was marked by a new design of wallpaper: red damasks and antique silver patterns raced past in a blur. It was as though an old-timey dining room, like the ones with china and stuff that you see in movies, had been stretched out into a labyrinth. If I could get enough space between me and the cops, I might never feel the stunner on my back. I shuddered mid-stride and tried to keep my path as erratic as possible.

Another, louder alarm sounded seconds later. I began pressing the buttons next to the doors, but nothing opened. Soon, I knew, whatever personnel was in the area would start to pop out of the rooms to see what was going on. Then they'd report on my location, and I'd be back in the frying pan quick enough.

I heard a group of voices behind me, including the silver-haired man, and I allowed myself a quick glance backward. There was no one in sight yet, but they were getting close.

I had just turned forward again when my body slammed into a solid mass of muscle and black cotton. Strong arms wrapped around me, gripping me by the shoulders, and this time, I couldn't stop the scream that followed.

Fourteen

"Shut up! Seriously." His tone was urgent and low.

Where had I heard that voice before? It didn't matter. What mattered was getting away. Surviving. I had to think fast.

My assailant had pinned me against his chest, facing him. My head reached the level of his shoulders, and one hand was still cuffed. I clenched my hands together into a big fist and slammed them up into his groin as hard as I could.

"*Unphh...* what the—" His grip on my shoulders vanished as he jerked back, giving me a face full of his short blond hair. I used that opportunity to bring my double-fist down onto his neck, just above the right shoulder.

"Wait! Don't," he grunted. I didn't stick around to hear the rest of his protests. The cops were closing in, their rapid footsteps muffled by the thick carpet in the area.

I took two more corners at lightning speed and came upon a room with a wide-open door. A quick glance inside told me that it was unoccupied, or that the owner was in the bathroom at the far back. Either way, it was good enough.

I darted in, hitting the button to close the door with my elbow while scanning every inch for a good hiding place.

Wait, no. For a weapon. First things first.

The room was beautiful, but not as ornate as the hallway décor had suggested. There was a kitchenette to my right, a black leather sofa to my left, and behind those, a yellow desk and a huge unmade bed. There were clothes lying on the ground: sneakers, jeans, dirty boxer-briefs, and of course, a few rumpled uniforms. The walls were painted steel blue, but covered with tons of neatly framed photographs depicting everyday scenes of life on Earth: a flock of gulls on the beach at sunset, a bird's eye view of a traffic jam at night, a forest at first light. There was an entire area of one wall devoted to flowers, which shared a border with a mural of people's faces.

It was a shrine to what we had lost.

I breathed slowly, trying to take everything in, but caught myself soon enough. It wouldn't be long before the cops swept the whole wing, going door-to-door. I couldn't go down without a fight, so I tore my attention from the scenes on the walls and continued my hunt for a weapon. The desk was completely bare, so I ran to the kitchen. There were a few packed boxes, but the drawers were still empty. No knives.

Time was running out. I'd bought myself a few minutes by closing the door. The soldiers would have no way of knowing it had been open moments earlier and had probably run past. But when they didn't find me, they'd have to conduct a thorough search. I'd need to be well out of sight by then, and preferably armed with something other than my wits. I glanced around, but my choices were distressingly limited. The closet, the bathroom, or under the bed.

My first instinct, the bed, was blocked by a long black case. I had seen cases like this when Kip and I had run the occasional job-for-hire on behalf of a mid-level criminal. Someone way up the food chain from us, for example. People like that had their everyday guns, and then they had the special stuff, which they kept in cases like these.

I had hit the jackpot.

I eased the latches off the case as quickly as possible and lifted the lid.

Then I frowned. Nestled in black foam was a long, shiny wooden tube, which tapered at one end and opened out on the other. It was scored every few inches with silver clasps. Or maybe they were buttons.

This wasn't a carefully packaged weapon. It was some kind of musical instrument. I groaned, but lifted it out of the foam anyway. At least I could use it as a club.

The door panel swished open behind me. My stomach dropped.

I threw myself behind the wardrobe, nearly tripping over a wad of t-shirts in the process.

The panel sucked closed. So the owner of the room was here, not the cops.

"Hey. I know you're back there. I just saw you."

Oh, awesome. So much for being stealthy.

I cleared my throat. "Don't come any closer. I have a weapon."

The guy who had grabbed me in the hallway came into view. When he saw me, he lifted his hands, as though to surrender. And either it was my imagination, or he was also suppressing a chuckle. "Seriously? You're threatening me with an oboe?"

"Just… just put down your stunner."

"Yeah, sure," he said, smiling slightly. He unclipped his stunner and placed it on the ground, then slid it toward me. "Don't, like, play me to sleep or something." He shook his head. "I honestly don't see how you've made it this far. It's impressive, really."

I rolled my eyes. "Right, 'cause you're so good at your job, too. How's the neck?"

He rubbed his shoulder before responding. "Fine, thanks. I see you found a change of clothing."

I frowned, then squinted at him. "Eren?"

He raised his eyebrows slightly, then settled himself on the couch with a sigh. "You didn't recognize me? That explains the nutshot."

This conversation was making no sense. "Nut—oh. Right. Well, you were asking for it."

"Sure. One minute I'm standing there, trying to figure out why the alarm was going off, then the next minute a highly dangerous fugitive in handcuffs runs into me and tries to leave me crippled for life. Definitely my bad."

Something about the way he said "highly dangerous" made me feel less remorseful about hitting him. "*You* grabbed *me*!"

"Fair enough. But you caught me off-guard and knocked the wind out of me, and plus, I wanted to see if it was you."

"What do you mean, me?"

"Look. I know your name isn't Magda, or whatever. And when I scanned your pass on the boat, it came up as belonging to a medical doctor with special clearance. So either you're a *lot* older than you look, or you had someone else's pass."

"It's… it's not what you think."

"I know."

"How could you possibly know that?"

"I just do. You don't seem the type to steal someone else's spot."

"You don't know that. You don't know anything about me."

"Maybe, but I know you're young, and I saw you save that kid on the boat. And I know that there are a lot more ways to get a valid pass than to steal one."

I cringed. I wasn't sure why I had pulled the boy back onto the deck, but I definitely wasn't the one who had saved him. That distinction belonged to the soldier who'd given up his starpass at the gate. But I couldn't explain that to Eren. I needed him to think I was a good person. It was my best shot at not getting turned in.

"If you knew I had the wrong pass, then why did you help me?"

"The doors were about to close, so it's not like I could change what had already happened. Let's just say I had seen enough of people dying for one lifetime."

I didn't have anything to say to that, so I lowered the oboe in silence. The stunner lay on the ground at my feet, but I didn't feel like picking it up.

"By the way, the officers will be here any minute. We should probably find you a place to hide. They're not going to be threatened by your musical prowess."

Eren stood and fished a thin piece of metal from his pocket. He moved toward me, stepping over the t-shirts, and reached for my wrist.

I jerked away. "Give it to me. I can handle it."

He looked surprised, but lifted the cuff key into the space between us. I felt myself blush a little.

"Sorry," I muttered. The cuffs snapped off, and I tossed them into his open wardrobe, on top of a pile of black uniforms. "You're quite the housekeeper."

He snorted. "Been a busy day, what with the manhunt for a cold-blooded criminal, and all. I think we should try the cabinets."

"In the kitchen?"

"Above the bookcase."

I looked around the room again, and saw that the far wall,

which held floor-to-ceiling shelves, actually had a long, flat storage space on top.

"They're totally going to look there."

"Okay, Miss Expert in police procedure. Where do you propose to hide?"

I bit my lip for a moment. "In the bed."

"They're going to look under the bed before they get to the cabinet ten feet in the air."

"No, not under the bed. *In* it." I hopped onto the mattress, which gave way under my hips instantly. I could not hide my surprise. "Holy cow. It's like a cloud."

Eren did not respond to this observation. His expression was pinched.

I smiled. "You don't trust me."

"I'm not even going to consider the ways in which that statement is absurd."

I raised an eyebrow at him before sliding underneath the enormous comforter, stretching out my legs and leaving my arms at my side. "Now bunch it up around me. Make me look like a wrinkle."

"A wrinkle. Okay." He must have been at least somewhat impressed, because the next thing I knew, he was carefully tucking the soft material all around my body. I was enveloped in feathers and darkness. This had to be my most comfortable hiding place ever. He was even more delicate around my head, sweeping my hair up and laying it lightly next to my neck. I was surprised that anyone wearing a uniform could be that gentle.

"Okay. Just don't move," he said, sounding tense.

"Um, duh."

"Okay."

"Stop saying 'okay.'"

"Ok— *fine*. They're coming."

"Relax. This will work. And put your stunner back on. And hide the cuffs."

I heard a click as he fastened the weapon onto his belt. "So, what *is* your name?"

"None of your business."

He gave a small snort. "I think at this point—"

I sighed roughly, cutting him off. "Why does it even matter? Just call me whatever you want."

"I want to call you by your name."

"I don't have one."

"Everybody has a name."

"No they don't. Not me."

"How is that even possible?"

"You really want to have this argument right now?"

"I really want to know your name."

"Well, like I said. I don't have one."

"Everyone has one!"

"Agree to disagree," I said in a bored tone.

"Fine," he said.

"Fine," I snapped back.

And then we heard the knock.

Fifteen

"Come on in," said Eren. I heard a soft smack as he hit the door button, followed by the hiss of the panel as it opened.

"Sorry, sir," came the first cop. "We're about to go door-to-door on the hall, and your room was flagged because the door was opened after the alarm went off. Protocol. You understand." The last statement sounded a little like a question, as though the cop were hoping Eren understood, instead of assuming he would.

"Some kind of trouble?"

"Same perp as before, but the Commander upgraded the threat to Level Three."

Eren laughed. "Level Three? I understood she was a stowaway. Now she's some kind of terrorist?"

"Yes, sir. Apparently she used deadly force on a guardian in the receiving dock, and there's evidence she might have brought some contraband from... down below. So we're to assume she's armed and dangerous."

"Really," Eren said dryly.

"Well, Commander says we can't be too careful. Same ending for her, either way. I guess you haven't seen her." Now he sounded downright deferential, and I had the momentary thought that maybe things would be different on the Ark to how they had been on Earth. I'd never known a cop to be so polite, except when they spoke to my father. Then I remembered the weapons cache in the cargo bin, and dismissed the thought entirely.

"No."

"We're required to search your quarters, sir, because of the flag. Do you mind?"

"Not at all." His tone was light, but I heard the note of tension in his voice. I slowed my breathing until my lungs began to burn.

There was the sound of several footsteps, followed by a few grunts, and I guessed that at least one of the cops was unused to a lot of crouching and standing.

"Nothing to report, sir," said an unfamiliar voice.

"Good. Fine. We'll leave you alone, sir. Sorry for the inconvenience. Everyone's been on edge lately, after what happened to Ark Five."

"Unbelievable tragedy."

"Yes, sir. Terrorism has never been this easy. Assuming it wasn't an accident, that is."

"Terrorism? I heard it was a leak of some kind."

"They're still looking into it, sir."

"Have there been any demands? Is anyone claiming responsibility?" Eren asked.

"Not yet, sir."

"Let me know when this, uh, threat is uncovered," said Eren.

"Oh, you will. Commander says we're going to announce the apprehension publicly, and broadcast the verdict as well." Eren didn't respond audibly, and the officer cleared his throat. "To show we're running things according to the Treaty."

"Of course. A good plan."

"Yes, sir. I'll keep you posted."

There was a swish as the door closed, and a moment of silence.

"All clear," said Eren, in a much quieter tone.

I allowed a moment to suck in as much air as I wanted, then sat up on the bed and chucked the covers aside, grinning. "Didn't I tell you? Easy as cake. Which end of the hall do you think they'll start on? I need to get moving in the opposite direction."

Eren was still staring at the door. "No. No way." He turned to me, and I saw that he was upset about something.

"What do you mean, 'no'?"

"You can't leave here. You're a Level Three threat, for crying... They'll have the entire floor locked down till they find you."

I frowned. I had no intention of staying put. Not that he'd be able to make me.

He continued, oblivious to my expression. "What were they talking about, before? How is it even possible to get a weapon past the bioscanner?"

"It's not, as far as I know. But someone sure did. I found an entire cargo bin full of assault rifles in the—"

"Assault rifles? That can't be true." He rubbed his neck and squinted at me, as though evaluating what he saw. I got the impression that he was trying to decide whether he'd been wrong to help me after all.

"No, I'm serious. There were rows and rows of them. It's in the cargo hold."

"You've been to the cargo hold? That's not exactly a safe place to be."

"Why not?"

"It's about forty levels down. Gravity is too strong there."

125

"Sure, there's that. And also *guns*."

"Mag—I mean, whoever you are—you have to understand. Those kinds of weapons aren't allowed anymore."

"Yeah. I kinda got that from the five thousand or so announcements since the Treaty was signed. Didn't stop someone from outfitting a small army up here."

He continued to stare at me. "Agree to disagree."

I snorted. "Fine."

"But," he said, brightening with the change of subject. "You still have to stay here for now. And I'm hungry. Grilled cheese?"

"Um, definitely. That sounds delightful." I could eat, then split. After all, I did need to keep my strength up.

He smiled and turned toward the kitchen. I stood and began arranging the sheets, suddenly conscious of the fact that I was hanging out in the bed of a strange guy.

"So. You don't have a name. Where did you grow up? Or is that classified, too?"

I considered that for a moment, then decided it would be safe to answer. "Manhattan, mostly." I didn't see the need to mention the fact that I'd probably done most of my "growing up" in various juvy halls, depending on how you defined the phrase.

"Ah."

"You?"

"Everywhere. Nowhere in particular." He produced some kind of blade and began popping the seals off the boxes stacked in the kitchenette.

"Military brat?"

"Yeah. Can't say I'll miss it too much. Before that, we had a farm."

"A *farm*?! Like, pigs and chickens and stuff? Did you milk cows?" I don't know why that struck me as funny. It wasn't

126

hard to picture Eren baling hay in the hot sun, or whatever it is you do on a farm. He definitely had the build for it.

"Goats, actually."

"You milked a *goat*?" I had seen pictures of farms in children's books. Farms were full of color. They had grass everywhere, and manmade wooden fences, and bright green trees full of red apples. Not a bad place for a childhood. A sight better than Manhattan, I was sure.

"We raised them."

I squinted. Real farms, like the ones Eren was talking about, had been illegal for several decades. They weren't efficient enough to warrant the space they used, unlike modern meat and produce factories. "How did your dad pull that off?"

"It was my mother, actually. It had been in the family for so many years that they had to let her keep it. She loved it more than anything, until she met my dad. We lived on the farm until he went into the service." His tone was light but careful, as though he wanted to tell me about the farm, and his mother, but wasn't sure how I'd react.

"She sold it?"

"She'd have done anything for him. He knew that." The way he talked about his mom was like hiking through the sand on a beach. Heavy, wearying work, but worth it, because of the view. He almost smiled, but there was bitterness in this memory, too. "I just never understood why he asked her to." He took a moment, cleared his throat. "She died the next year."

"I'm sorry."

He paused again, holding the pot he'd unpacked in midair. "They both made their choices. And I got along with the other kids on the bases. I mean, it was a different group every time we moved, and my mom was long gone by then. I didn't have siblings. I just wanted…"

I didn't press him to finish the sentence. Instead, I took extra care in making the bed, tucking the end of the dark blue comforter under the enormous mattress and pulling the far corners until every wrinkle had disappeared. When I glanced back at Eren, he'd located a frying pan and was rummaging through the icer for cheese. I took a small breath. "You wanted something permanent. You wanted to belong to just one place."

He closed the door of the icer and stared at me. I got the same feeling as before, like he was trying to decide what to think about me. Finally, he nodded. "Yeah. One place. I assume you want double cheese on this."

"You assume correctly, *sir*."

He laughed. "They say that to everyone."

"I can promise you they don't." I suppressed the urge to touch the bruise on my face. "In my entire life, a cop has never called me *ma'am*. I'd probably die of shock if they did."

"I'll be sure to steer clear of it, then. And we prefer "guardian," up here, *Miss*."

I giggled. "Well, that changes everything, then."

"What's your problem with cops, anyway?" He plopped a healthy-sized pat of butter into the skillet and looked back at me while it sizzled. "Oh, right. But, before all this."

I picked up the small stack of plates he'd left next to the boxes and chose a spot for them in the empty cabinets. "Let's just say, I've been told I have a problem with authority."

"You? Impossible." Eren laid a piece of bread in the buttery pan and began stacking layers of cheese on top of it. I inhaled deeply, allowing my stomach to growl. The smell was heavenly.

"I can see why that would be hard for you to believe."

He shrugged and flipped the sandwich. "Some people are naturally rebellious. I just never saw the point. Nothing wrong with that."

"That *is* the point. If you don't question the rules, they'll just make you do whatever they want."

"Who exactly is 'they'? And why is that such a bad thing? Rules are meant to protect us."

"Some rules, maybe. Other rules only protect a small group."

"Like what?"

"Like, rules about who can use a museum, who can apply to public colleges." I stopped for a moment, filling the silence by clanging a package of silverware into an open drawer. "Who gets to go on the Ark, for example."

"You don't seem like the type who cares a lot about museums."

"Maybe I would have, if I'd been allowed to go there."

"And the Ark. They tried to make it as fair as possible. It's not like they could save everybody."

"Fine. But they could have saved more than they did."

Eren looked pained. "I can't really argue that. It's like, you can always fit one more person. I guess they just had to draw the line somewhere. But they did everything they could to make the best new society possible."

"That's exactly what I'm talking about. Someone made up all these rules, but no one could really question things because then they wouldn't get a spot on an Ark. And now there's a bin full of weapons in the cargo hold. Makes you wonder what else they're lying about. But as long as everyone just lets it happen, whoever's in charge is only going to get more and more powerful. Doesn't that scare you?"

"Maybe the person in charge isn't so bad."

"Maybe they're worse than you can imagine."

"No, they're not."

"How would you know?"

"I just… I just do. Not everyone is out to get you."

"Spoken like someone who never had his face broken by a 'guardian.'"

Eren stopped for a moment. "A *guardian* did that to you?"

I touched my cheek and regretted bringing it up. He was staring again. "Of course he did."

"I wasn't going to ask. Now I wish I hadn't." He shoved the sandwich onto a plate and looked down at it for a moment. A muscle in his jaw worked back and forth before he spoke again. "What was his name?" His voice was overly casual, as though he wanted me to answer the question without thinking about it.

"I have no idea."

He shook his head and held the plate toward me with a lopsided smile. "*Bon appétit.*"

"Don't mind if I do."

Three grilled cheeses and two apples later, I lay on the couch, groaning. "I've never been so full in my life."

"That last round might have been overkill, in retrospect," said Eren from the armchair.

"Who says *retrospect*?" I tossed a cushion at him.

"I do. You should, too. It's a perfectly good word."

"Hmm. I prefer to look forward."

"Yeah." He glanced around the room, presumably at his photographs. "That makes a lot of sense these days."

"Speaking of which, we need a plan."

"For what?"

"For getting me out of here."

"Uh, not sure if you noticed, but we're on a spaceship. So 'out of here' is *space.*"

130

"No, I mean, out of this area. There are a hundred thousand people on this ship. I should be able to disappear without too much of a problem."

"But it's not safe."

I laughed. "I've never been safe. Ever. And besides, I've been thinking. They're probably going to catch up with me sooner or later. I have to make my peace with that. And the only way to do that is to make something of the time I have left. So I'm going to figure out what's going on with those weapons." I didn't tell him my other goal, which was to find my family. That would lead to too many questions, and I wouldn't have known the answers.

I don't know how long the silence lasted, but when he spoke again, my mind was a thousand miles away, with West. I tried to picture what his new life must be like. In the Ark's biosphere, the air would be hot and humid, like in his beloved greenhouse back home. I wondered whether he'd get into mock battles with his coworkers using garden hoses and spray bottles, the way we used to do. I'd been gone from his life for many years, even though his memory was constantly a part of mine.

I hoped he had someone to goof around with. He was far too serious when left to his own devices.

"Fine."

"Uhn?" I did not open my eyes. I could still see West's face, barely.

"Fine, I'm in."

"In what?"

"I'm going to help you."

Now I was focused. "You don't have to do that."

"I know." He twisted the corner of the cushion I'd thrown at him, then caught himself and tossed it to the ground. "But you're serious. If you found weapons, then we have no idea how far this goes. And they're looking for you, Mag. Really looking. You won't last a minute out there. You need help."

I didn't know whether I agreed with that last part, but he made a good point. I could use a hiding place and a steady supply of food. And hey, if he was willing to help me out, who was I to tell him otherwise? He'd already saved my life twice, though something kept me from acknowledging that out loud.

Plus, he knew way more about the layout of the Ark than I did. Information had been filtered in public, but as a member of the staff, he'd have a wealth of data: everything from the layout of each level to the names of the highest-ranking cops. Or *guardians*. Whatever. I could use this guy, at least for awhile.

I nodded.

"You'll stay here?"

"For now."

"Okay." He looked relieved. "Okay. Partners."

"Partners." I smiled. "So tell me about the ship."

For the next couple of hours, Eren ran through the organization of humanity under the Treaty of Phoenix. I knew far less than I let on, but he patiently explained everything from the beginning.

I perked up when he started talking about Commander Everest, the most powerful person on the North American Ark. In the continent-wide election, Everest had barely edged out the American president, who had then been left behind due to his age.

"And there's almost no one over forty on any of the ships," he finished. "To maximize our reproductive capabilities. Once we land on Eirenea, and get it terraformed and stuff, there's going to be major bonuses for everyone who has a baby."

"That just seems... wrong."

"About the babies? Or the elderly?"

"The elderly. I mean, it's not like forty-five is even old. We lost multiple generations with the swipe of a pen. Doesn't that seem... crazy?"

"The whole thing is weird. But it helps to remember that the main goal in all of this, the *only* goal, is to save the human race. So many people had to die, and there wasn't time to build more Arks, or they would have. The people who wrote the Treaty understood that." He paused, as though trying to process everything all over again. "It's the only thing that kept me going, down below. Just knowing that it all meant something; that we would survive, as a species.

"Anyway. They don't know exactly how long it'll take to get to Eirenea, so they figured young people are their best bet."

I snorted. "They obviously don't know the same young people I do."

He ignored that. "And it matters now more than ever, because of Ark Five."

I recalled that Five was the Afro-Australian Ark. "What do you mean? What happened on Five?"

"You didn't hear? I knew they kept some stuff from the public, but... wow. Where have you been?"

"Doesn't matter. Tell me about Five. Some kind of leak, right? Did they fix it?"

"Magda, the whole thing was destroyed. Either a leak, or a bomb, or something. There *is* no Five."

Sixteen

Four hundred thousand. There are four hundred thousand human beings left. In the entire universe. And none of us can ever go back to Earth again.

I tuned out most of the rest of the conversation after that. He talked about Universal Time, which meant that all of surviving humanity kept to basically the same schedule, sleeping during the night and working during the day, even across different Arks. I guessed that helped save electricity and made communications easier among different ships. There was something about the changes in the education system, which now ended at the age of nine, since ten-year-olds were such an important part of the workforce. Obviously.

I paid more attention when he mentioned that this level housed guardians only. That explained all the offices I'd run past. "So, all the guardians live on this floor? Including Commander Everest?"

"Yeah."

"I think we should start with him."

Eren shook his head. "Uh, no. That doesn't make any sense."

"Sure it does. Who else has the authority to sneak in a bunch of weapons?"

"It makes no sense because it's *his ship*. Why would he want to hurt it?"

"Who said he wanted to hurt the ship itself? I found guns, not bombs. Maybe he just wants to make sure he stays in power permanently. Either way, it's against the Treaty."

"Mag, he'll stay in power anyway. The only way his term can end is if the Tribune calls for a referendum, or we land on Eirenea, in which case the government starts from scratch. Or if he retires, of course."

"I don't know. Sounds to me like he has a lot to lose."

"We can't just start somewhere else? As one half of this partnership, I think the Commander is a waste of time."

I sighed. "Alright. Who else on this level has a high enough clearance to arm an army?"

"We don't know it's an army."

"Eren, wake up. What else do you need guns for? No one's going hunting up here."

"We can't ignore the obvious possibility."

"Which is?"

"Maybe someone wanted to save them for a museum, or something."

I suppressed the urge to roll my eyes. "In which case, they'd need the Commander's permission."

"Can we just focus on someone besides the Commander?"

"Then tell me who else had control over what gets cleared through cargo."

"Okay. There's Jorin Malkin, Head Guardian. He's the Commander's lieutenant, sort of like a second-in-command. The heads of InterArk Comm Con and IntraArk Comm Con probably had access, and maybe Transit Control–"

"Wait, what's a comm con?" I asked.

"IntraArk Communications Control. It governs communications on board this ark. InterArk Comm Con deals with communications from ark to ark."

"Oh. Right. So four other people?"

Eren paused. "And the Tribune Liaison. That's, uh, me."

I knew enough about the Treaty of Phoenix to recognize the reference to the Tribune, a shadowy group of thinkers tasked with making high-level judgments that even the five Commanders couldn't influence. Their identities were a secret, and no one even knew which Ark, or Arks, they lived on. It made sense that they'd have a liaison on each Ark. "Oh, fancy, fancy. Tribune Liaison, huh. So five people."

His blue eyes took on a new intensity. "Magda, no. It's four. I'm not seriously a suspect, right?"

I didn't answer that. "I'm not counting you; I'm still counting the Commander. But we can focus on the other four."

He sighed. "Great. So what's the plan?"

"You go to work during the day, like usual, while I search their rooms. Then at night, we'll canvass the offices, control rooms, and anywhere else we can't get to during work hours. You know how many guardians patrol this floor at night?"

"Not really."

"Well, they won't suspect you anyway. And we'll have to split up."

Eren looked pained.

"Look, if we're seen together, they'll know where I'm hiding. Then it's game over."

"Okay, fine. We'll split up. But we can't go out tonight; they'll be looking for you everywhere. You should stay in for the next few days. And when you do leave, promise me you'll be careful."

I smiled. "Always. So, when's lights-out?"

*

I can't say I didn't enjoy the next couple of days with Eren. I unpacked his stuff while he was at work, carefully leaving the piles of clothing and rumpled bed sheets untouched, in case I needed to hide. In the evenings, we cooked together and played video games from Eren's extensive collection. My favorite game was one about a chase through a forest. The graphics were so realistic, right down to the sound of tiny twigs snapping underfoot, that I started dreaming that I was walking with Eren through the dark, quiet woods. He'd point out different kinds of trees, and explain how you can tell the species of an oak by the pattern of the veins on its leaves. I would smile, nodding, and inhale the crisp scent of pine all around us.

Or maybe my dreams were about West. When I awoke, I was never sure.

"You must be going crazy, all cooped up like this," Eren said one night during my turn in the chasing game.

I didn't look away from the screen. It was my favorite part of the game, where you could climb inside a giant redwood to hide from the hunters. "It's not so bad. I'm kinda used to it."

"Don't get out much, huh. Sheltered girl?"

I snorted. "'Sheltered' is one word, I guess."

"So, what was your life like? I mean, before."

"Just… normal, I guess." I missed the redwood, and the hunters closed in on my little fox character onscreen. My red tail swished into view, then disappeared as I started running again. The first arrow missed its mark, and I scrambled to find another place to hide before the hunter could nock another arrow.

"School, homework, all that?" Eren leaned his head back against his recliner, eyes closed, as though reliving some moment of his own life on Earth.

"Uh huh." I hadn't seen the inside of a classroom in years.

"Did you have a job after school or anything?"

The second arrow must have landed true, because the screen filled up with red, signaling the end of the game. I tossed the controller onto the couch. "No job."

"Lots of friends?"

"Uh, sure."

"Boyfriend?"

"Seriously? Why the third degree?"

His eyes popped open. "I'm just trying to get to know you. They say it's good to talk about Earth. Therapeutic, or something."

"Not for me, it's not."

"Did he get left behind?"

"Who?" I could feel my voice rising.

"Your... never mind."

I set my jaw and stared straight ahead at the crimson screen, which read "Continue? Quit?" in bright letters. Only when Eren reached for the controller and restarted the game did I speak. "I'm going to start looking tonight."

His blue eyes focused on mine. "Magda."

"Don't. It's time. I did everything you asked."

"I'll come with you."

"Too dangerous. This way, if I'm caught, you'll be out of trouble."

"Mag. Please. Why can't you stay here with me? I can protect you. After awhile, it'll be obvious that you're not a terrorist. People will stop looking. You can apply for citizenship, or something."

"That's, like, years from now. And the law would have to change. They could catch me anytime between now and then."

He swallowed. "But you'd be safe."

"I'd be worthless. I'd be the person who found a stash of illegal weapons on a ship full of helpless people and did nothing about it."

"You don't even know why it's there."

"And I never will, unless I start looking." I paused. "Look, I appreciate what you've done for me. And I'll do everything I can to keep them from knowing you helped. But I can't live with myself anymore if I take the easy route. I'm finished with that part of my life."

"The easy part? Or the safe part?"

"The part where I do what feels good. Where I only think about the next day, or the next hour." I took a breath, and looked directly at him. "The truth is that I'm not the kind of girl you want to get to know."

He looked at the wall, then back to me. "Agree to disagree."

I smiled, in spite of myself. "Fine."

He returned my smile, just a little. "Fine."

A few hours later, Eren was asleep on the couch, and the clock above the door panel read "00:00 U.T." I was impressed by Eren's sleeping skills. He could lose consciousness at a moment's notice, and stay asleep however long he wanted. I, on the other hand, generally spent the first hour or so in bed tossing and turning, and would jolt awake, heart racing, at the slightest noise.

I didn't even glance back at him when I slipped out the door. I knew he wouldn't hear me.

My first choice of rooms to search was the Commander's office. But I'd promised Eren I'd focus elsewhere, and for some reason, that had begun to matter to me. Plus, I'd rather search the Commander's bedroom anyway, and I'd have to wait until "daytime" to do that.

InterArk Comm Con was as good a place as any to start, so I headed "east" out of Eren's room. I brought with me a detailed copy of the map Eren had drawn when he'd finally explained the basic layout of the Ark. He'd carefully marked down everything he knew, and included a second page of specifics on the Guardian Level, where we were. I made my own copy, then destroyed his. If anyone caught me, the only handwriting they'd find was mine.

The Ark was shaped like an enormous doughnut with a huge, cut-out circle in the center, or "torus," as Eren had called it before I threw another pillow at him. To create gravitational pull, the doughnut spun like a wheel, with the floors being concentric circles expanding out from the hole at the center. That explained why gravity was stronger in the outer, "lower," levels and lighter on the inner ones. The Ark was also divided into ten sectors by barriers, like the spokes of a wheel.

The Guardian Level, complete with any mission-critical operation centers, was at the sweet spot of the ship, where the amount of pull most simulated the gravity of Earth. The general population lived and worked in the levels above and below it. Cargo was stored in the outermost rims, along with greenhouses and the aquaria, where the force was considered too strong for people.

The panel slid open with the access code Eren had given me, and I stepped into a huge, round room. He'd explained that the room was generally unguarded at night, except for the security panel, and only high-ranking guardians had access after hours. I had broken into enough places to question this. In my experience, the easier the job, the less the payout. Surely the Commander had some kind of eyes on a room like this, unless there was nothing here worth finding.

But Eren was right. Row after row of desks and empty chairs surrounded the central space, like an amphitheater. The screens at each workstation were locked onto the same moving image, a rotating blaze of fire and stars.

My attention was glued to the space in the middle of the room. A delicate hologram stretched up from a raised panel to slightly above eye level. It was beautiful. Tiny dots of white light flitted across the space in random bursts, like an intricate meteor shower.

I fought back a flush of jealousy. What kind of life had these people led on Earth to land a position like this? I crept toward the holo, all but invisible in the darkness. I had the feeling that something more than its beauty was pulling my attention toward the dancing lights, but I couldn't explain it.

After several minutes, I refocused. There were no buttons or controls near the holo, so I turned to the rest of the room. The circles of desks containing identical screens would be for the lower-level engineers, who probably each managed smaller, more detailed amounts of data. I wanted the desk that controlled *everything*.

My search was rewarded when I reached the lowest row in the amphitheater, which housed a desk the size of my parents' banquet table. This desk had a couple of small screens built into its surface, but when I sank into the chair, I had a perfect view of the holo. Whoever sat here oversaw the whole enchilada. Bingo.

I leaned all the way back, fighting the urge to continue staring at the rushing lights, and studied the controls in front of me. There was a normal keyboard, but pressing the keys didn't do anything. Then there was a series of other buttons, including one in the corner of the desk that looked promising. I held it down for a few seconds, and the desk was suddenly illuminated from underneath the wood, and a small hologram of moving lights floated up to the level of my chest. I reached out to touch them, and the lights on the giant holo jumped back.

That was interesting.

I lifted my hand a second time, but instead of thrusting it into the dancing lights, I slid my palm along the edge of the projection.

The lights in the giant holo shifted in the opposite direction.

I reached out with both hands, as though grabbing the smaller holo, and turned it on its head. The big holo flipped upside down. Dots that were bright had gotten dimmer, and dots that weren't visible twinkled into view. I spun the tiny lights a few times, watching the bigger holo react and enjoying the feeling of control, before reminding myself that I had a mission to accomplish. I was in the communications room. If Ark Five had really gone down because of foul play, then someone involved had to have communicated about it. If so, there was probably evidence somewhere in this room. *Think, Char. Think.*

But something about the lights continued to hold my attention. It's not that they were dancing, exactly. More like, they were flying. In a formation. I twisted them again and kept watching.

Frustrated, I grabbed an errant dot of light between my thumb and forefinger. The lights of the holo blinked away, replaced by a single straight line of dots and dashes. I had seen a pattern like that before. It wasn't Braille, exactly, but something even older.

Morse code.

The lights weren't meteors, or even stars; they were communications. There were limited points of origin for the dots, and only a few destinations. They were flying from ship to ship, in real time, right before my eyes, like moving dewdrops on a giant spiderweb.

Something was still off, though. Countless smaller lights went from one invisible point to another, but the biggest and most frequent lights seemed to fly from one of four places, which were flung farther apart than the smaller ones. The smaller lights only flew back and forth from these larger destinations. If I didn't angle the image just right, I couldn't see the direction of the lights that were headed straight for my face. They would just appear to be a pinprick that disappeared an instant later. From the side, though, they had a clear starting point and a destination.

I figured that the big lights were communications coming from Arks, and the smaller lights came from Arkhoppers, the smaller ships that transported high-level citizens between the Arks. They probably only sent flight-related communications with whichever Ark they were about to dock with. I watched a moment longer, until I had identified the locations of the four remaining Arks based on the origins of the biggest dots of light.

Just as I was about to turn away, a large dot of light glinted near my cheek, then faded. It was too big a dot to have come from an Arkhopper, but it wasn't coming from one of the four Arks, either. I pulled the image around, hoping to get a better glimpse of the next light from that source, but none appeared.

A small, still hope rustled in my stomach.

But it wasn't possible, was it?

Surely I had imagined the size of the dot. After all, it had appeared close to my eye. Maybe it was just a minor com from an Arkhopper.

Or maybe it wasn't.

I settled myself back into the chair and waited, motionless. If another light left my mystery point, I would be ready. When I was eleven, and just beginning to lash out against everyone but West, my mother had tried to teach me about meditation, in the hopes that I would learn control over my reactions. I hadn't listened to much of what she'd said, but a little of it had sunk in. I focused on the blank space in front of my nose and made myself completely calm.

Not a minute later, another light caught my eye. This one wasn't coming from my mystery point, but headed toward it. When it came within four inches of the space near my face, I grabbed it.

As the holo shifted into Morse code, the door panel slid open to my right. I threw myself from the chair but kept my grip on the pinpoint between my fingers.

This was idiotic. I had to let go and find a way to hide. Using every ounce of my non-existent meditation skills, I homed in on the dots and dashes with laser focus, searing them into my memory, and released the light. At the same time, I launched myself past the gap in the row, landing behind one of the minor workstations nearby.

The code disappeared, ceding the screen to the dancing lights once again.

My best bet was to get the intruder away from the door panel, then make a blatant run for it once I had a clear shot at leaving the room. In order to do that, I'd need to make some kind of noise happen on the other side of the room.

In normal lighting, my plan would seem absurd. But in the half-light of the comm room, I figured I had a fair chance. I lifted an object from the desk nearest me—a small, portable screen—and chucked it toward the far side of the room, carefully avoiding the rows of desk-sized screens along the way.

There was no way the screen survived the crash that followed. The intruder, no more visible than a shadow, turned toward the noise, giving me a chance to make my big escape.

My palm was inches from the "open" button when I heard a quiet voice several feet away. "Mag? Magda?"

"Eren?" I let out a breath I hadn't known I was holding. "Seriously? What are you doing here? Something better be on fire."

"It's not. I mean—" he paused, cutting himself off. "I just couldn't do it."

"Do *what*? Sleep?"

"You know what I mean. I woke up; you were gone; I kept thinking you'd get caught, and you'd need me."

"So you thought I'd be better off with a heart attack?"

He moved toward me in the darkness. "No, I just thought—"

"You thought wrong. And I don't need you."

He was silent for a moment, and I grimaced in the darkness. That had come out harsher than I'd meant it.

"Okay. I'm leaving," he said.

"No, Eren. Wait. Let me show you what I found."

His frame straightened a bit, and I thought I saw him nod. An inexplicable relief flooded through me, and I was glad he couldn't see my smile.

"So, this is a three-dimensional map of all the interArk communications."

His shadowy face turned toward the big screen. "It's kinda pretty."

I considered that for a second. "Yeah. I think so, too." I cleared my throat. "Anyway. There are four big blank spots, one for each remaining Ark. Their communications are the big dots of light. Then there are smaller spaces, for the Arkhoppers. They make the little dots."

"Got it."

"That's not all. A few minutes ago, there was a big light coming from over here." I waved at my mystery point. "It was too big to be from an Arkhopper, so I waited for another one. It came from that Ark—" I indicated a huge blank spot in the center of the screen—"and headed straight for the mystery spot."

"Okay."

"I caught it. It was in Morse code."

"What did it say?"

"I have no idea. I don't know Morse code."

The shadow standing next to me perked up visibly, and I caught a glimpse of the white of his teeth reflecting light from the screen. "I do."

"Give me your hand. I'll show you what it said." I reached for his wrist and spread his palm out over mine. Even allowing for the darkness, I was clumsier than usual once his skin touched mine. "Okay. So this is the first word." I began tracing the dots and dashes. The skin of his palm was soft and warm against my fingertip, with a neat row of calluses near the knuckles. I was sure he could see my blush in the darkness.

"Right. That's '*reste*.'"

"Um. Great. I'll just keep going."

"Okay," he said. "That's '*froid*.'"

"So 'rest fwa.'" This was discouraging. "That's nonsense."

"No, it's French. It means 'Stay cold.'"

"'Stay cold'? Still sounds like nonsense."

"Do the rest," he said. I touched his palm again.

"That's '*l'oiseau*.' Bird. Keep going."

"Then this."

146

"*Volera. En.* X," he finished. We stood there, holding hands, for a moment longer. And then his hand was suddenly heavy in mine, and I dropped it abruptly. He took a step back and rubbed his neck.

I realized all at once that I had stepped away from him, too, and regretted it. "Uh, translation? This wasn't my strongest subject in high school."

"It means, 'The bird will fly on X.'"

"That doesn't mean anything."

"Yes it does! If you'd remembered it wrong, the bird wouldn't be flying. He'd be swimming, or something."

I considered that. "It would have been nonsense, like tly-ing. I mean, it's not like you'd have a totally different word in perfect French." He nodded, and I realized that we were standing next to each other again. "But anyway, don't you see what this means?"

Eren leaned back against a nearby desk. "Not really. What bird are they talking about? I don't see the point."

"The point is that this Ark sent a message to Ark Five! Ark Five isn't gone after all!"

There was a long pause. "Mag. You can't seriously believe—"

"Of course I do! I'm telling you, it was a big dot, not a little one."

"The bird is probably someone's helicopter or something, and it won't work in space. It was probably just a random message to an Arkhopper pilot from his commander."

"Look, Eren. I don't know what bird it's talking about, but that was *not* a message to an Arkhopper. It was too big."

"Even if you're right, and the big dots are from Arks, then this one would have been big, too, right? If the European Ark, or whichever one it was, was talking to an Arkhopper, then it would have been a big dot."

"No, I'm telling you. The first dot, the one I didn't catch, it was big, too."

He sighed. "Whatever."

"Eren, you have to believe me. Ark Five is out there."

"So now you suddenly care if I believe you?"

I stared at him. "What does that even mean?"

"You won't tell me your name, but somehow it matters whether…"

Flames rushed up to my face. "Let's get this straight right now. I owe you *nothing*. Not my name, and especially not my life story, and every single thing I ever did wrong, and every person I lost, and how it made me feel," I said in a mocking tone. "You don't get that from me."

Eren didn't respond. Good. Let that sink in. It would serve him right for thinking he was so superior to me that he didn't have to believe anything I said.

But I knew, deep down, that I didn't deserve his trust. I had lied to everyone I'd ever known, at some point or another. Why would Eren end up being any different? He was smart to be skeptical.

But then the silence continued, and a twist in my gut pulled my chest tight. He'd been so kind to me, these past few days. Why was I being so mean? Had I gone too far? An overwhelming urge to see his face stopped my breathing, and the twist deepened.

Had I hurt him?

I turned toward him, wishing I could see his expression, and his frame loomed closer. I took a step back involuntarily. In the shadows, he seemed twice my size. Was he angry? Without thinking, I lifted a hand toward him.

He did the same, and I flinched. But instead of hitting me, his hand moved lightly behind my head, barely touching my hair. Its warmth in the cold air was the only way I was completely sure his hand was there at all. "Okay," he whispered. His voice was deeper than I'd ever heard it, and his mouth was an inch from mine. "I believe you."

"Oh." I couldn't think of anything else to say, but this silence wasn't so weird as before. Neither of us moved. His hand rested softly on my neck, and a slow shiver worked its way down my spine.

And then we were kissing. His mouth met mine, impossibly gently, and I kissed him back. His lips were much softer than I expected, and fuller. I smiled against his mouth, and he smiled back. I laughed under my breath, slightly. That was one way to read his expression.

I think I would have stayed there forever. I think I could have told him everything he ever wanted to know about me, and then I would have asked him everything I could think of about him. Everything.

But I never got the chance, because at that moment, there was a soft *click* behind us, and the room was flooded with light.

Every alarm in my head started screaming, like a full-on symphony. Eren was caught. He'd be taken in for harboring a fugitive. He would lose his job, and probably his freedom. And that was the best-case scenario, at this point. My life was over, too, of course. But I couldn't handle the thought that Eren had sacrificed everything.

Without thinking, I twisted around in his arms, so that we were both facing the door, and yanked his hands down around my shoulders. I crossed his forearms over my chest and pretended to struggle against him.

"You have to arrest me. *Now*," I said, my jaw clenched. I threw a glance over my shoulder. Eren's brow pulled down above his eyes, which were wider than usual. When he didn't respond, I opened my mouth to speak again, but couldn't find the words.

Blue-clad figures armed with shields and stunners raced through the open door and spread out among the rows of desks. I allowed myself one more second of alarm-ringing panic before fully committing to the charade.

"Ugh! Let me *go!*" I pitched forward but kept my grip on Eren's arms, so that he came with me. He struggled to regain his balance against my back. The effect was perfect: anyone would think he was trying to control a difficult prisoner, instead of the other way around.

We continued like that for a second longer, until the same thought occurred to us both: The guardians weren't doing anything. They had surrounded us, stunners raised, but they had not attacked.

They were waiting.

Unnerved, I stopped wrestling with Eren. He tightened his grip around me, and for one fleeting second, it felt safe, like I was protected. But I knew that feeling never lasted.

"Well done, Ambassador! I see you've apprehended our little space rat." A vaguely familiar voice boomed into the comm room, followed by a black uniform with a chest full of medals. I tilted my chin further up to take in the smooth face and gray hair of Commander Everest.

Eren straightened. "Father. I've been meaning to talk to you about something."

Seventeen

Commander Everest strode toward us. Eren was like a statue, and I had long since dropped the fake-struggle routine. The Commander took in the scene with a calculating nod, pausing only on Eren's face before turning on his heel to leave. "I'll take your statement in the office, Ambassador. Bring the girl."

Eren's arms left my shoulders, and I suppressed a shiver. His hand shifted to my elbow, and we followed the Commander out into the hallway. The guardians filed in behind us, like some kind of parade.

That was when I noticed the cameras.

Three women at the end of the line of guardians sported video equipment aimed squarely at Eren and me. I glanced at his face; it was like stone. That was unsettling, and the fact that I couldn't control my own expression made it worse. I was mad enough to spit feathers, and I hadn't recovered from my shock enough to hide it. Eren was the Commander's *son*?! I had gotten into some bad situations in my day, but this was by far the stickiest.

At least it explained his relentless questions about me. I should have known there was a darker reason for his curiosity.

On our trip down the hallway, I mentally catalogued every bit of information I had given Eren about myself. He knew I grew up in Manhattan, and that I liked grilled cheese. From my starpass, he knew I had lied to him. Not that he had fallen for it, which was more than I could say for myself.

And that was about it. Eren's report to the Commander should be fairly thin. At least if I died, no one would know my real name. It was sort of a final consolation prize for my family.

I allowed myself a small moment of pride for having kept him at a distance, but it tasted sour. About five seconds longer, and I'd have given him anything. I had thought I was so smart, that I was the one person in the room who always knew the score. What had happened?

Whatever it was, it would never happen again. That much was certain. I pulled my shoulders back and tilted my chin up and away from the camera. I'd had enough of screwing up. I would be a stone vault from now on.

The plush rugs of the hallway gave way to dark wood, and I focused on the steady tap of the Commander's leather soles against the floor in an effort to prepare for the scene ahead. It hit me that the soldiers and camera crews around us were doing the same thing: matching their pace to the Commander's. Even Eren deferred implicitly to his father, pausing as we turned corners, so that the Commander entered each hallway first, perfectly flanked by the rest of the entourage. If the Commander could influence the way people walked, what else was he capable of?

By the time Eren ducked his way around a particularly ornate and low-hanging chandelier, I had more or less gained control of myself. My anger was a hot, bright secret buried under my skin, and it would be strong enough to keep me afloat for several hours, at least.

When we neared the end of the corridor, Eren squeezed my elbow, and the procession halted. The Commander turned to face the guardians behind us, carefully positioning himself so that the camera could catch every inch of his face.

"I'd like to thank the brave men and women who made this apprehension possible. Your time and effort over the last several days have made our ship a safer place." He laid a hand on the exposed wood of the door before him, which was reinforced around the frame with thick iron paneling. "Rest assured that the suspect will be brought to justice, and we'll be providing updates at regular intervals from now on." The door swung back, like a door on Earth, and we stepped into the Commander's office.

The room was enormous, with rounded corners paved by pale, intricately patterned wallpaper that was reflected in the white marble of the floor. The room had no fluorescent lights. Instead, a series of colored fixtures hung low from the ceiling in a wide semicircle, creating an arc of light. The farthest light shone on a heavy desk. The arc of light swept through the room and ended with a small square lamp over a thick red couch.

The effect was staggering, but the most unbelievable feature of the room was located perfectly in the center of the floor: a soft, low fountain. The fountain was lit from underneath the water. It bubbled and changed shapes slowly.

The Commander reached behind us to secure the lock on the door. "I see she appreciates my little memorial," he said. He crossed the short distance to the couch and sank into it, throwing an arm across the back of the cushions. "Welcome. I've been hoping to have you here for some time." He crossed an ankle over his knee and regarded me frankly, then spoke to Eren. "She's younger than I expected."

"Father, about that. I'm not convinced—"

"Doesn't matter, son. You can spare me the time." The Commander frowned at Eren, then pursed his lips and continued. "Although I must admit that I was impressed with your display in front of the cameras. You might have learned a few things in spite of your folly of the past few days. I had hoped as much, which is why I allowed the soldiers to enter before the cameras. I scarcely thought you'd have the wits to shape up before they arrived, but you've done at least one thing right. Combined with my influence, it should be enough to keep you from prosecution." He cocked an eyebrow and looked from me to Eren. "Do we have a name?"

My mouth clamped shut. I hadn't even realized it was open.

Eren released my arm. He tried to meet my eye, but I looked away, and he turned to his father. "No. Only Magda, so far. But she's just a stowaway. She was looking for a way out. Millions of people did that."

"Maybe. Maybe not. Most of those millions of other people lacked the resources to pull it off as she did. We can't rule out the idea that she's connected to the tragedy on Five, either. There may be one on every ship. A shadow team of misguided souls grieved enough to carry out a grudge mission. They're likely working from a master plan to overthrow us and invalidate the Treaty. We don't know how she got her hands on that poor doctor's OPT pass, but I can assure you that Cecelia Turner didn't give it to her willingly. The truth is that she's a killer at best, and at worst, a threat to the safety of the Ark. We will be wise to handle her accordingly."

"You can't possibly believe in the Remnant. Those are just stories."

"Stories like that have a way of complicating things for people like me." The Commander glared at Eren. "So do people like her. She's dangerous, Eren."

"She's not involved in that stuff on Five, and you know it."

"If it were up to me, I'd execute her right here, in all possible haste. Fortunately, the evidence against her is sufficiently compelling, and the Tribune isn't known for dragging things out."

"Father—" Eren began, but his father jumped up from the couch.

"That's enough, son. I knew you were impulsive, but this is an embarrassment, even by your standards. She's a traitor to our species, not to mention my command, and you harbored her. In your *bedroom*. Then you lied to the search team." Eren looked at him in horror, and his father smiled. "Yes, I knew about that. I've set my screen to monitor your door panel's activity ever since the alarm. I couldn't afford the humiliation of arresting her in my own son's living quarters, but I knew that it was only a matter of time before you did something stupid." He came within a few feet of Eren, and I was obliged to watch.

Eren stood a good six inches taller than his father, and his blond hair was ruffled forward, in sharp contrast to the perfectly coiffed black-and-gray of the Commander, who raised a single finger. If they started fighting, there was a chance I could find another door out of the office.

The Commander looked from me to Eren, and shook his head. "You always were weak. Now, I'm going to tell you how this is going to go. You're going to march your little friend straight to the holding cell, in front of God and the cameras, and you're going to leave her there until her trial, at which time you will publicly retrieve her from the cell, and take her to the Courtroom, where the Tribune will officially relieve you of your charge."

Eren glanced at the floor, but the Commander was undeterred by his hesitation. He crossed the room and whacked the door sharply. It popped open a second later, and a bulky figure in a black uniform swayed into the room.

"Jorin will assist you, to ensure that there are no… complications," the Commander finished. "You may go. Now."

Jorin reached for my arm, but he was too slow. I jerked away and threw myself toward the door. Jorin swiped air once, but his reflexes turned out to be far more advanced than I'd estimated. His foot blocked the frame from opening before I could reach the handle. Meanwhile, his grip landed squarely on my right arm, twisting it backwards.

A sharp pain wrenched through my shoulder blade. The pressure from Jorin's hold on my wrist combined with my forward momentum, and my face hit the door. Behind me, Jorin sneered into my ear. His breath was hot against my neck.

"Have a care, Jorin. We can't afford to have her look damaged," said the Commander from behind us.

After what seemed like an eternity, Jorin untwisted my arm and shifted his hold to my elbow. Eren reached out to touch my other elbow, then slid his fingers around it, so that his grip mirrored Jorin's. All the while, Eren just stood there, watching me, his expression stupidly blank.

I hated him.

Eighteen

Five steps forward, six steps right. This cell was even smaller than the one I'd had in juvy. And it smelled funny, like acetone and eggs. I stretched out on the bare bench, then changed my mind and curled my legs up against my chest. There was no light switch, so I shut my eyes against the harsh fluorescence of the ceiling. But I did not sleep.

I can make it till breakfast.

I could lie there, and not freak out, until food came. Then I could eat. Then I could sleep. I had done this before. The only thing new was the Tribune at the end of the tunnel, instead of a juvy court judge, so I figured the trick was not to think about them. I could handle this.

But food never came. And consequently, neither did sleep.

The hours trudged on. I might have slept eventually, but I couldn't tell. I was tired, and above all, hungry, when the cell door swished open.

I frowned. "What are you doing here?"

Eren nodded, as though he understood me already. "I wanted to tell you."

"Gee, if only you'd had a chance. Like, I don't know, three days alone in a room with me, or something."

"It just didn't sound right."

"I'm sorry to hear that, Ambassador *Everest*."

"Why do you even care who my parents are? It doesn't change anything."

"It changes everything! It definitely explains all the questions."

He tilted his head, like a puppy. "What questions?"

"You know. When you asked all about me. Research."

"You can't seriously believe…" Eren trailed off. When he spoke again, his voice was less mellow, more staccato. "Fine. I'm being watched. I brought you something."

He pulled a bag from under his shirt and plopped it down on the bench next to me. Then he left.

I stared at the sealed door panel for a few minutes before turning to the bag. It was still warm from his body heat.

No, wait. It was warm because of its contents. I pulled a pair of melted grilled cheeses from inside the bag. They were carefully wrapped in plastic, which stuck to the cheese. There was also part of an apple, cut into flat slices, in a separate piece of plastic.

I had to smile.

I had barely finished the apple slices and the first grilled cheese when the door swished open again. I opened my mouth to apologize to Eren. I knew what it was like to tell the truth when no one seemed to believe you. Our friendship, or whatever it was, was over. Soon, we would never see each other again. But I didn't want to end things like this. Once again, I never got the chance.

Commander Everest, not his son, stood before me. For a second, it was hard to believe that he even fit in the cell. He was too… large, or wide, to be contained by a place like this. He looked down his nose at the bench. I had to tilt my chin all the way up to see his face. His skin was tight, too tight, as though he'd gone in for a facelift just before boarding and told his doctor to really make it count, but he hadn't dyed his hair.

That was smart. He'd managed to retain some of the authority that comes with age without appearing too much older than everyone else on board. I bet every move he made was calculated in advance.

He stared for a split second longer than he seemed to have intended, once he saw the sandwich. I glared right back, steady as a rock. He grunted. "Take her food."

The Commander stepped aside, revealing the impossibly tall frame of Jorin. I actually stopped chewing, so that I could wonder how they both fit in the cell at the same time. My heart sped up, and I looked from one man to the other.

It was almost funny.

I shoved the second grilled cheese into my mouth and continued chewing as fast as I could. Jorin leaned forward and grabbed a handful of my hair. He hadn't even needed to take a step forward in order to reach me. His hand was on the exact same spot on the back of my head where Eren had touched me the night before, right before we kissed. The thought was comical, somehow, and I heard myself make a wild giggling sound. It probably sounded different to Jorin and the Commander, though, since my mouth was completely stuffed with sandwich.

Jorin tightened his grip on my head, and some of my hair tore out in his grasp. Then he jerked me backward, and the top of my head hit the white brick of the cell. When I gasped, his hand was in my mouth, sweeping out the rest of the cheese. It hit the floor with a wet splat.

The Commander watched without emotion. "No bruises where the camera will see. Top of the head is an excellent place to start." He frowned, thinking. "But maybe not the best."

I looked down at the blob of cheese on the ground and made another noise. The Commander nodded, as though I had said something intelligible. "Let's start with your name. Would you care to share that with us?"

I clenched my jaw shut. It was the one thing I would never tell. This one, final time, my father wouldn't have to hear about my troubles. He wouldn't get the phone call.

He wouldn't have to worry about how it would reflect on him.

The Commander shrugged. "We can come back to that. There are more pressing matters. For example, how many of you are there?"

I frowned at him, then frantically began shaking my head. "No. No, there's no one else. I swear."

"Jorin." The Commander spoke without breaking his gaze on me.

Jorin pulled a long stunner out of his belt. In the cramped space of the cell, its barrel was inches from my face.

"Have you seen one of these before?" the Commander asked. "Ah, of course you have. During our first encounter. Although I'm not sure you've had the honor of fully witnessing it in action."

Jorin twisted the dial near the grip and pulled the trigger. A sharp buzz filled the room, and my mind, as a white bolt leapt from the end.

The Commander waited a beat before continuing, then cleared his throat. "Last time. How many are you?"

I wrapped my arms around my chest, in an effort to stop shaking. "Really. I got the pass, and I got on board. That's it. That's all I know."

160

"And Ark Five just blew up, all by itself?"

Something about this question rang a bell in my mind, but I couldn't think about that right now. "I don't know anything about that!"

He nodded, and the room exploded with light. I was on the floor, and my mouth was open, but I couldn't even scream. The pain was too much.

Jorin smiled and pulled the stunner away from my side. He kept it where I could see it.

"Back on the bench," said the Commander.

Jorin picked me up under my arms and slung me back to my seat without releasing his grip on the stunner. I let out a moan when the weight of my ribcage slumped down into my belly.

The Commander continued. "That's the lowest setting, which means that this is as good as it gets, young lady. Your name, please."

Not that question. I wouldn't answer that one. That's the one I owed to my family, so that they would never again be associated with me. The room exploded again, but I must have already taken a breath before he got me, because this time, I screamed. Loud.

"Unpleasant every time, isn't it?" the Commander asked Jorin, who shrugged. I got the feeling he rarely found someone else's pain unpleasant. "Doesn't matter what brand of scum you're dealing with. There's something so... *human* about suffering." He turned to me. "Which Ark is your leader on? How did he coordinate the attack on Five?"

I struggled for breath, for the words that would keep him from nodding to Jorin again. But I couldn't think of any. "No leader!" I gasped.

"Then how did you get on board the Ark? You are obviously not Cecelia Turner. Any guardian would have caught that."

161

"She did catch it! That's... why... I ran." I wanted to close my eyes, but I was afraid not to see them. So I forced them open, as hard as I could.

"Not until you got to the Ark. Someone had to help you before that."

"No one questioned my pass. It was valid."

"Yes, we know that. It still doesn't explain your interest in my weapons."

"I didn't even know there were weapons! I thought they weren't allowed anymore."

"My dear, it's *my* ship. It's allowed if I say it is. Take our current situation, for example. This kind of questioning might not fly under the terms of the Treaty *per se*, but there is literally nothing up here, in reality, that can stop me."

"Eren can stop you." The words escaped my mouth before I even realized I was thinking them. I almost regretted it, until I saw the look on his face. His face was suddenly red, and his mouth shook before he started speaking. It was almost worth one of the stuns. Almost.

"Continue. Raise the level every time she says my son's name. Monitor the heart. Report to me immediately after. I hardly need mention that this must not reach the news feed."

He swept out the door, leaving me alone with Jorin, who broke into a wide grin.

Nineteen

"*Who is West?*" That was weird. The pounding in my ears was making actual words. "*Who is this West? Your leader? Which Ark is he on?*"

"Nooo." The word drifted around my head, long and drawn out. Not West.

"*Say his name again. Errrrrren. I dare you.*" The words were tinged with a slight accent and more than a trace of enthusiasm.

I coughed, moaning, and opened my eyes. Jorin's face swam before me. I shut them again. The silver lining was an easy one, this time. Before, I had dreaded meeting the Tribune. Now, I longed for it.

Not that I could totally recall what they were. I only knew that they would sentence me to die, and that would end the pain.

And that calling for Eren somehow made it worse.

Either I was hallucinating, or I had opened my eyes, because the barrel of the stunner waved in front of my face. Oh, no. Not again. I tried to tighten up, in preparation, but my muscles no longer responded to my commands.

Jorin lifted it, then made a big sweep with his wrist, so that it faced downward. He shoved it under my collar, where the mark wouldn't show on camera, and I let out a helpless whimper. Maybe this one would kill me, and I wouldn't have to meet the Tribune after all. Another silver lining.

But the pain didn't start.

Instead, the door panel swished open, and I heard the sound of flesh against bone. The stunner clattered to the ground.

Eren's voice cut through the fog in my brain. "Magda! Are you okay? Can you walk?"

"She does not say much. Not like the others. She cries for West and Eren only," said Jorin. He looked down at me, then flashed a smile at Eren. "Two boyfriends?"

Eren ignored him. I stood, then fell, and Eren grabbed me.

Then I saw that he had a syringe. He stuck it in my thigh, and the ugliest scream of my life bellowed out from deep in my belly.

Eren had a wild look in his eyes, and I recoiled, suddenly able to stand. My heart pumped faster, and my injuries dissipated. I was suddenly powerful and unwieldy. He reached for me, and I jerked away so hard that my back hit the wall of the cell behind me. When I finally focused on Eren's face, I saw that he was terrified. He spoke in a rushed voice. "It's adrenaline. I needed you to be able to run. It won't last long. They're coming for you. You're to be executed. Let's go!"

I brushed his hand away. "Stop it! Don't touch me."

He spoke to me with the kind of tone you might use if you encountered a wolf in your living room. "Magda, please. We don't have much time. We have to leave."

"You think?" I huffed, stumbling toward the door.

But Jorin stumbled to a standing position, effectively blocking my exit. "Your father," he growled, pausing for breath, "will not be pleased."

Even now that I was standing, he seemed fifty feet tall. He made a move for the stunner, but Eren kicked it out into the hallway just before he reached it.

Jorin lunged, but Eren was ready. He dodged a blow, then threw a punch that sent Jorin sprawling. I was barely conscious of the sound of footsteps. I grabbed the stunner and, without a moment's hesitation, hit Jorin over the head with it as hard as I could. He fell, finally.

I looked up at Eren and shrugged. We were already in enough trouble, the way I saw it. One more unconscious guardian wouldn't make much of a difference.

Eren made a commendable effort to catch his breath. "Here, let me help you," he said, reaching for my arm again.

I brought the stunner toward his face and pulled the trigger. The electricity snapped off the end. I tried not to take too much satisfaction in the shocked look on his face. I may not have hated him anymore, but I was definitely still sore about his deceiving me. That might have been the torture, though. It was hard to say.

"I'm going alone, Eren. Don't follow me."

"You've got to be kidding me right now. Did you miss the part where I just broke you out of this cell?"

"We can't be together. And anyway, I can't hide you. You're the Commander's son. He'd never stop until he finds us."

"You don't know my father. He's never going to stop anyway."

"Yeah, but he'd never hurt you. Not really." The Commander was capable of plenty, but I was pretty sure he'd never seriously harm his own son. "You're safer with him. No one's ever safe with me."

I snapped the stunner one last time, and Eren's expression changed. He looked hurt, angry. He looked like he understood that this was goodbye.

I turned and ran.

Twenty

Footsteps pelted along the hall behind me. I was certainly outnumbered. Just when I thought my lungs would tap out, I found the door to the stairwell. I wanted to make it to the cargo hold. My plan was far from perfect. There was no way out of the hold, for example, and it would be easy enough for the guards to search every bin systematically. But that would take time. The hold was huge, and somewhat familiar, and there were plenty of places I could hide.

Oh, right…and there was an unsecured cache of weapons roughly the size of a military takeover.

At least I could go down with a proper fight. If they arrested me in the weapons bin, they'd pin its existence on me. But by then it would be impossible to hide the weapons. Everyone would hear about them.

I slid the door open and gently guided it back into place behind me. With any luck, the guards wouldn't catch where I'd gone. Then I started running, breathing harder than usual because of the extra gravitational force.

I wove indiscriminately among the bins, many as tall as a house, abandoning any attempt to remain quiet. I'd worry about stealth when the guards entered the hold. Right now,

I had to worry about distance. The bin with the weapons was farthest from the door.

The corners of bins brushed past in bursts of color—red, red, yellow, blue—until I nearly tripped over a pair of figures standing in the near-darkness. I stepped back to size them up. They were unarmed, without even so much as a stunner, and more importantly, they weren't wearing uniforms.

We locked eyes. A boy, maybe twelve years old, stared back at me. Beside him, a younger girl gaped openly, and my thoughts began to race. *They had no uniforms.* They must be stowaways.

Something deep in my soul shook itself awake and assumed a shaky perch in my heart.

Maybe they weren't alone. Maybe, just maybe, there were more of them. Outlaws, like me. Maybe they could hide me.

I lacked the courage to finish the thought, but it persisted, folding and unfolding its wings... *Maybe I could belong with them.*

But my hope served no purpose, so I ignored it even as it hopped up and down, testing the branch that held it.

I forced myself back into escape mode. "You guys better run. I think the guards are coming." They exchanged a glance. The girl's eyes widened for an instant. "My bad," I added as an afterthought. "But seriously. *Run.*"

They did.

It is common courtesy, when running from the law, not to follow directly behind one's cohorts. You scatter, and the sooner, the better. Even the greenest criminal knows to split up when the chase is on. Makes you harder to catch. Gives the cops a decision to make, which might slow them down, if you're lucky. It almost always ensures that one of you will make it out. In general, it makes things more interesting.

But all that was irrelevant now. I was far from green, and I never broke the code without a good reason. I followed them, flush with hope, and flew through the aisles in their wake.

As it turned out, I didn't follow closely enough. When we'd made our way nearly to the edge of the hold, the pair rounded a corner and disappeared into the wall. Or into a door in the wall, I supposed. It slid shut behind them, leaving me in silence and darkness. I stopped running, and my fledgling hope stopped flying.

"Wait!" I banged on the wall where I guessed the door to be, then thought better of it, due to the noise. "Please! Let me in!"

There was a beat, and I pictured a brief argument while they decided whether to trust me.

The door clicked, then slid open a crack. I heard a grunt and realized it had opened manually. Someone must have disabled the power in this part of the wall.

"State your name," said the boy.

My name wasn't Magda. It couldn't be. Like countless other aliases before her, Magda had died in a holding cell. She died with my mother's picture, with my mother's name on her lips. Magda was a lie. Magda was a liar.

The boy's voice was more urgent. "Come on. Your name."

Magda died on Earth. Magda died in space, in Eren's arms. Eren was a liar, too.

If there were more of them, more free people on board the Ark, I didn't want to lie anymore. "My name is Char."

"Wrong answer."

"What? That's my name."

"Your *real* name."

"It's Char. As I may have mentioned, I am being chased. Open up."

168

"Wrong answer." He took a breath. "It doesn't suit you, you know."

My hands went cold. "What did you say?"

But he didn't answer again, and I thought I might go mad before the guards reached me, just to save everyone some time. I gave an exasperated sigh and started working on another plan. I wasn't sure whether I could overpower the boy, but I was definitely stronger than the girl. Not that it mattered, if I couldn't get the door open.

At length, the girl spoke. "We can't open it until you tell us your name."

I paused. Somewhere behind me, the door from the hallway opened again. More light spilled into the cargo hold in long streaks broken by the bins. "They're coming for me," I breathed.

"Come on," she said, her voice stronger than mine. "You're supposed to know this. Your *name*."

The footsteps focused in our general direction. The guards must have heard me pounding on the wall. What kind of game was this? I began to panic. "I have no idea what you mean! It's Char! Charlotte! It's Charlotte."

There was a moment of silence, then the door slid open.

A mismatched pair of hands pulled me into the wall, and I traded the near-dark of the cargo hold for an inky blackness so thick that I coughed, just to make sure my other senses were still working.

"They can't hear us here," said the boy, but his voice remained quiet nonetheless.

"Well, they definitely can't *see* us," I said.

"Amiel?"

There was a rustling of fabric. "Hang on, hang on. It's coming." A plastic *click* popped through the air, illuminating it, and the darkness pressed back several feet. "A flashlight." Amiel smiled at me.

The boy rolled his eyes, betraying his status as her older sibling. "No kidding. It's not like she's blind."

"Adam!" Amiel looked genuinely surprised by her brother's choice of words.

He sighed. "C'mon, Ame. I didn't mean it that way."

"Still," she said, pursing her lips primly. I liked her, suddenly.

I took another moment to consider the boy. Something about him put me ill at ease, like a pit of quicksand I had barely avoided walking into. My guard was up, and I didn't know why.

He turned to face me in the light. "Do you want to carry it?" he asked. His face was so young, so innocent, that I was caught off-guard and quickly declined.

He shrugged. "Okay. We're supposed to ask."

"It's my turn anyway," said Amiel.

The boy nodded. Adam. His name was harder to plant in my mind than Amiel's. He reminded me too much of West. Not in any specific way, necessarily, but his eyes followed me, widening slightly when I slid practiced hands across the nearly undetectable seam in the wall, to check that the door had sealed behind us and make sure the lock was one I could trust. I knew that look. It meant that from then on, whenever he passed this way, he'd do the same. West had been like that. Eager to watch me, to learn from me.

Until he wasn't.

Deep down, West had never been like me. I'd always known that about him. About *us*. West was good and smart in all the right ways. I was smart, too, but not in the ways they gave out trophies for. He deserved better than me for a role model. For a sister. All along, I understood that, but

I didn't act on it until it was too late. And by the time I'd started pushing him away, for his own good, it had been too late. He'd discovered that fact for himself. He never saw the need to follow me again.

I shook my head, trying to free myself from that particular train of thought. One day, West and I would meet again, but as equals. I just had to find him first.

"It's this way," Adam was saying, but Amiel insisted on taking the lead. He smiled, helping her past him, and together, we set off into the darkness.

We trotted along the inside of the wall, me tagging several feet behind my new companions. It was an easy pace, without the urgency of pursuit. They spoke in hushed voices in spite of their apparent confidence that we were no longer being followed. After a few unsuccessful attempts at eavesdropping, I gave up and focused instead on getting my bearings. I didn't think we'd made any turns, so I figured we were still against the wall of the cargo hold, maybe half a mile away from the hidden door, when they stopped.

The boy rounded on me suddenly. "Were you really in jail?"

"Down there? Or up here?"

"Both."

I thought a moment before replying. "Yes. Why do you ask?"

"How'd you get out?"

It was too easy. All I'd have to do is give a knowing smile, maybe even a wink, and say something mysterious, and he'd be mine. He'd follow me anywhere.

Given his status as a stowaway, Adam almost certainly didn't have citizenship. There was no bright future here that my influence would threaten or destroy. One instant of conspiratorial scheming could pass between us, with nothing more at stake than the breath it took to speak the words.

But I had no room in my heart for another West, and certainly no capacity for further heartbreak. So I bit back the kindness I could have extended him and offered a dismissive shrug in its place.

After a moment of silent staring, he turned from me to face what must have been another secret door. His hands pressed into the seal, and a keypad appeared. I glanced over his shoulder with interest. It was old school, with separate physical buttons, the kind they used nearly a hundred years ago. Adam made an awkward but deliberate attempt at hiding the code from me as he punched it in. We wouldn't be planning any heists together anytime soon.

At last, he turned back to me. "This way."

The room was warm. That's what I noticed first. The rest of the ship was cold, like a museum. Like space. But here, you could almost picture a summer breeze. Not that that was possible. But for the briefest instant, I was nearly able to forget that there was no longer any such thing as a summer.

Next, I noticed the light. It, too, was warm. There were no open flames, of course, but somehow, the bulbs here seemed to burn more gently than the harsh glow of the cargo bin, the holding cell, and even Eren's room.

But that's not why I noticed them.

I noticed the lights because they burned more precisely here than in the rest of the Ark. I shrugged off the idea that a light could be discriminating in its choice of target, but there I stood, watching the scene. The people before me ranged greatly in age and race. They were dressed differently. There were some who could not walk. They could not have been more firmly or obviously placed outside of the ideal demographic for the Ark. And as I approached them, mouth agape, they appraised me as well, and I adjusted my posture in an attempt to convey the confidence I lacked. The enormous room seemed to shift, and a path was cleared for me. People stepped back, displaying friendly smiles, and the light came to bear more intently upon its subject.

He sat on a chair in the middle of a raised platform. His posture was large and easy, and as I studied him, barely able to breathe, I came to understand that it was more of a throne than a chair.

I approached uncertainly, and he stood. The room fell silent. Despite his blindness, he had always known when I was near.

Isaiah broke into a grin. Then a beat, and he began to laugh, as though the pain and terror of the last several days had been some excellent joke between us. At last, he paused to speak.

"Char, baby. Welcome to the Remnant."

Twenty-one

I have no memory of running toward him, of the embrace that must have happened. I was far too engaged in the series of mental acrobatics necessary to process the fact that Isaiah was here, on the Ark. Isaiah was part of the Remnant.

Isaiah was King of the Remnant.

Now, there was a title I would never get used to.

"King? Really?" I followed behind him, almost beside him, anxious to explore my new surroundings, but unable to ignore the fact that our hands kept touching, then not touching. "You didn't want to go for Emperor?"

He laughed again, and I concentrated on relaxing my arm. I had a hard time picturing how it should hang naturally. As soon as I softened, his hand fell away from mine. Whatever we'd been back on Earth, it was never this awkward.

I took a breath and continued. "I hear it comes with a new wardrobe."

"Ah, yes. The one people can't see? I've got my excuse all worked out already."

I gave a little laugh, grateful for the joke. . He slowed his pace, intending me to walk closer to him. I fell into step and soldiered on, convinced we would find our rhythm again.

"Supreme Dictator for Life wasn't available? Honestly, where is your ambition?"

"I didn't much care for the retirement plan," he said. His hand quested out toward mine again, and after a moment's consideration, I left it unanswered.

In response, he stopped walking. I stumbled to a stop, then turned to face him. I could feel the corners of my mouth tightening. Whatever part of my brain was responsible for acting casual had clearly not recovered from the stunner.

"Char," he began. "I suppose we should call you that. You will get used to the extra weight. I promise."

The pull of gravity, despite being an ever-present burden down here on the cargo level, was the furthest thing from my mind. How many years must he have known about the Remnant? It wasn't like we'd been close back on Earth, exactly. But we'd always been friends. Or so I'd thought. "You can't just—"

"I know." His hands brushed both my arms at once. His touch was light but deliberate. "I know. But let's not talk about it right now."

I stared at him. When I spoke, my tone was low and level. "What should we talk about, Ise?"

"The future! Look around you, baby. We made it. Here we are. And there's more." His hands slid down my arms to cover my hands. It wasn't unwelcome. But it wasn't friendship, either. "Char. We're gonna get it right this time."

Had we been wrong before? I shook my head so slowly that he didn't see my hesitation.

"Everything is in our power, now. Schools, food, hospitals. Everything. And we can make sure we use them equally."

I blinked. Of course. He wasn't talking about *us*. He was talking about everyone else. His hands tightened, and I managed a smile. "That's great, Isaiah. Really great."

"I mean, now we can make *sure*. No one will be left behind again. We control half a sector! Right under their noses! We've been taking in the stowaways, of course, but the rest of the group was already on board."

His excitement was a hard, solid thing. I couldn't slow it down, nor could I match it. He seemed to flit from one issue to another, bound to a thread only he could follow. "On board the Ark?"

"On board with the plan. We chose them from all over the world. They've known what it's like to live like we did, Char. If that's going to be your name. You can choose a different one, if you want. Not because you're a fugitive. No more hiding. Because now, you are free. We're *free*."

I was cold. His hands, like the rest of the room, were warm against my skin. It wasn't enough. "You chose them?"

"Inmates. Political prisoners. Convicts. Refugees. We chose them. And then they chose me."

"As King," I amended. "And when was that, exactly? How long have you known about all this? Your cage was never really locked, was it? Still, you were cutting it kinda close, if you ask me."

He sighed. "Char, this path don't lead nowhere. I know you can see that."

"All I see is an old friend who had a way out, but for some reason, he decided not to take me with him." Another thought hit me, and I jerked my hands away from his. "Is that why you came back to juvy? To recruit the Remnant?" I was awash in pain, anger, fear, and even jealousy. It was too much at once, so I grasped onto the one emotion I'd always understood best. Anger. "And what? I didn't make the cut?"

He raised his brows, as if to say, *Are you sure you want to challenge me?* It was not quite a question, not quite a threat.

I had never seen his anger. Not out in the open. Isaiah was always careful. Calm. Assured of the world, and his place in it. He was always in control. Of himself first, and everyone else tended to follow. I doubted he'd lost his temper once in his life.

I wasn't afraid to change that.

I opened my mouth, intending to push further, but his hands were suddenly against my cheeks, and his face loomed in close. And then he kissed me.

I gasped, surprised, and the kiss seemed to freeze. He did not back down, and I didn't pull away. It was a different sort of challenge than the one I'd been expecting. It was bright, and fast, and over too soon.

"Charlotte. Maybe you prefer I call you that? Nobody needs to know but us." His voice was calm. Tender. I'd have to wait for another day to see Isaiah angry.

Too soon, the frozen moment lifted, and my thoughts forced themselves on me all at once. *I am safe. Finally safe. I will have friends now, and family. I will have Isaiah. I will have happiness.*

That's what I should have been thinking.

Instead, all I could feel was confused. Had he betrayed me? Had he betrayed his own brother? We had both lost so much, but did we even deserve a second chance? Was such a thing possible?

And most of all: What about Eren? He had definitely betrayed me. But in his arms, I really had felt safe. But that was stupid. Eren had been loyal to the Commander all along. Not that everything between us had been false. Some parts were definitely real.

Then again, I had never been the best judge of character.

And underneath it all was a small, quiet voice, the one I hated myself for listening to, but ignored at my peril. It was the part of me that had named me Char and never stopped trying to win. This was the part of me that had ruined my family, that had lost my mother to the burning sky and my brother to his better judgment. The part that had almost let Meghan die alone. This voice was the only thing that had ever made me strong. It was the part of me I would never be rid of, because deep down, I knew it was my truest self. I loathed it—I loathed *me*—but I listened anyway. And right now, it was practically screaming.

You can't afford to refuse him.

It's not like there was another Remnant, one Isaiah didn't control, or another life I could pick up and carry out, like an open closet full of someone else's clothes. This was it. The rest of the Ark was closed to me, and Central Command wanted me dead. But here, I could make my own path. And Isaiah would be part of it. This was surely a good thing.

So it surprised both of us when I pulled away.

Isaiah stepped back instantly, releasing me from his embrace.

My mind filled with the memory of his hand on mine as I drove down the interstate, Cassa's gun at my neck, Kip careful not to intervene. I remembered how, in that moment, I had been drowning, and I had needed Isaiah more than air. And he had not wavered.

I wrapped my arms around him, confused, hoping to feel him pull me toward him again. I felt no fear, and no anger, so I spoke honestly. "Isaiah. My mother was down there."

I didn't finish the thought, at least out loud: *And you could have saved her*.

But his response, uttered after a long moment, answered what I couldn't ask. "Mine, too. And Abel."

The horror of the meteor was heavy around us, pressing us toward each other. At length, he returned the embrace, and we were finally still. My body relaxed, enveloped in the warmth and safety of my old friend.

My mind, however, continued to race.

Isaiah had never doubted that I would make it this far. I'd come to him in desperation, and he'd helped me. I'd thought we were helping each other, but I understood now that Isaiah had been in control the whole time. He'd always had a plan. He might have changed his course, slightly, once I'd approached him in his cell. He must have decided there was room for me in the bigger picture he was working to create. I looked up at his face, and he tilted his head so that my hair grazed his cheek. It was tender, but was it also calculated? Did he have other, bigger plans I'd yet to discover? I looked over his shoulder, wide-eyed, and it hit me.

I didn't know him at all.

The next several days were a blur of new sights and sounds. Life among the Remnant was everything the rest of the Ark was not. Instead of carefully assigned quarters, we shared bunk rooms in no particular order. There was an abundance of blankets. Those who preferred to sleep alone certainly did, but most people piled themselves into heaps of three or four. After a week, I found myself doing likewise, and the cold, constant pressure of space receded slightly during the nighttime hours. Often, people slept in different places and with different groups each night, but I felt myself pulled toward a certain set: a boy and girl about my age, and a woman old enough to be our mother. We did not talk or even really touch, but we shared a large, soft mat, a pair of cotton-stuffed comforters, and an unspoken agreement not to exchange names.

Instead of ration cards, we had a stockpile of food and a dedicated team of cooks. Everyone took what they needed.

We had enough to last a year, according to Amiel. Adam wasn't as certain. I was never sure how to ask Isaiah which sibling was closer to the truth. Something thick and quiet grew between us, and I never brought it up.

My plan, if you could call it that, was to bide my time until I could find my family. Second to that, I'd become intrigued by the enigma that was Isaiah, and increasingly worked to understand his game. Surely he wasn't planning for the Remnant to remain quietly hidden until we reached the new planet. It was unthinkable that the Commander didn't realize we were here. The mystery of Ark Five, along with the cache of weapons, took a distant third seat.

I resolved to play my hand cautiously.

Isaiah asked a thousand questions about my time in the part of the Ark under the control of Central Command. He was warm enough toward me, but it was clear that I was never his priority. Once he was content that I'd settled in, I went days without even seeing him. Then he would appear, suddenly, wanting to know more about this or that aspect of the holograph, or the layout of the Guardian Level, or some such thing. Always, he was kind. Always, he wanted to know if I needed anything.

Always, he was evasive. My questions to him went unanswered, and the mystery deepened.

Not that I could blame him completely; I kept secrets of my own. I never mentioned Eren to Isaiah, for reasons I couldn't make clear even to myself.

Everywhere, there was work to be done. Dishes to clean, vents to maintain, laundry to wash, and, of course, toilets to scrub. I threw myself into the labor crews with my whole heart, working long days alongside chatty children, quiet teenagers, and adults who only wanted to talk about life on Earth, or not at all. I rotated often, so that I never got to know anyone too well. At night, we slept soundly, or at least I did. It was the first honest work I'd done in years.

And the work was just the beginning. In the mornings, informal exercise groups sprung up all over the place. In the evenings, those who knew, taught, and classes for foreign languages, computer building, literature, ninjitsu, plumbing, music, lock-picking (which I carefully avoided), history, and even needlepoint cropped up in every corner. About the only thing we scheduled was the late evening entertainment: guitarists, comedy troupes, opera singers, dramatic monologues, you name it.

On my second night, I finally heard Handel's "Messiah" in its entirety. The choir hadn't had sheet music, but there was a man who'd spent years as a conductor, and he'd painstakingly taught each musician the parts they performed. The result was solemn and joyful and loud, all at once, and I had to swallow several times in order to keep calm at the end. But I clapped as hard as I could and found that the swell of applause was almost as heartrending as the performance had been.

Technicians worked around the clock to give the lighting the quality it had on Earth: sunrises bathed us in pale blue and yellow, and every evening, the dining and sleeping areas were ablaze in orange and red. Star patterns, visible only in the darkness of night, adorned the ceilings.

There were no curfews, no assignments, and no rules. Everyone did whatever they thought best.

I came to love the Remnant in spite of myself. It was the resurrection of everything I'd believed lost. The rest of the Ark may have salvaged Earth's art, but the Remnant had saved the artists. The rest had libraries full of history books.

We had those who had lived in the world long enough to understand them. They had the recipes, and probably most of the food, along with most of the surviving copies of music and movies, but we had chefs, writers, actors, and thinkers. They had the politicians.

We had the dreamers.

The rest of the ship measured its passengers carefully. Here, among the Remnant, we cared only that you were, in fact, here. You had survived. They had survived. We were bound together by the common thread of *life*, and little else mattered.

I discovered I had a knack for gardening, and increasingly spent my waking hours among the careful rows of dirt containers in the rooms that comprised our greenhouse system. One morning, I asked the caretaker, a man whose tanned, deeply lined face was accented by a shock of wild white hair, what kind of plant a potato grows on. He shook his head and took my hand, leading me to a particular row in a room coated in UV light. When we arrived in front of his chosen series of plants, he reached deep into the soil and produced a single, dirt-encrusted russet potato, which he placed in my hands without comment. He went back to the lettuces, but I stayed behind to stare in wonder. Here was food. From dirt. I turned it over in my hand for a few minutes, then carefully placed it back in the garden.

I visited him every day after that.

Twenty-two

It's totally weird to date a friend. But when that friend turns out to be King of a secret world of rebels and outcasts, maybe weird is exactly what I should have expected. Maybe I was lucky it wasn't worse.

Now there's an epic friendship for you. *Lucky it wasn't worse?* When had I become so cynical?

Oh, right. Roughly seventeen years ago.

I didn't have to work to find the silver lining. I truly loved the Remnant. For the first time ever, I felt like I was becoming a whole person, instead of just someone's idea of a cautionary tale.

But underneath it all was a sense of loss. I missed my mother so much that, at times, it hurt to breathe. It wasn't like I'd had a lot of quality time with her in recent years, so I didn't know why it hurt as much as it did. I missed West, too.

And Eren.

It was several weeks before I could admit that last part.

I didn't deserve to miss him. We barely knew each other. And he definitely didn't deserve any pining from me.

But my feelings of loss were mirrored in the eyes of everyone around me. No one who was still alive—literally, no one—hadn't experienced catastrophic pain. We were all looking for some kind of healing, for the right steps forward.

Adding to the weirdness between Isaiah and me was our apparently mutual decision to avoid defining exactly what we were to each other. We never kissed again. As far as I knew, which wasn't all that far, Isaiah never planned time alone with anyone else.

My respect for him grew even as the mystery deepened. He had so many ideas and dreams for our future. "Our" meaning all of humanity, not me and him. I told him honestly that I believed in his dreams, too, and that I knew they'd come true. He tolerated no inequality among the Remnant, and, although he never spoke about it, I came to believe that he was working tirelessly to ensure its survival.

That the Remnant had chosen the right King was indisputable in my mind. Whether I'd chosen the right boyfriend, less so.

One night, everyone decided to learn the tango. There were more than a few people who'd danced before, and plenty of musicians. Someone gave a short lecture on the basics, the technicians lowered the light levels, and then, we danced. It was slower and weightier than I'd imagined the tango to be, possibly because of the relentless pull of heightened gravity we had come to view as normal. I knew instinctively that Isaiah would be in attendance, and that he would find me.

Within minutes, I was in his arms. We slinked around, not taking anything too seriously, and ended up making passable small talk. Unsurprisingly, he was a better dancer than I, but I liked to think I could hold my own.

Or, I would have, if the self-appointed instructor hadn't kept yelling out directions. He was a small man, but his voice carried, and he had the annoying habit of punctuating random words by shouting them more loudly than the rest. The effect was highly distracting.

"A tango only truly happens when the MUSIC has pulled you into its power. The tango will own you, but when you understand its strength, it will already be TOO LATE. You will tango. Those who dance the tango have no choice but to TANGO.

"Step, step, *lunge*, and pull, now. Lunge and pull. Feel the music. She is SLOW, very SLOW. So you must be slow as well."

I tightened my grip on Isaiah's hand, and he led me through the thick crowd. It goes without saying that we never bumped into anyone. That could have been because we were all so in tune with each other, or, more likely, because people were watching us, and tended to give us a bit more space. In prison, Isaiah's merest presence had commanded attention. Here, he was King in name as well.

But I had never been one to back down from a challenge. I threw myself into the dance, trying to match my steps to the long, wandering pull of the music without thinking too much about it.

It was exhausting, to be honest. But fun, too.

I made my next lunge, and Isaiah's face drew close to mine. The instructor continued shouting. "The tango is Earth! She is loss and beauty. Sneak, be stealthy!"

Isaiah snorted.

I glanced at him in surprise, and caught the end of an unmistakable smile.

"No, no, no, do not observe your partner. FEEL his presence in your heart." The instructor, like everyone else, was watching us. I doubled my effort, but this, too, was met with criticism. "Do not think. NO THINKING."

Isaiah turned to the instructor and continued dancing. "This one's always thinking, man. The day she stops thinking."

"That's funny. I'd have said the same about you," I said.

In response, the instructor directed his considerable volume in our direction exclusively. "YOU MUST RELAX! There is no wrong in the tango! Only the MUSIC."

"Unless you look at your partner, apparently," I muttered.

Isaiah smiled. "I mean, come on, can't you sneak any better than that? They used to say you were stealthy." He pulled me toward him and lowered his voice even further. "Your TANGO must not be from the HEART."

I snorted. "Oh yeah? Where is it from, then?"

"The legs? I don't know, baby. The arms, I reckon." Isaiah smiled, and I risked chastisement to steal another glance.

"Speak for yourself. My arms are absolutely sneaky."

"Mine too. Don't know about my legs, though. They do a lot of thinking."

"What do they think about?" I let him spin me in a slow circle. When he pulled me around, I was slightly off-balance and had to scramble to catch up. We both tripped. "Not the tango, apparently."

I suppressed another fit of laughter as we composed ourselves. The instructor hurried toward us. "NO! Again you are THINKING! Stalk. *Stalk* your partner!"

At this, we lost it.

Our laughter began silently, rocking us back and forth until it escaped, and we laughed out loud until we gasped for air. The instructor, clearly taken aback by our appalling indifference to the sacred TANGO, regarded us coldly for a moment before giving a small, dignified sniff and returning to the podium.

Long moments later, still in each other's arms, we returned to the dance.

Our laughter was spent, and the music was slower than before. The instructor pointedly ignored us. Isaiah's hand on mine was as steady as ever.

We tangoed.

The music swept over us, and together, we pressed a path through its currents.

Soon enough, Isaiah swept me into another spin, and I emerged off-balance once again. This time, instead of scrambling to catch up, I let myself fall into a long, straight dip, supported only by his arm behind my shoulders.

I was barely upright when we slid into the next steps, and his face came near to mine. I wanted so much, in that moment, to believe that Isaiah would always catch me. The heat of the dance had given chase to my fears, suspicions, and most of all, my usual abundance of caution, and I leaned toward him, careless and very nearly happy.

But Isaiah didn't kiss me. Instead, he whispered, "Hey, little bird. We need to talk."

Isaiah led me to an empty room with an enormous porthole. Windows, however small, were extremely rare on board the Ark, since they compromised the integrity of the hull. But there were a precious few, and it seemed that one of them was within the half-sector controlled by the Remnant. I took my first look out at the sky since being on the OPT.

I waited for Isaiah to speak with a growing sense of dread that had little to do with the nothingness of space. Conversations beginning with "We need to talk" never ended well, in my vast relationship experience. I knew what was coming next. At least, I thought I did.

"I want to make something clear, to start with," he said.

I alternated between looking at Isaiah and looking out at the infinity of stars and blackness that surrounded us.

He continued. "So I'm going to tell you the whole truth: I love you. But we can't be together. Not now."

I stared at him in silence.

"The day is coming when I can be with you, and there won't be anything to stop us. But right now, it's all wrong."

He waited for me to speak, but I wasn't feeling generous enough to help carry this conversation. It was a lot to process. For one thing, I didn't share his optimism regarding our future. How could I? Wasn't he breaking up with me?

For another, love? This wasn't love. I was suddenly sure of that. Whatever Isaiah and I had, it needed some other name. But he kept waiting for me to speak, so I finally said, "Okay."

"I don't expect you to understand. I don't even expect you to wait for me. But the day is coming when we will be together. Our story doesn't end here. So that's that."

I shook my head slowly. "That's that, then."

Isaiah cleared his throat. "Char, baby, I have to ask you something."

The hairs on my neck began to stand on end. This felt dangerous. "So ask."

He nodded and took my hands in his once again. He was as confident as ever, or so I thought. But the tone of his voice betrayed him. He knew the gravity of what he was about to say. Even if he couldn't have possibly predicted everything that would come from it, he surely knew what he was asking.

"I need you to steal something for me."

Twenty-three

"I don't. I don't steal anymore."

He didn't respond to that, so I continued. "I'm not that person anymore, Isaiah. Don't you remember talking about my cage, and how it was bigger than the prison walls? That was my cage. And I'm done with it. Let me help with the food, or the children. Heck, I'll scrub the toilets. I can work hard, so let me do honest work. There are plenty of thieves among us. They can do the stealing. I'm out."

He breathed. "I'm so sorry, little bird. I really am."

"Don't be sorry. Just don't make me go back there."

He frowned. "I don't have a choice. You're the best. We need the best. You want to live here, right? You want to belong? You can't just go around learning about potatoes and expect that to be enough."

It was like falling through the ice on a frozen pond. I felt myself slip, like I'd missed a step, then my stomach dropped. "You know about that?"

"These are my people, Char. I have to look after them."

My hands went cold, and my fingers began to freeze. "You've been spying on me?"

"These could be your people, too. You can belong here,

little bird. You can be safe. There's a program on the Ark's system. You can access it from Central Command. It has... it's important. You have to get it for me. For *us*."

I didn't answer. I was numb.

So this is how a heart breaks. Not with a betrayal of kisses, or declarations of indifference, but like this. With a request I couldn't refuse.

Couldn't I?

The threat was there. In his hands, Isaiah held everything I wanted. If he told me to leave, I would have no home. No food, no shelter, unless I stole it.

So if he told me to steal, I had to steal.

"I'll leave you now. I'll send you the details later. You can sleep on it." Isaiah slid off the ledge we'd chosen and strode out of the room.

I stayed behind to stare at the stars.

When I left the room, I didn't want to go to sleep. I returned to the common room and found a new dance partner, some boy who worked in the kitchen. I did not ask his name. I didn't speak at all. My new partner held me well enough while the music played. Around us, those who were still dancing were also quietly weeping.

I cried, too. I didn't know why, but it didn't matter. The best part about the tango is you don't have to think.

The package arrived early the next morning, while I stumbled, barely awake, toward the mess hall. It was delivered by Adam, of all people. I didn't know the exact nature of the war Isaiah would wage, but I thought Adam was awfully young to be a soldier.

"Where's your sister?"

"Amiel's around somewhere."

"Does she know about this? Or is she a bit young for the cloak-and-dagger bit?"

He failed to pick up on the irony in my tone. "The King said I'm not supposed to tell her about it. I'm just supposed to give you the package and tell you we'll be waiting for your orders."

I stopped walking. "Wait. We? Orders?"

"Yeah," Adam shifted uncomfortably. "There's a group of us," he said, finally sensing my disapproval.

I made no effort to lighten my tone. "Well, Adam, you can tell them to stop waiting. I work alone."

"But the King said—"

"Oh, you don't have to tell him anything. I'll deal with Isaiah myself."

I was granted the satisfaction of seeing Adam's surprise at hearing me call the Mole King by his name. Once he left, I slipped into a side closet, leaning against the door so that no one could surprise me, and sifted through the package. I had to be impressed with Isaiah's work. There were a solid number of details: the guard schedule in Mission Control (around the clock), the exact location of the access door, and complicated instructions on how to get back to the Remnant if the cargo hold got locked down.

I frowned and flipped through everything again. There was nothing about what that program actually was, or how to download it. I must be on a need-to-know basis.

Isaiah didn't trust me.

I thought about that. If anyone on the Ark could understand me, it was Isaiah. His family had divorced him, too. That was a pain that never went away. It receded further and further into the skin until it melded with bone. It lay down with us at night and whispered truth in our ears. *This is who you are: abandoned children. Bearers of heartache. Rebels who got what you had coming.* Whatever became of my life, should I live, it would always be tainted by this thing that clung to our skeletons, defining our destiny over the course of a thousand subtle changes in the way we saw the world, interacted with it.

So he understood that when he asked me to go back to the person I used to be, what he really meant was, *be the person who ruined everyone who ever loved you.* No one could understand that like Isaiah. There was no mistaking it. The only thing worse than knowing your mother cries herself to sleep at night is knowing that she finally stopped crying, and the only difference between the Mole King and me was that his family had died on Earth, and mine was still out there somewhere, blaming me. Hating me.

My arm burned, and I saw that I had crumpled the blue-prints into a tight ball, my fist a steel trap around them. I smoothed the pages against the door and willed my throat to relax as well. I had no use for tears.

I cleared my mind, and only this remained: Isaiah had always had good instincts.

He was right not to trust me.

He found me within an hour. I was pulling potatoes, a task the head gardener usually left for me. It suited me, of course, so I was grateful. I yanked a big one out and shook off some loose soil, then tossed it across the row into a box with the others. It was a long shot, but I made it on the first try, and allowed myself a victory smile.

It's the little things.

"Char." His voice sounded less melodic than usual. He was all business, this morning.

Maybe he had always been all business, and I'd been a fool to think otherwise.

I made my voice pleasant. "Isaiah."

"Adam says you're not taking a team?"

"Adam shouldn't be doing this stuff, Ise. You know that."

"That has nothing to do with you," he said.

"Until you send me *children* to break into Mission Control! You know, and I know, that that's exactly what happened to me. There was Kingston, then Kip. I learned from the best, until I became the best. Then there was nothing else I could do. No other path to take."

"The kid has talent. And like you say, you're the best."

"All the more reason to keep him away. Teach him to do something else. Anything else. One thing I've learned here is that nobody is good at just one thing."

Isaiah remained impassive. "You're gonna need backup."

"Either you trust me or you don't. I work alone."

He tapped the table, and I saw that he no longer carried a cane. He must have memorized the layout of most of the half-sector by now. "You never did before."

"I'm not the same person I was before, am I? Look, that doesn't matter." I jerked the packet off the small of my back, where I'd taped it for safekeeping, and waved it at him. "You won't tell me what the program does. You just want me to steal it. Fine. But everyone has to draw a line somewhere, Ise. This is my line. No kids."

Isaiah smiled. "Good thing I do trust you, baby. You and me, we've been through some things."

I softened, thinking of his hand on mine in Meghan's car, Cassa's gun at our necks. Why did I have to be so angry all the time? Maybe I was just plain broken.

"You got to take Adam," he said. "You're good, little bird, but you know nothing about computers. Too many years on lockup. And this is one serious computer. Adam's the best."

I considered that. "No one else, then. Not his little sister, for sure."

"I'll tell Amiel. She'll be mighty disappointed. Reckon she'll live, though."

"That's the idea," I said dismissively. I plunged back into the potatoes. There was nothing left to say. Isaiah had won. I was a monster, so I would act like a monster. And this kid would be right behind me.

Later that day, I went to see Isaiah in his bunk. He kept himself separate from the day-to-day stuff. I understood that; it made him a better leader if he remained above the minutiae of our existence. No one wanted to know whether the King left toothpaste on the bathroom mirror or not.

But it wasn't like he lived opulently. Nothing could be further from the truth. Isaiah's room was small and sparsely furnished, but it had a warmth that kept it from feeling like a cell. There were bright, thin tapestries on the gray walls and a shaggy red rug underfoot. His bed, smaller than a single bed in the main part of the Ark, was draped with a heavy handmade quilt. He'd told me once that he liked the idea of being surrounded by color.

Isaiah was sitting on his bed with a book, his long fingers transforming the careful rows of Braille into images only he could see. I had a flashback to our last day in juvy.

We'd come a long way.

Not everything had changed, though. For example, Isaiah spoke before I had a chance to identify myself. "Char, baby."

"Let me guess. Eyes in the back of your head?" The idea that anyone could know me so well gave warmth to the little thrill of being found out. "I don't know why you keep calling me that. Not anymore."

He returned my smile in spite of his serious tone. "And here I thought I wasn't getting through. You never cared before. When you're ready, you can pick a better name."

I grimaced. "We'll see. Maybe when I'm not stealing."

His fingers stopped. "Now, don't get like that."

"I'm not. I just needed to talk to you first. Before I go... do this. I have questions."

Isaiah paused, then laid the book aside in a deliberate motion. "That's fine, that's just fine. But first, let me show you something." He crossed the small, spare room and felt his way to the latch of a small cabinet and shifted a few things aside. He spent less time rummaging around than most people. I guess he kinda had to know where things were. As a result, he barely made a move he didn't need to make. The effect was intimidating.

So was the gun he produced. It was suddenly shiny and *present* between us. I felt myself reeling. "How did you get that? No, don't tell me. You brought it up here."

He held it up for me to see. "We couldn't bring guns. Had to get through the screening process to get here. Take another look."

I paused, suddenly full of a thousand new questions. "I know that gun. Is it from the cargo bin I told you about? Wait, how *did* you get here?"

Isaiah sighed. "Same as you. Used a starpass. Although, ours weren't real. We had a few connections. Once we got up here, we met up."

I'd been doing some figuring. By my estimate, there were at least two thousand people in the Remnant. We were never all in the same place at the same time, so it was hard to say. The truth is that it could have been twice that many. "How did you get that many fake starpasses through unnoticed?"

"Now Char, baby. You're not asking the right questions."

Isaiah raised his eyebrows. This was the only response I was going to get, apparently. When I nodded, conceding defeat, he sensed the change in the atmosphere. He had been in control the whole conversation, but now I was aware of that.

His voice was gentle, though. "All right. Look here." He pointed the top of the gun at me, pulled the chamber back, and pumped a bullet out.

I caught it, reflexively. But when it hit my palm, I frowned. "It feels weird."

"It do, don't it."

I turned it over in my hand. "This isn't metal."

His head did the tilty thing again. "*That* is a steel-plastic polymer. The scientists tell me it's harder than flesh, but not as strong as—"

"The rest of the stuff on the ship," I said, understanding. "In other words, it's not going to break through the hull and suck us all out into space. It's a safety bullet."

"Nothing safe about it. They got all the molecules stacked up in a certain pattern. If it hits glass or steel, it stops. If it hits skin or fabric? Now, that's a different story."

I pressed my thumbnail into the bullet. It dented slightly. I was on the verge of figuring something out, but I couldn't put my finger on it.

I looked at him, expecting more, but Isaiah just sat there, patiently waiting for me to draw my conclusions. "So, where did this come from?"

"You already know that, now."

"It was engineered on Earth, obviously. Brought here by someone who was already looking for a fight. It'd have to be the Commander."

He crossed his arms and leaned back a little. "Wouldn't *have* to be. But I think it probably was."

"So he brought the armory up here with him."

"I'm thinking he brought a lot more than that."

"You think he brought an army."

"There are a hundred thousand people on board this Ark, little bird. He didn't have to *bring* one. They were already here."

I turned the bullet over in my hand. "How many of his guns did you get?"

"Just that one. They got away with all the others."

"Isaiah. They're *armed*. You can't hope to win this."

He pursed his lips. "This?"

"This." I spread my arms. "Whatever game you're playing. Whatever war you're planning."

"It's not a war, Char. Can't you see that? This is a revolution."

"Either way, we're gonna lose."

"Hmm." Isaiah leaned back again the wall, frowning. He had the look of a guy who'd tasted something he didn't like. "I may not have the weapons. But I have you. And you're gonna steal that program."

"Not if you won't tell me what it is."

His voice was suddenly distant, careful. "I'm afraid I can't do that, little bird."

A flush of anger rushed over my skin, and I turned to leave.

When I reached the doorway, Isaiah gave a sharp rap against the rail of the bed, causing me to jump, and stop. "All right," he said. "It's the algorithms for the lighting patterns in the other sectors."

I raised an eyebrow. "The lighting program? That's it?"

"Yeah. If we have that, they can't throw us into the Dark Ages."

"And they keep this program in *Mission Control*? Are they paranoid much, or what?"

"That's what I hear." Isaiah scratched behind his head. "Space is a big, dark place. We all know that, but we don't want to *know* that, you understand. That's why they light the place up like a theme park all the time. They can't afford the dark. It makes people crazy. If we get our hands on it, we could turn the tables easy enough."

"That's the plan? Turning the tables?"

"Not just now, Char. Don't you worry about that. You just come home with the program, and then we'll talk about the plan."

"Is that a promise?"

He pursed his lips almost imperceptibly. "Yeah. It is." Isaiah stood suddenly. "You got any other questions for the Mole King?"

I was taken aback. "No. I guess not."

"Good. 'Cause I got some questions for you."

I straightened. That was when it occurred to me that he hadn't asked me to sit, or anything. I was still just standing there, too stiff to be considered a guest.

I wasn't a guest, though, was I? I was an underling. More like a soldier than a friend, or a girlfriend.

No, not a soldier. A thief.

I squared my shoulders. Isaiah would never, ever hurt me. So there was no reason for the small curls of nerves that began to stir in my belly.

I cleared my throat. "Go ahead, Ise. You can ask me anything. You know that."

"This gun's been fired."

I nodded.

"You're the one who fired it."

"Yes."

"You said there was a whole bin, at one point. My spies tell me there was a blast, and the guards started moving. But they got there first."

"Adam?" I asked.

"Yes. And Amiel, among others. They were close enough to see you running, but we didn't know who it was. I had my suspicions. Made me happy to think you were out there. Helped me get to sleep some nights. Anyway, they grabbed the gun off the ground and got outta there before the guards saw them."

"That's not a question, Ise." I took a step back, and then another.

"No, it's not. Be patient, little bird. We'll get there. Seems there were hundreds of guns. Now, the Char I used to know would never have left a weapon behind. And I know you're not armed now."

"Okay," I said. I was near enough to the door that I didn't worry about getting away. Not that I had anywhere to go.

But surely that didn't matter, because like I said, Isaiah would never hurt me.

"And the Char I know wouldn't have kept all this hidden from her old friend Isaiah, would she. So here's a question: Where were you?" He rubbed the back of his neck, then looked at me again. "Where were you hiding? Do I wanna know the answer? Here's a better question: What changed?"

I opened my mouth to answer, but he spoke again, taking a step toward me.

"You know what? I don't care. Because this is my real question: Why are you so afraid of me?"

My belly tightened, making me overly aware of how I held my face and hands.

"Look, Isaiah—"

"He knows, baby. He knows about the Remnant."

"The Commander? How? Wouldn't he attack?"

"He sure will. Central Command is coming after us. Thanks to you, we know he's armed. *That's* who you should be afraid of."

Isaiah took another step. I was unsteady. "I know. I mean, I am. This isn't easy, what you're asking."

He stopped, gave an easy shrug, and sat back down on the bed. It was a much less threatening stance. "We all been through a lot."

I shook my head, forced my hands to relax. He was right. The Commander was our enemy. I was being ridiculous. I had never understood how normal people were able to trust each other. Maybe I would never have a solid grip on anything, and I would always feel this sliding suspicion about anyone I cared about. Maybe I would never trust myself, either. That was what I deserved, anyway.

"It's nothing compared to what will happen if we fail," I said shakily.

Isaiah, on the other hand, was as solid as ever. "We're not going to fail. We got you."

Adam was in the Big Room with the lighting techs, running a prototype for a storm simulation. I entered the half-lit room just as a bolt of lightning struck, followed by a deep clap of thunder. The techs jumped.

Adam smiled from his perch on a metal platform welded to the wall about ten feet up. "Nice entrance."

I took a moment to admire their work. "Nice storm."

"Yeah," he agreed. "Lightning needs work, though." It was an attempt at modesty, but his youth and excitement were written all over his face.

I returned his smile. My ears popped. "Oh, the room's pressurized."

"It was until you opened the door," he said, decidedly less modestly. "Look up."

I did. Gray tendrils swirled far above me, and the air became chill against my skin. "Oh. Are those… real clouds?"

He shrugged. "Depends on what you call real."

I raised an eyebrow. It was going to be a long day, at the rate this kid was going.

"Okay, yeah, they're real," he conceded. "It's technically a nimbus cloud. But we can't make it gather right without using up a lot of the life support system."

I was suddenly less inclined to stick around. "Sounds dangerous."

"It's actually pretty cool. The ions have to be—" He broke off when he saw my expression. "I'm guessing you don't care about the science."

"No, it's fascinating," I deadpanned. "But we have a job to do."

"Now?" His voice had the slight tone of a kid being told to leave his friends and come home for dinner.

Which made me the mom. As grating as that was, it was a dynamic I could use. We'd be breaking into one of the most secure places in existence, so it was in my interest to be in control of things. "Yes, now." I chucked a blue uniform at his head.

Adam caught it easily and sighed as he slid off the platform, then ducked into a closet to change.

"Do you want to carry the light?" I asked.

He shrugged, but took the flashlight from my hands and secured it in his pack until we reached the edge of the sector.

*

As we crossed the threshold into the black space between the sectors, Adam stepped aside to let me go first. I smiled at his youthful gallantry, and he caught my eye as he followed me, shadows eclipsing his impish grin. The air was instantly cooler, and my pulse quickened as absolute darkness closed around us. The tenor of our relationship had changed, too. We were partners now, and the job had begun.

I had almost forgotten how much I enjoyed this.

"Aren't you going to turn on the flashlight?" I asked.

"You scared or something?"

I laughed. "Nope. Just checking to make sure you didn't need it."

"I heard you pulled all your best jobs in the dark."

"People like to talk," I said easily. His footsteps quickened, and I followed apace. This kid wouldn't have the best of me.

"So it's all talk?" he said after a moment. We were fairly sprinting, but he wasn't even short of breath.

"What is?"

He snorted. "You know. All the stories."

"I don't know what you mean," I said, trying to hide my breathlessness. "But if you want stories, you're better off with Isaiah."

"The King? They talk about him, too."

"What do they say?" I asked.

"They say he broke you out of jail."

I nodded, forgetting that Adam couldn't see me. "Yep. Broke himself out first. Then he came back."

"And that's why you love him," said Adam. "But you had another boyfriend."

"I didn't have a boyfriend. And Isaiah is just a friend."

"You're the only one who can call him that."

202

I paused to consider that, and to force Adam to slow down a bit. "Friend? Or Isaiah?"

"Either one," he said. From the sound of it, he was still smiling. "But I meant his name."

"Names can be tricky." I clucked my tongue against my teeth, and the sound echoed in the darkness.

"Some people say your boyfriend blinded him. They got in a fight, but the Mole King won." Adam's voice was now far ahead of me. I sped up, hoping I didn't trip over a pipe or something.

Something in his voice made me press further. "But?"

He spoke like a child, freely and honestly, unfettered by concerns for any possible reaction on my part. "But most people say it was you. That he wouldn't show you the way out, so you blinded him. That way, he had to take you with him when he left."

The chilly air thickened, like a draft around a bonfire. There was danger here.

I spoke carefully, in contrast to my companion. "So why would he still be with me, if that were true?"

"Because you're the best. Everyone knows that."

"So he's using me for my tricks."

"You used him to get out," said Adam. "According to the stories, I mean. And maybe he loves you."

"Well, the stories are wrong." I could have explained further, but I might need the shroud of uncertainty Adam had spun around me. He, on the other hand, was proving to be a fount of information. And information was more valuable than any of my other tricks. "What else do they say?"

"That you can crack any safe and hack any house. That you never came back from a job without the goods. That your family disowned you. You're crazy fast, faster than the cops even." He barreled through the list, oblivious to its sensitive nature as only a child could be. "They say you're not afraid of anything."

I thought of Jorin, and the bin full of weapons. I thought of a war big enough to break a bioship, and the emptiness of space. I remembered the feeling of a stunner cracking through my body, and I shuddered.

But the darkness was my ally, and Adam was blind to my reaction. So I lied. "They may have a few things right, then."

"Then why *is* he blind?"

"That's not my story to tell." We had arrived at the entrance to the cargo bin. My focus returned to the mission at hand. "And besides. We have a job to do."

We slowed our pace as we cut a path among the cargo bins. I couldn't look toward the corner where the weapons bin had been. Adam trotted along gamely beside me, clearly enjoying the adventure so far. He reminded me so much of West that I had to look away.

Except that, when it came right down to it, West had been smart enough not to follow in my footsteps. Not that I would have let him. His easy grin flashed across my mind, and I endured a moment of heartache so intense that I had to dig a nail into my palm just to keep moving. The wrenching in my heart lessened as the pain spread through my hand. In spite of it all, my legs never stopped moving.

I gritted my teeth. I really was cut out for this. And West was cut out to be a good son. My father's son. The thought was oddly comforting.

"First, we need to get to the Guardian Level." I shouldered past the corner of another bin, this one chalk blue. "Not a lot of space between these bins," I observed, by way of distracting myself from further thoughts of West. "On Earth, you'd stack them far enough apart to get one out, if you needed."

Adam threw his head back, eyes wide, taking in the vastness of the room and its contents. "There's nowhere for them to go. It's not like we can take them outside until we get where we're going."

He was a sharp kid. "I suppose not."

"So, what's the plan?" he asked.

"Well, my young cohort, we need some way to get there unnoticed."

He perked up at the challenge. "Food delivery?"

"*Everyone* notices food, grasshopper. Especially halfway through an eight-hour shift."

"Laundry bin?"

I shook my head. "I'm betting guardians don't do their own laundry. So the bins would go in the wrong direction."

He was silent a moment. "Prisoner transport?"

"That would be the most noticeable thing of all. Criminals are not exactly the norm in this part of the Ark. Plus, trust me. People stare at you if you're in handcuffs."

He sighed. "Fine. Medical emergency?"

I raised an eyebrow. "Are you offering to take one for the team? Good ideas, but that's going to stand out. Think about it. Put yourself in their shoes. They're bored and tired."

"All right," he said. "I give up. How do we do it?"

I let the question hang before answering. "We walk."

He looked at me incredulously. "That's the worst idea ever. They will definitely catch us."

"No, they—" I started.

"We're totally going to jail."

"No, Adam, we—"

He broke into a grin. "This is awesome! You can show me how to break out!"

"We are not going to jail. Jail is not awesome. *Space* jail is *absolutely* not awesome. Besides," I said, pulling him into the last bin before the door to the stairwell. It was full of seedling trees, and probably close to the door because they needed to be watered. "I have a few tricks up my sleeve."

Adam stared excitedly as I unzipped my pack. When I angled it away from him, hiding its contents, I realized he had done the same thing with his own bag when he'd stashed his flashlight. I put the thought out of my mind, though. We both needed to focus. Giant supercomputers don't exactly rob themselves, after all.

"What is that?" said Adam. "Scissors?"

"Nothing gets by you." I took the flashlight and laid it on a shelf, positioning it so that the light hit Adam's head.

"What for?"

"For not going to jail, mostly. You need a haircut."

"I really, really don't."

I clicked my tongue and gave a disappointed sigh. "That right there? That's you not trusting me. Bad move, if we're going to be partners. Now, I don't know how much time you've spent in the rest of the Ark, but believe me, *no one* out there needs a haircut. Hold still. I'm not planning to lose the game because you insist on looking like some kind of space rat."

Adam puffed his cheeks, but held still while I started trimming his bangs, then the rest of his hair.

"Isaiah said this is some kind of supercomputer?" I asked.

"It's literally the strongest computer ever built," he said. "There's one on all five Arks, but they're all different. They were all designed by the continents that own them. This one, for example—"

"Does it know everything?" I interrupted, thinking suddenly of my family.

"Nothing knows everything. That's not possible. But this one knows where to look."

I pursed my lips, concentrating more on the computer than the haircut, and looked over my handiwork. The result was something in between a bowl-cut and a total mess. I wouldn't be fighting off haircut requests from the rest of the Remnant any time soon.

He noticed my grimace. "How bad is it?"

"It suits our present purposes," I said, in as dignified a manner as possible. "Uh, you can always get someone to clean it up when we get back. Let's move."

We made our way through the bins as quickly as possible, easily avoiding the guardians on night patrol by keeping out of the longer aisles whenever possible.

The stairs were as daunting as before, but I pressed on, knowing gravity would decrease as we approached the sweet spot of the ship.

Adam, on the other hand, seemed unaffected by the climb. His voice piped up the stairwell ahead of me. "Not that I don't trust you, but how are we going to take them out?"

"We don't," I said, struggling to keep my breathlessness from showing. "I really can't stress this enough. We don't take anyone out. We just need to slow them down for a minute, assuming you're as good at this as Isaiah seems to think."

He scoffed. "Don't worry about me. Everyone says you're going soft."

"Everyone has vastly overestimated my feelings about their opinions."

Adam turned back, his hand on the rail. "Aren't you a wanted fugitive? I mean, I'm pretty sure those guards were about to—"

"Details, details." I waved at the blue door at the next landing. "This is where we get off. Now let's go."

Our key card unlocked the door to the Guardian Level without giving us any trouble. I stuffed a rubber band into the hole for the deadbolt, effectively assuring our safe re-entry to the stairwell in case the floor were locked down.

Adam started jogging down the hallway. "Hey. This way," I hissed.

"The map says it's this way," he said.

"The *map* isn't taking into account the fact that we need a diversion," I whispered, possibly more loudly than necessary. "Also, chips."

"Chips?"

"Or whatever they have in stock. The Remnant is awesome, but we are seriously lacking in junk food." I rounded a corner and used our hall pass to access the commissary.

"Whoa," said Adam. "Whoever owns this pass must be a pretty big deal. This place isn't even open, and the pass still works."

"Makes sense, I guess," I said. "They run the computers at Mission Control. Hand me that rack of chips." I waved at a metal stand with rows of puffy, family-sized bags of potato chips on display.

Adam selected a bag from the top shelf and tossed it over to where I stood in the doorway.

"No, not the bag, sorry," I said. "The *stand*. I can't move; I'm keeping the door from closing behind us."

"Oh," said Adam, as understanding lit his face. "Got it."

He wrenched the potato chip stand from the wall with surprising strength—or maybe the stand wasn't as heavy as it looked; I couldn't tell—and wedged it into the doorframe as I hopped out of the way.

I did a quick check of the room and bar area to make sure we were alone. "Isaiah says you're some kind of a genius with them."

"He said that? Nice."

I smiled. "Yeah, well. Don't let it go to your head."

Adam laughed at that. I was just thinking that things were going pretty well, and that Adam and I might even make a fair team, when Adam caught a glimpse of himself in the huge mirrored wall where the snack stand had stood a moment earlier. His hand went immediately to his scalp, and what was left of his hair. His voice went up at least an octave, along with his eyebrows. "What did you *do?*"

"Oh, stop whining. It's not that bad."

"Not that bad? I thought you used *scissors*, not your teeth! I look like I had a run-in with a pack of hyena barbers on their way back from a middle-school playground."

"You're a bit dramatic. You know that, right?" I selected a few items from the food rack and tossed them into the top of my pack.

He ignored me, his grimace deepening as he turned his head from side to side. "*Stoned* hyenas. Just, massively high. Are you—are you stealing potato chips?"

"And gum." I zipped my backpack closed.

"I thought you were... like, more serious than that."

"Watch and learn, Grasshopper. Gum should be the first thing in your pack on a mission. Any mission. It has a million uses."

"You're expecting our ears not to pressurize or something? What about the chips?"

I paused. "I just really like chips."

Adam sighed and, with visible effort, removed his hand from his hair and his gaze from the mirrored wall. "I can respect that." His eyes slid back to his reflection. "Maybe I'll look okay with a buzz-cut."

"That's the spirit!" I said brightly, giving him a light slap on the shoulder before hopping over the counter and pressing the alarm button. I took a split second to enjoy the shock on his face. "Now get going. Cops are on their way."

We vaulted over the food rack jammed in the doorframe and sprinted down the hall, then slowed to a casual walk when we turned our first corner. I popped a stick of gum in my mouth and slid the wrapper into the pocket of my uniform. It was an old trick of mine. Or of Kip's, actually. When I started chewing, I blocked everything from my mind except the mission at hand. Spearmint flooded my mouth, and in response, I was utterly calm. I could do this.

When we saw that no one was in the hallway, we sped to the next corner and repeated the process, slowing to a casual walk as we rounded the bend. This time, a woman in a blue uniform was swiping her card to enter a room on the hall. She took in our black uniforms, gave a small, deferential nod, and slipped into the room. Adam let out a breath.

Isaiah's intel was spot-on. The white door marked "Mission Control—Danger! No Unauthorized Entry" was exactly where his team had promised it would be. "Moment of truth," I said, indicating that Adam should try his key card on the panel.

He popped the card into the slot and the door sucked open.

Well, that was easy.

Before I followed Adam into the room, I paused to fold my silver gum wrapper into a thin rectangle, which I stuffed way down into the key slot. There. That should slow the guards down if they tried to access the room while we were still in it. When they stuck their access card in, it would only pack the wrapper tighter into the slot. I couldn't suppress a smirk, and a small thought that maybe, just maybe, I'd missed this kind of thing.

I rushed into the room, then stopped cold. Mission Control was *tiny*. There were two stark white walls and a white ceiling. The floor was an intricate swirling pattern of stark white and black reminiscent of a galaxy. A third wall contained a porthole, complete with a view of the star-studded ever-blackness of space, and facing us, on the fourth, smallest wall, was a single desk with a computer.

Adam stood, frozen, in the center of the room. His hands were raised.

"What's the hold-up?" I asked.

"Funny you should ask," he said, through gritted teeth.

The answer came from a robotic voice located somewhere in the room. "I-repeat:" it said, sounding far more metallic than human. "State-your-name-and-credentials-for-further-access. Bioscan-in-progress."

"Oh, that's going to be a problem," I breathed. Isaiah's team hadn't mentioned anything about more security, but that shouldn't have surprised me. If they'd been able to get inside the room, he wouldn't have needed me.

"Identification-not-recognized. You-are-under-arrest. If-you-attempt-to-leave-or-make-any-other-movement-I-shoot-to-kill."

That was when I noticed the jointed white pipe protruding from the wall panel above the computer screen. It reminded me instantly of a creepy robot arm, but instead of fingers at the end of its thin hand, it had small, straight barrels, all trained on us.

I spoke without moving any part of me, including my lips. "Let me guess. A gun? Five guns? Does *anyone* still pretend those are illegal here?"

"No, not a gun," Adam muttered back, barely intelligible. "Worse. It's a laser."

I didn't see how lasers were worse, but whatever. It wasn't good, anyway. "So, if we move, it shoots us?"

"Pretty much. See the panel in the middle of its palm? That's a motion sensor. We have to hold still until they disarm it."

I resisted the urge to bite my lip while I wracked my brain for a viable plan. "They?"

"The guards." He swallowed. "We're going to jail. I mean, unless you want to die a fairly painful death."

"Pass." I was still standing in the doorframe, out of habit, so that it had not been able to shut yet.

"Jail, then." Adam's voice cracked, betraying his adolescence.

"Pass on that, too. Now, don't move." Without another thought, I threw myself out of the room. The laser fired almost at the first twitch of muscle, nicking my leg. I landed on the floor in the hallway, one fist around the edge of the door. If I let go, the door would close, and I'd never get back in.

"What are you doing?! You can't leave me here!" Adam's pitch crept higher and higher.

My leg was numb where the laser had hit it, but a second later, the pain began. A white-hot jaw clenched onto my thigh and refused to let go. With my free hand, I yanked the bag of chips from my pack and ripped them open. The pain was unbearable. "Calm down," I growled at Adam.

But Adam was too young, too scared of being shot. Worst of all, he was inexperienced. "Don't leave me!" he whined. "Please."

212

This was why I really needed to work alone. "Seriously, shut up. The door is still open." I dumped the chips onto the floor of the hall and turned the Mylar bag inside out. It was silver, and shiny enough that I saw the rough outline of my facial features in its surface.

It was reflective.

Adam's panic crescendoed. "I'll tell! I'll tell them everything if you leave me here!"

I blocked him from my mind along with the pain in my leg and took a long, slow breath. Working as fast as possible, I pulled my old black shirt out of my pack and twisted it around my hand, which I then slid into the inside-out bag of chips, shirt and all.

This really was an awful plan. But it was all I had at the moment, and the guards would be there within a minute. "Just a friendly reminder that the laser will kill you if you move, Grasshopper. So stay. *Still.*"

I bit down hard on my gum and leaped into the room, pointing my covered hand at the laser. All five fingers fired, hitting the silvery bag ten or fifteen times. My hand in the bag felt some heat, but most of the deadly energy from the laser was deflected onto the walls on either side of us.

My weeks in the Remnant had not dulled my ability to move as fast as I wanted. The adrenaline pulled the sting from my thigh, and I crossed the room in a flash. A second later, I had the bag over the creepy laser hand, silver side in.

I secured it to the thin white wrist with a wad of gum. Inside the bag, the white hand jerked around, firing repeatedly, but the gum held. For now. The deadly shots were reduced to nothing more than a reedy, high-pitched *twiptwiptwiptwiptwip.*

I turned to Adam with a smile. "Okay, you're up. Start hacking. Hack like the wind."

To his credit, he snapped himself together and slid into the chair. He clicked the key pass into the side of the screen, popped his knuckles over the keyboard, and got to work.

"Technically, this isn't hacking," he said. "I'm sitting at the actual source; no more break-in necessary."

"I wouldn't get too smart with me, if I were you. Not after what just happened."

"That *was* pretty cool." His fingers flew across the keypad.

"I'm talking about what you just said, Adam."

There was a long, awkward pause, but his hands never stopped working, and his eyes didn't leave the screen. "I didn't mean it," he said at last. "I was scared."

"We'll talk about it later." Above my head, the Mylar bag crinkled furiously as the laser hand fired impotently. "The guards should be here any time now. They have a hundred twenty second response time for this room, right?"

"Okay, first, yes. I am going as fast as I can. Second, you're not helping. Third, it's the most important program on the entire Ark. It may take a minute, you know?"

I cocked my head to study his face. "Most important?"

"Done."

"What?"

"I'm done. I got it." He popped a tiny slice of metal from the side of the computer and tucked it into the strap of the black leather band on his wrist. I had to be impressed with his speed.

Unfortunately, it wasn't fast enough.

The sound of heavy fists pounding the door made me jump nearly out of my skin. "You!" The accompanying voice was equally heavy, and easily as angry as the fists. "You're under arrest! Come out with your hands up!"

"Blast," I muttered, hopping toward the door. It had no window, so I couldn't see how many guardians we were up against, and I couldn't tell how much progress they'd made against my little stunt with the gum wrapper. "That is not ideal."

I paced in a quick circle, then put my ear to the door. The voices were muffled, but fairly worked up. Whoever was on the other side of that door was not planning a friendly welcome party. "You got any ideas?"

"Just one," said Adam. "Move to the side of the door and hold still."

I turned back just in time to see Adam reach for the bag over the robot hand.

"No!" I shouted, understanding his plan. "Adam, STOP! They'll die!"

His calmness froze my blood. "People die in a war," he said grimly. "Don't move, starting *now*." He ripped down the bag, exposing the deadly, thin barrels.

The white fingers clicked and popped, as though attempting to realign their gears, and then were still.

We were still, too.

I was frozen, my hands still out toward Adam, fingers splayed in a universal sign for *stop*, a horrified look on my face.

Adam's eyes were locked on mine. His face held a mix of determination tinged with fear. And... anger?

Maybe we had more in common than I realized.

Outside the door, the guards continued to pound away, oblivious to the fate that awaited them once they opened the door.

"Don't come in!" I shouted. My eyes were wide enough to feel dry, and I tried not to blink. "The laser is armed! Stay away from the door!"

They either didn't hear me, or, more likely, didn't understand. A moment later, the door popped. I screamed motionlessly as it sucked open.

Three guardians entered the room. The robot hand began firing.

Three guardians fell.

Everything was suddenly silent.

My mouth was still open, but my scream dissipated into a cold, pale cloud inside my skull.

Adam flipped the bag easily back over the hand, displaying a deftness I hadn't known he was capable of. The hand began firing again, a useless series of *twips* and clicks against the Mylar.

Adam crossed the room, stepping over the body of a guardian on his way to the door. I followed him, very like a robot myself, willing my mouth to shut and my brain to reboot.

My stomach fell with every step as we descended into the heavy part of the ship. The wound on my leg didn't appear deep, but the laser had effectively cauterized it, so it was hard to tell. The pain made me sick.

Or maybe it was the look on the face of the guardian who died nearest me.

Isaiah had lied. This was absolutely a war, and we'd fired the first shots.

Ise would say that they fired first, when they kept stacking the deck against us. We were only fighting for what was right.

Were we right? I thought there was a chance that we were, and that it might be a war I could believe in. Maybe this was my fight, too.

My thoughts were a fast-swirling haze. I needed to see the medic. I hadn't finished digging the potatoes this morning.

I shook my head, aware that my breath was coming hard, and tightened my grip on the rail. Those guardians—two men and a woman—were dead, and we were to blame. But we'd gotten the lighting algorithm. I hadn't let anyone down.

I was still the best.

Kip would know it was me if they announced the bit about the gum wrapper on the news.

Wait, not Kip.

Not Kip.

I reached another landing, and another, and I finally started grabbing the rail at each landing as far below me as I could reach, and just letting my body swing around that anchor and onto the next flight of steps. I needed time, space. I hoped my leg was not infected. The wound had already sealed. Everything was so *heavy*.

Something else was making me sick. And it wasn't the pain in my leg, or even the look on the face of the guardian. It certainly wasn't Kip. I needed to clear my mind, but my gum was all the way back at the entrance to Mission Control, along with my pack. Something slippery was snaking its way through the nimbus cloud in my brain, leeching away my body's life support...

"Adam."

He turned, and when he saw me, his expression morphed into one of shock and concern. "Okay, okay, hang in there. We're almost there." He looped a skinny arm under my shoulders and slumped us toward the door. "See? No more stairs. Man, you look rough."

"Adam." I closed my eyes and let him guide me.

"Hey, that's my name. Don't wear it out. Come on, come on." His face was impossibly young as he pulled me past the cargo bins. They went on forever. How had we ever made it through so many bins? Adam kept up a constant, quiet chatter in my ear as we hobbled along our crooked way, but he didn't need to worry. I wasn't faint. I was *sick*.

After twelve eternities passed, we reached the last bin. I slammed myself into the far wall, grateful for its stability. But that was a lie, too, because nothing was stable. We were spinning and spinning. We'd only ever been spinning on Earth, too. I swallowed a wave of nausea.

I looked at Adam, who was busy opening the secret seal to get to the Remnant, the lighting program tucked safely away in the band at his wrist.

"Adam."

"*What?*"

"That program isn't for lighting, is it."

He looked at me in the peculiar half-light of the cargo hold. "Oh. Of course it is."

"It's the 'most important program on the ship,' right?"

"People don't want to—" he began to quote Isaiah.

"To be in the dark. No, they don't," I said pointedly. We regarded each other, and his concern melted into something harder. I rubbed my face. "It's life support, isn't it."

His new expression told me everything I needed to know.

"He's going to do it. Isaiah plans to suspend life support on the rest of the Ark until he gets what he wants."

"This is a war," he said.

"This is the *end of everything*. We just have to survive until we get to Eirenea. *Then* we start a revolution. Give me the program."

"I can't. You know I can't do that."

"Adam, my brother is out there on this ship somewhere. I can't let you take that program."

"With all due respect, you can't stop me."

I started to lunge at him, but stopped short. He stood, one foot in the black space and one in the cargo hold. In his hand, pointed at me, was a gun.

My gun.

Oh, Isaiah. It is the end of everything between us.

He motioned me forward with the barrel, his voice far less steady than his grip on the weapon. "Come on. I'm not going to hurt you. We'll get you to a doctor."

I thought of West suffocating in the blackness of an Ark without life support, his body spinning through space forever. I stood testily, leaving the weight off my injured leg. "I'm not going with you. And you're not taking that program."

I lunged again, forgetting that Adam had already killed that day. Forgetting that unlike me, he had found something to believe in. Something he was willing to fight for. He leveled the gun at my chest.

He shot me.

Twenty-four

There was a dull pain below my collarbone where the bullet had landed. I placed the tips of my fingers on my neck, then cautiously swept them across my chest. A heavy bruise was blossoming out around the bullet.

But the bullet hadn't killed me. In fact, it hadn't even penetrated the skin.

The ship continued to spin, and I retched onto the black floor. When I was done, I looked around me, wiping my face on the sleeve of my black uniform. Adam was long gone.

I thought back to when I'd handled the bullet in Isaiah's room. It wasn't as hard as steel, but it had been harder than plastic, and I'd been shot at point-blank range. By anyone's measure, I should be very, very dead.

I sat up.

The bullet dropped into my lap. It hadn't even made it through the uniform.

I looked around, thinking. Had the Commander, or whoever owned the weapons, engineered the polymer *and* the uniforms? Isaiah said the molecules were stacked so that they wouldn't damage the ship. Maybe they couldn't damage the black fabric of the uniforms, either. It was a smart move by the Commander. Everyone on his side would be armed and fully protected from the bullets they carried. Everyone else would be helpless.

I was sick again.

This time, I stayed seated afterwards. I gathered my thoughts like errant wisps of steam in a thunderstorm and ran through every scenario I could think of. They were all terrifying, but the ones that scared me the most were the ones where West was in danger. And my father, too, if I were being honest. Perhaps there was something I could fight for, after all.

I needed to get to the Remnant and stop Isaiah from using the program. I'd never catch up with Adam, especially with the head start he had going. So he would get there first, and he would warn Isaiah about me. But I had to try, so I reached for my pack. Breaking into places I wasn't supposed to be had always been a tough habit to kick.

My pack wasn't there. I must have left it in Mission Control. Either I was slipping, or a room full of lasers was bad for my concentration.

Wait. Adam couldn't warn Isaiah about me. He thought I was dead. He was nothing if not a good soldier, so he'd absolutely tell Isaiah what happened. He'd explain that I had tried to stop him, to recover the program, and that he'd shot me. Isaiah's suspicion that I couldn't be trusted to carry out the mission if I knew what was really going on would be confirmed.

Even if I could break through the seal, my chances of success were slim. I still hated the Commander, but I wasn't sure whose side I was on. Maybe there was another way to stop Isaiah. I couldn't go back to the Remnant. Not yet.

And once I carried out my new plan, I could never go back.

I was going to warn the Ark.

The interminable length of the cargo hold gave me plenty of time to think. It didn't do any good. I didn't exactly have access to hordes of high-ranking officers. Heck, most of them would probably kill me on the spot. Which left precisely one option. Eren.

By the time I got to the Guardian Level, I still hadn't come up with a better plan. It was probably too much to hope he'd be happy to see me, but I pushed that thought from my mind. I had no future with Eren, because I had no future at all. I was about to burn my last bridge. Central Command wanted me dead, and I was well on my way to betraying the Remnant, as well.

A cacophony of warning bells tolled in my mind as I strolled down the carpeted floor as casually as possible, considering the searing pain in my chest and thigh. I ignored them. My pulse beat faster and faster, but I kept my pace the same. I wasn't trying to run anymore. There was no escape at the end of this tunnel.

Eren's door was open. You'd think they'd have things a bit more secure, what with a dangerous fugitive on the loose. I walked right in. Eren was bent over a screen at his desk, giving me a generous view of his bright yellow hair and full shoulders. My throat tightened. Some bridges are harder to burn than others. I gave a little cough.

Eren stood up at his thin yellow desk, his eyes wide, looking for all the world as though he had no idea what to make of me. It was an uncomfortably familiar expression, albeit a new one, coming from him.

"What are you *doing* here?"

I didn't know what I'd wanted him to say until disappointment bit through me. I guess I'd used up my last warm greeting in the holding cell. I told myself that it didn't matter what he thought about me, or even what I thought about him. That wasn't why I'd come.

I rolled my eyes. "It's great to see you too, Ambassador."

A muscle worked its way through his jaw. "Magda. Tell me you didn't come back for *me*."

"I—I didn't realize that would be such a problem. Good to know."

"No." He leaned forward over the desk. The strain in his voice was evident on his face. "It's not that. I wish I could say I'm glad to see you, but frankly, this is—"

"Oh, don't worry. I'm not here to sweep you off your feet."

"I see." His face relaxed into an unreadable mask. He glanced around the room. "What do you need?"

"I have to tell you something. Can you, could you just calm down for a minute? You're making me nervous. This is important."

Everything in his body was telling me *stay back*. His words were clipped. "I would imagine so."

"Eren, there's a program on the ship that controls *everything*—the lighting, the doors. *Life support*."

"The Noah board?"

"I don't know what it's called." My tongue wanted to freeze, to save what was left of my friendship with Eren, despite his present demeanor. But there was no getting around this. I willed myself to speak, to ruin *us*, to save what was left of the world. "I stole it."

He strode around the desk and crossed the room in an instant. "You must be kidding."

"Well, I helped steal it. And I thought it was something else. You know what? It's complicated."

Eren stood there, a confused look on his face. "Whom were you helping?"

I took a deep breath. "The Remnant."

"Magda."

"Eren," I echoed sarcastically. Why did he have to be so sharp? I mean, I knew we hadn't left things well, but it wasn't like he'd wanted me to stay and die.

"The Remnant."

"They exist."

Eren looked around the room, as though struggling for the right words. "You shouldn't have come here. You need to leave."

"Didn't you hear what I just said? The Remnant. Has. The Noah board. You're under attack, Ambassador. You just don't know it yet."

"Even assuming that there is a Remnant, this makes very little sense. First of all, you wouldn't still be here if you had broken into Mission Control."

"Oh, you're referring to the barrage of lasers? Fair point." I ripped open the hole at my thigh, exposing the burn from the laser. "They did slow me down. Slightly."

He looked sick. And impressed. And I'd be lying if I said I wasn't a bit gratified to see those two emotions battle each other across his face. "Oh, Magda. Why didn't you—"

"Tell you? I'm not here to talk about my leg, Eren. There's a war on. Do try to keep up."

"You really, *really* shouldn't have come here." He glanced around the room one last time, then back to me. At long last, something inside him seemed to break. His stony façade melted into a furrowed look of concern.

He crossed the room in four giant strides and, an instant later, wrapped me in his arms. My legs went weak, but his grip was strong enough to keep me on my feet. "So you keep mentioning."

"We don't have much time."

I sighed into his neck. "And here I was beginning to think you weren't paying attention. Look, they're going to threaten life support unless Central Command surrenders."

"And then what? Anarchy?"

"*Equality.*"

"Is that what they're calling it? If they shut down life support, they'll definitely achieve that goal. We'll all be equally dead." He twisted away from our embrace so that he could look squarely at me. "Why did you come back? You had to have known they're looking for you."

"I just... I don't want anyone to die. Surely you can tell Central Command to change the access codes for the Noah board, or whatever it is, so that the system can't be hijacked."

He bit his lip, still holding me.

I squeezed his arm, just below the shoulder. "Like, now. Right now."

He let out a long breath. "We can safely assume that Central Command is already aware of everything you just told me."

I froze, except to straighten slightly as an errant thought crept slowly up my spine. "You mean—" I was about to say *they're listening to us right now*, but Eren cut me off.

"Magda, you have to go back to the Remnant. If they succeed, it's the only place that's safe for you."

"I just betrayed them. Plus, I'm pretty sure they think I'm dead. They know I tried to keep them from getting the Noah board. They're about to realize I've warned Central Command."

He considered that for a moment, presumably formulating a response. None came.

Instead, he kissed me.

*

I kissed him back, this pale son of a powerful man, and allowed my mind to race. He was different from his father, in many ways, but he had his own brand of power. And danger. So I kissed him with my eyes open. He must have thought the same thing about me, because a moment later, Eren opened his eyes, too.

Blue. All I saw was blue. Cornflowers in a yellow field. The endless sky on a perfect day. My mother's favorite sweater. So many things that were gone forever lived again in Eren's eyes.

And his arms moved against mine. I had a million reactions ready: I wanted him to stop, because he was dangerous, this quiet son of an angry man. I wanted him to stop, so that I could freeze his gaze into mine, and drink in more blue.

I wanted him to keep moving.

The tips of his fingers brushed past my neck, impossibly gently, to sweep back my hair. His mouth moved to whisper in my ear. I stopped breathing.

But Eren spoke, as softly as his pulse. "Magda. *Run*."

Twenty-five

I was out of breath almost immediately. In my defense, it had been a rough day. I veered left, then right. And then I stopped. I had no idea where to run to, but it wasn't in my nature to stand still before they caught me. A door sucked open ahead of me, and the sound of heavy boots on thick carpet flooded the corridor.

That was when I noticed Eren, who'd apparently been trotting along behind me. "Turn left. Keep running."

"Are you *following* me? Don't you have somewhere to be? Like, I don't know, *Mission Control*?" I hissed over my shoulder. My leg burned, but I forced myself to keep moving.

"Magda, *everyone* is following you. You just don't see them yet. Left again."

I banked left. My mind reeled. It wasn't like I'd expected to be ignored, but I hadn't planned on quite this level of surveillance. "You know, your dad can be kind of intense. No offense. Where are we going, exactly?"

"None taken. To the only hiding place I could think of. But don't get your hopes up. It's not a very good one."

"I'm all ears."

"What a pleasant surprise. Go straight." Eren pulled ahead of me and swiped his access card against a random door panel, revealing a maintenance access closet. "In here," he whispered, pulling me inside. "Look, anytime I use my access card, he knows where I am. So we can't stay here. They'll have gotten to my room already."

"I hate to break it to you, Ambassador, but there is literally nowhere for us to hide."

"Not us. You. Magda, I'm not coming with you. That's what I'm trying to explain. Even if my father weren't following me, I have obligations now."

"I thought you said they already know about the Noah board?"

"They do. They knew as soon as you started talking. My room has been bugged since you left. And maybe before that; I don't know." He looked directly into my eyes and squeezed my shoulders. The blue pierced through me. "But I will not abandon my post. This is my fight."

I stared at him. "What do you mean?"

"If what you're telling me is true, it's an act of war."

"Why does everyone keep *saying* that?" I shook my head, confused. "It's not much of a war if you can't breathe, Eren. And if you stop them from using the Noah board, they're practically defenseless. Why not let them have their sectors?"

Eren looked as confused as I was. His grip on my shoulders tightened. "Because they're dangerous! Look at what they've done. They need to be secured until we get to Eirenea. I mean, not all of them will have had a hand in this. We need trials, reintegration programs for their civilians. It could be that we could disperse the more innocent ones among the other Arks. I don't agree with everything my dad says, but he's absolutely right about the Remnant being a threat. I just didn't know whether to believe they were real until now. It's not like we can ignore them."

"So you're going to fight them."

He set his jaw. "I'm going to stop them."

I stood there, staring into the blue of his eyes for as long as I could. But I couldn't conceal my hurt. "Meanwhile, I'll be executed."

"No." His grip on my shoulders slid around my back to an embrace I didn't return. "I'll never let that happen to you. I know I can stop my dad from doing that, especially now that you've warned us. Worst case, you'll be locked up until we reach Eirenea."

"But that's years away!" How could he be so cold? Tears stung my eyes, but I was far too proud to let them fall. It wasn't like he had a choice.

"We don't have much time. Magda, I can protect you in prison. I'll make sure you have everything you need. Then one day—"

"Does it hurt to be this naïve? No one is getting a fresh start on Eirenea. Can't you see that? They may say we'll start over, but in the back of their minds, no one wants to unleash a convicted felon on society. Besides which, you are seriously kidding yourself if you think your father won't kill me the first chance he gets. This is the end of the line, Eren."

He closed his eyes. Our time was up. "Okay. Okay. There may be one place you can go. But it's not as safe as prison."

I waited for him to speak before shrugging at him. "So tell me! As you may have observed, I am open to suggestions."

"I found your family." He cleared his throat awkwardly. "Charlotte."

Twenty-six

I spoke through gritted teeth. "Except that one."

"Do what you want. I hope you'll surrender, so that I can keep you safe. I can see how that may not appeal to you. But if you hide with your family, at least I'll know that someone is looking out for you."

I snorted. "You don't know my family."

Eren looked at me. "No. I don't. But they can't be any more screwed up than mine."

"Your father would do anything for you. My father, on the other hand, knows I'm set to stand trial and be executed, but he still can't be bothered to come forward and say that the starpass wasn't stolen. Do you really think he didn't see me on the screens?"

"He may surprise you. How do you think I found them? I ran a search on the woman whose starpass you were using. She never even attempted to board. On a hunch, I pulled the file on her family. It listed a husband, son, and… a daughter."

"A daughter." The words swirled around me, but they made little sense. How could there be a daughter listed? I'd been in prison for years. They had to have known I wasn't getting out.

"Named Charlotte. Who was never issued a starpass."

I looked at him. "It's not like they were just handing them out."

"No, they weren't. How many times did you apply?"

"Uh, never? I was a bit… otherwise occupied." I had the dizzying sensation of standing on the edge of a high cliff and trying not to slip, the wind increasing around me with every word Eren spoke. The more he knew about me, the closer he was to finding out about my past. I had the feeling I couldn't stand up much longer.

Then he gave me a little shove.

"According to the database, someone filed an application in your name every single day for the last five years."

I shook my head slowly. "But that's, like—"

"Almost two thousand applications. Maybe you don't know your family as well as you think you do."

"It was all her. My mom." And she was gone.

"Maybe. Seems like a lot of work for one person. And it's unlikely that—" he consulted a sheet of paper on his desk—"a *doctor* would have the clout to break the number of rules required to do that." His tone changed. "In any event, Charlotte, being up here, after everything we've been through, has a way of changing people. Lots of time to think, and all that."

His lips hovered near mine, but I was still too confused to kiss him, and the almost-kiss passed us by. "Sector Seven, Level Twenty. Room B-17. No one else knows. I'm going to open some more doors. Throw them off the scent."

I could only look at him helplessly.

"They'll follow my access card. So I'm going to go use it. We have to go," he said. "Unless you want to surrender, of course."

I would never surrender. I shook out my shoulders. "Okay. Go. Fight. Open doors. Maybe when this is all over, we can find each other again."

"I'm counting on it."

"Just be careful. Don't take the Remnant for granted. They're smarter than you think. And... kinder, too."

The door swished open. "Goodbye, Charlotte," he said. And then he was gone.

Twenty-seven

I took off in the other direction, taking stock of my situation as I ran. I'd lifted just about everything I could off Eren while his arms had been around me. Except his access pass, obviously. I didn't know how he'd react to finding out his stunner was missing. I told myself it didn't matter. He was about two steps away from finding out everything I'd ever done, if he hadn't already. The thought was so sickening that I slowed my pace until the moment passed. There was nothing I could do about it now.

By some miracle, our plan to draw the guardians away from my path appeared to have worked. I turned corners cautiously, making sure every upcoming hallway was clear before barreling down it and pausing before taking the next corner.

I nearly made it all the way to the stairwell before I encountered my first hiccup in the form of a pair of guardians, reflective shield masks down, standing at the end of my final stretch. I approached casually, or as casually as I could with my pulse pounding through my temples. I was about halfway there when they made me.

The bigger one figured it out first. The visor covering his face tilted down, and I pictured my injured thigh catching his eye. His black-gloved hand slid to his stunner, a move I mirrored back to him.

His other hand extended toward me, palm out. The second guardian drew her stunner.

"That's her," the second guard said.

Now, how many times had I heard that phrase in my life? It had a different ring to it, though, up here. Her tone set me on edge, probably because without citizenship, I had no rights. It wasn't like the Commander was itching to send me to a fair trial, exactly.

"It's me!" I responded sarcastically, quickening my pace.

"Stop right there," the first one said. Something about his voice made my hands begin to shake, which I ignored.

I took a deep breath and pressed forward. "Let me guess. 'Hands where I can see them?'"

The first guard answered. "Wouldn't make much difference, little bird."

At that, I did stop. I stopped so hard I nearly tripped. "Isaiah?"

He nodded to his companion. "Arrest her."

"I can't! I can't go with you," I said.

"That's kinda the point of getting arrested," the female guard said, moving forward. "It's not optional."

She'd had plenty of training, judging from the way she held the stunner. Possibly a former police officer, or maybe a prison guard. I'd had enough of both. I drew my own stunner.

"Put that on the ground and raise your hands," she said.

I rushed her, wielding my stunner like a sword. Hers cracked to life, barely missing my face. Relief flooded through me in place of pain. But I was outmatched, and the feeling was short-lived. Her stunner swung back immediately, with a force and speed I hadn't counted on, and its black edge connected to my arm. The tip flamed white again, inches from my ribs, but failed to connect for the second time.

A bright slash of pain nestled itself into my bicep where she'd hit me. I added it to my mental inventory of physical injuries and tackled her, taking special care to grab her face mask as we went down.

It came off too easily to do any damage, revealing a girl about my age with a shock of red hair. Fake red, the kind that reminds you more of the actual flame than the warmth from the fire. She flipped around immediately, both hands on the stunner, and brought it around my throat. Her knee dug into my back. She may have been better at this than I was, but I couldn't afford to lose. I was wild and angry, and in a moment, I'd broken her grip on the stunner's handle, relieving my neck of its pressure. I gained the advantage and used the moment to pull her stunner out of her grasp. I'd soon be past her and on my way to my family's bunk.

Or, I would have been, if I hadn't discounted Isaiah so readily.

CRACK. Blinding pain seared through every molecule of my existence. The memory of pain doubled together with the pain of the present moment, and my body convulsed, pressing a scream out from deep inside me.

CRACK. I saw nothing but white. Terrible, blinding white. The screaming increased.

A moment later, I realized the screams weren't just coming from me.

"Stop! It's me! You're stunning—*NO! me!*" The girl shrieked, her pale, heart-shaped face contorting in pain.

CRACK. This time, I felt no pain and heard no screaming. The guardian had passed out. I spared a moment to envy her, then turned my eyes to Isaiah's. To his mask, rather.

He lifted me wordlessly, grunting slightly at the effort as he straightened. I realized with a shock that I could not resist. My body twitched, but failed to respond to my increasingly panicked suggestions that I start kicking.

"Put me down, *Isaiah*," I growled through gritted teeth. "You don't understand."

He shouldered through the door to the stairwell and trotted down the first flight of steps. "I understand you warned the Commander," he said evenly. "Adam had to reprogram the Noah board because of you."

The adrenaline that had flooded through me during the brief fight was tapering off fast. Isaiah's mask filled my vision, swimming before me. "No, Isaiah, please. Let me go."

His voice was velvet in my ear. "Now, you know I'm not going to do that. You can't stay out here, is all. I sent them to retrieve you, but you'd already gone. Can't blame that boy for leaving you, though. Or for shooting. He's a good enough soldier. Carried out the mission, anyway."

"Isaiah, my family! Please, my family."

At this, he stopped. "Your family."

I nodded weakly. "I love the Remnant. But I don't want this war, Ise." I continued to struggle in his arms. It did no good. "This is wrong. Too many civilians."

I could almost hear his face tighten behind the mask. "They should have thought of that, *Char*."

I fought for words and the strength to speak them. "But my family. They're out there."

"This the same family that left you to die in that prison cell? Don't sound much like family to me." He huffed down another flight of steps. His grip was gentle but unyielding, and I lacked the power to fight him.

Time passed like some kind of shiny, slippery eel, impossible to grasp. I opened my eyes, and we were crossing through the door to the cargo hold. I opened them again, and the bright primary colors of the bins slithered around me.

I found that my legs could work. I began to kick.

"Now, stop that. We're almost home." Isaiah's voice, like his grip, was firm and gentle at once.

I'll never be home, I thought.

Isaiah stopped to turn his face to me, as though he could see me, and see through me. As though he could read my thoughts. I saw that his mask had come off, revealing the tension and concern that knotted his forehead. He spoke slowly. "I gave you a home. I thought that's what you wanted. I gave you a family, Charlotte. You belong with us."

"Family doesn't shoot each other! Family wouldn't—" I kicked again, hard—"*kidnap* me!"

Pressed against his chest, I felt him stop breathing.

"Is that what you think I'm doing?" he said quietly.

"You *stunned* me!"

"I'm blind, Char! I was stunning the girl."

"I'm not sure I believe that."

"That I'm blind?" he asked sarcastically. Disgust replaced the concern on his face, but his voice betrayed only sadness. "She shouldn't have stunned you. I was rescuing you."

"No. I never asked you to do that."

"Look here. We reprogrammed the Noah board. We're overriding Central Command. There's a war on, baby. And you're picking the *wrong side*."

"You're shutting down life support for everyone but the Remnant. What if the Commander won't surrender and everybody dies? I have to find my family."

"Your family?" he scoffed incredulously. "Take it from me, little bird. That word only means something when they want it to. I'm the one who broke you out of that prison!"

A long, cold moment passed in silence, and I knew that we were through shouting at each other. Our anger had abandoned us, along with whatever other things we'd been nurturing, slipping away into the darkness like a shadow.

I steeled my voice and spoke as deliberately as I could. "I'm not coming with you, Isaiah."

He looked like I'd slapped him. His voice was low and quiet, and it betrayed a world of pain. "I can't let you leave, Char. You know too much."

"I'm going to my family, not to Central Command. Please, Ise. Let me go. Just this once. For old times' sake."

He remained frozen for another moment. Then his head moved back and forth once, a weird little shake, as though finally computing what I was saying. He set me down, and his voice matched his robotic movements. "I hope you think of me when you're gasping for air, and how I tried to give you a place to breathe. How I tried to save you."

"No one can save me, Ise. That's what I keep trying to tell everyone."

He turned to leave, and his hands clenched and unclenched. To my surprise, I saw that his neck was still tense. I had been wrong about his anger leaving him. It had been outweighed, briefly, by his pain, but that was no longer the case, judging by the tightness of his mouth.

He spoke one last time, without looking back to me. I knew, as surely as I could feel my own heartbeat, that every word was the absolute truth, and that his mind would never change. "You've betrayed us, Char, but we're still going to win. If you survive the battle, don't come back. When we find you again, you'll be arrested, and tried for treason by the Remnant itself. You are our enemy now."

238

Twenty-eight

I must have run. I must have banged on my family's door, identified myself. I must have waited, breathlessly, for my father to decide whether to let me in. But I don't remember any of that.

I only remember seeing him standing there, looking much the same as he had on Earth. He was a bit grayer than I'd realized, a bit thicker around the middle. He was older. Maybe he noticed I'd gotten older, too. We'd had so many of these wordless encounters on Earth, when he'd been away on an extended, work-related trip, and he'd come in the door to find me curled up on the couch. Or, during the years I was inside, when Mom would drag him to visiting hours. We'd weigh up each other's little changes, update our mental image of each other, and continue on our separate ways.

But we weren't on Earth, and everything had changed.

My dad.

He just looked at me, like he had to decide whether to know me or not.

Actually, that couldn't be right, since the last thing he'd said to me was, "I can't know you anymore." The words burned through me every time I remembered them. Which was way more often than I liked to admit.

I looked around the room, because eye contact sharpened the sting.

I immediately wished I hadn't. His room was different from Eren's in a million ways, and not just because it was designed for a family instead of a single person. The beds were built into the walls, with an enclosure like a tiny garage door over each one. Then there was a small living space that ended abruptly, with a counter containing a microwave, sink, and toaster. Pressed leaves, carefully mounted on clean white paper, adorned the walls. That was West's work. My mother's picture was taped to the wall next to the bunk.

It was a *home*, my family's home, and there was no place in it for me.

The pain of this realization washed over me slowly, relentlessly. Our home on Earth was gone. My mother was gone. And here was a home I'd never be a part of.

I sat down, right where I was, in the hallway. My arm and leg hurt so much.

My father stared a moment longer, then surprised me by crossing the room to extend a hand out into the hallway. I surprised myself by taking it. My father's glance alighted on the laser burn on my thigh, but he simply led me to a chair in silence. A metal chair in the kitchenette, not a seat in the living space.

Once I was again seated, the next thing I noticed about my family's bunk was that it wasn't as nice as a room on the Guardian level. There was no ambassador living here. I wondered how that felt to my father, who'd always been important in some way or another.

Only then did it occur to me that West wasn't there.

Dad continued to stare at me. A long time ago, in another life, I might have felt angry at him. Why couldn't he just *love me*, the way he loved West? But my anger had burned off somewhere in space, like a candle whose wick got too short, its flame suffocated by its own melted wax.

I turned back to my father. "I don't have much time. They're looking for me."

My father looked away. I believed, then, that I would never recover from that moment: not because he was ashamed of me, exactly, but because he no longer cared enough to hide it.

And then, it hit me. I had said everything I could possibly say to him. I had already apologized. Everything was different, but nothing had changed.

"Where is he?" I asked.

Dad stared back, blankly. He looked so tired.

I was tired, too. I made a vow to myself, then and there. Our sick little ballet was over. I would no longer try to be his daughter. He would no longer have to listen to my pleas for forgiveness, or for anything else, for that matter.

When I spoke, my voice conveyed a strength I didn't feel, alongside a harshness I wished I could conceal. "You need to find him as soon as possible. Where's your emergency kit?"

His gaze slid back to my leg. Something strange crossed his face—something I hadn't seen there before. I couldn't read it. I leaned in, forcing my mind to ignore the pain for a few more moments, so that I could focus.

"Dad. Is there any way to communicate with other citizens? Do you have a comm device in here? You need to find West. Get ahold of your emergency kit. You're about to need it."

My father finally spoke. "Why are you here, Charlotte?"

To my chagrin, I flinched at the coldness in his tone. It was mixed with some other emotion I couldn't place yet.

I told myself again I wasn't here to make nice. I was here to warn them, to try to save them. "The Ark is about to be

241

attacked. You're going to need everything in the emergency kit. Especially the oxygen."

He looked away from me. "Okay."

"Okay?" I repeated, confused. "That's all you have to say?"

"To you? Yes."

One by one, my emotions had been stripped from me. I could no longer feel sorrow, or pain, or even my old standby, anger. There was numbness deep inside me, and I gave it full rein to my heart, hoping it would protect me. I had the sensation, suddenly, of being composed of nothing more than flesh between skin and bones.

The man before me was nothing but the same.

He clearly wasn't going to respond, so we were done.

I stood and turned to leave.

But my father had one last move.

"Char. Do they still call you that?"

I stopped, answered carefully. I did not turn back. "Depends on whom you ask."

He scoffed. I continued walking.

"Wait. Char." He tested my name again, clearly conflicted about using it. "He's gone."

I turned to him. A faint sense of dizziness crept into the back of my skull.

"What do you mean, *gone*? Gone where?"

"He ran off to find the Remnant."

"You know about the Remnant? Then you have to believe me—"

"Everybody's heard of them. It's Central Command's best trick yet. It gave people hope back on Earth. Made them think there was a chance. Keep them from rioting in the streets."

"It's not a trick. The rumors are true."

My father scoffed, began fiddling with a pen. It clicked in and out, in and out. He glanced around the room, then toward the door. Click, click. Click, click. I shook my head in disbelief. My father was nervous. And chatty, like he wanted me to stay at the table. Normally, he couldn't wait to end our conversations.

Suddenly, I understood the look on his face. It wasn't just nerves, or exhaustion. It certainly wasn't anger. It was guilt.

I shook my head in disbelief, surprised at how shaky my legs were. He looked at the door again, cementing my suspicion into a dense brick that pulled me down, down, into the space beneath the ship.

"Oh, Dad. You told them I'm here."

My mind snapped into survival mode.

I made my father nervous. That was good; I could use that.

The next thing I planned to use was the stunner Isaiah had thoughtfully let me get close enough to steal as he carried me. Old habits and all that.

I slid it out from its hiding place in my sleeve, ignoring my father's look of disgust.

"You're not going to use that."

I looked at him. "I'm absolutely going to use this. Not on you, obviously."

He looked at me as if to say there was nothing obvious about it.

I knew my dad wouldn't want any part in the confrontation, other than his hand in bringing it about. He'd never put much stock in physical struggles. As far as I knew, which, admittedly, wasn't very far, he'd never even been to a football game outside of an election year.

So I could count on him to stay out of it.

That left at least two guards I'd have to fight. I doubted the Commander would spare more than that if he knew the Remnant was about to attack. I kept my father talking while I searched the room, mainly because I needed to know if he moved from his seat at the table while my back was turned.

"So he's gone to fight the Remnant single-handedly." I jerked open a bed panel and found a tab marked "Emergency Kit—Family." I pulled, and a box fell onto the mattress.

My father scoffed from his position at the table. "Hardly."

"I thought you said he—"

He carefully avoided saying West's name, and it hit me that I'd done the same. "Your brother thinks they're starting a war. He wants to fight *with* them."

I regarded my father, who finally met my eyes. His gaze was accusatory. Unlike mine, his anger had not yet burned away in the time that had passed since the OPT. Or it was new anger, nursing new wounds.

"You must be joking," I said.

"I wish."

I rifled through the kit, snatching up the three long, deflated oxygen helmets. "Well, he's right." I slid one flattened helmet into the shirt of my uniform, where it couldn't be pierced by a bullet, and tossed the other two to my father. "And it's not a bad place, assuming they make it through the battle. Do you know if he found them?"

"What do you mean, he's right? What battle? What kind of nonsense—"

"Dad, he's right. About everything." I took a position near the door, stunner ready. "The Remnant exists. They have a code that will stop life support on most of the Ark. They're planning to—"

The door sucked open.

244

The guard entered the room, armed with a gun. My father's eyes widened, his hands raised. His mouth opened, a silent O of disbelief.

From my position behind the guard's back, I had the advantage, barely, as long as I didn't blow it. The guard was armed. He meant business. I shifted, trying to get a useful angle, and extended the stunner toward his exposed neck.

The guard was much faster.

He grabbed the stunner and jerked it away from me. He flipped it in his right hand, aiming the gun at me with his left. The stunner flipped in the air, and its handle landed in the guard's waiting grip.

My mouth went dry. "Jorin."

His face twisted into its familiar sneer, and I felt my stomach turn to liquid. "Magda. Or should I call you Miss Turner?"

I raised my hands slowly. "Okay, okay. I surrender."

Jorin's sneer took on a hint of a smile. "I think not. I think maybe you give me a little trouble first."

CRACK. The stunner sparked, and I backed into the wall next to the door panel. When my back hit against it, a stupid, helpless whimper escaped my mouth. I doubted I could survive another stun.

He took a step forward, crowding out my view of anything else, and I crouched down, covering my head with my arms. I wished there were some other way to die. I wished Jorin's awful sneer weren't going to be the last thing I ever saw.

Instead of a jolt to my neck, he started with a blow to my face. I fell sideways, already halfway to the floor, and hit the ground. My vision blurred, but I saw a streak of red against the cheap blue and brown carpet.

The stunner sparked again, but he still hadn't used it on me. Jorin grabbed my collar, clearly enjoying himself, and slammed the back of my head into the wall.

"Where are they?"

I looked back at him. Some part of my mind understood the question, but most of it was preoccupied with absorbing the pain in my jaw.

At length, he raised the stunner.

I shook my head. "No," I garbled, my mouth filling with blood. "I told you before. There's no one else."

"That's not what you told your boyfriend."

CZZAACKK. The room ceased to exist, replaced by a field of darkness and pain splintered by lightning. Somewhere in the back of my mind, I knew I wouldn't have to go back to being conscious. I relaxed, relieved of every burden I carried, and surrendered myself to whatever came next.

What came next was the last thing I expected.

CRACK. My father's voice floated across the black field on which I lay. "Aagh! No!"

CRACK. "Please, stop! Aah!"

I shook my head, but only my dream-head responded. In reality, I must still be lying on the floor of my father's bunk, immobile.

"AAH! No!" That was definitely my father screaming.

Breathing. Breathing came first. I pressed my chest in and out as hard as I could, and found myself leaving the comforting embrace of darkness. A bright light split my vision, and I felt my lips move, just barely.

The pain came next. It was unbearable, relentless. But my father's desperate shouts didn't stop, and I forced my eyes to focus.

I was flat on my back, looking up at the ceiling. Somewhere above my head, Jorin must be stunning my father.

Beside me was a chair. It took me a moment to realize that it was oriented correctly from my perspective, so it must be lying on its back, too. I moved, and my neck began to protest, followed by the rest of my body.

I pressed onto my hands and knees, heavily and clumsily.

At the sound of my stirring, Jorin turned back to me.

We remembered the gun at the same moment, but I was about eight feet closer. I beat him to it, barely, pointed it at his chest just as he loomed over me again, and fired.

Jorin fell.

In my first bit of luck that day, he didn't land on top of me. I was glad; it probably would have knocked me out again.

I yanked the stunner from his grip and scrambled away from him as fast as I could.

Nearby, my father was pulling himself up via the thin, metal table in the kitchen area, which was bolted to the linoleum. I looked around, still too weak to stand, taking stock of the situation.

I struggled to piece together what had happened. The answer was obvious, but made no sense. "You hit him. With a *chair*."

My father leaned against the wall of the kitchen, looking down at me. "Seemed the thing to do," he said, with obvious effort.

"Thanks."

He rolled his eyes and gave a little shake of his head. "Stunner hurts even worse than it looks," he grunted.

"He's not dead," I said, nodding weakly at Jorin, who remained splayed out on the carpet. "Grab the stunner. We have to be careful."

"You shot him at point-blank range, Charlotte. Let's not be paranoid." Dad lifted the stunner between three fingers, as though it might ignite in his hand at any moment.

"He's wearing a black uniform. The bullets don't penetrate it. Hurts like a monkey, though."

Dad gave me a strange look, but seemed at a loss for words. His ruse uncovered, Jorin shifted.

"Stay on the floor," I barked. "I have a clear shot at your head. Dad." I glanced at my father, who was massaging his neck, jaw slightly open. "Maybe you should get out of here. Take the oxygen." Honestly, he was taking all this a little better than I'd expected him to.

Dad thought about that for a moment, then sighed in resignation. "No. I don't intend to run from my problems, Charlotte."

I ignored his tone, my mind racing. I didn't think I could even stand up yet. "Fine. Whatever. Jorin, get up and cuff yourself to the chair. I'm basically looking for a reason to shoot you right now. Just so you know."

Jorin smiled, understanding our conundrum at the same time we did. He moved slowly, though, and did as we said. I grunted, partly from the pain, but mostly out of frustration. I had no plan. None. From the looks of it, neither did anyone else in the room.

Finally, I spoke. "So then, what do you propose we do now?"

My dad shook his head. "There is no *we*, Charlotte. This doesn't change anything."

I took a moment to absorb that. Of course. My father had defended me because Jorin had been interrogating me about the Remnant, and West had joined the Remnant.

Actually, Dad hadn't defended me at all. He had defended West.

As that realization hit me, a long, low rumble pulled itself up from the ground and through my legs. My father's hand went to the wall, and I realized he'd felt it too, so it wasn't my pain making me shake. Rather, it wasn't *just* the pain.

The familiar female voice rang out through the hallway and the speaker in my father's room. "Warning. Level Three Alert. Partial system failure. Citizens, return to your assigned room and locate your emergency gear. Prepare oxygen apparatus. Remain calm and do not attempt to unseal your door. Life support will reboot shortly."

There was a pause, during which the hallway began to fill with panicked voices, followed by people rushing to find their rooms, but the voice spoke again, silencing the burgeoning chaos.

"All guardians report to Sector One, Level Fifteen immediately. Repeat. All guardians report to the Guardian Level immediately."

The battle had begun.

Twenty-nine

The effects of the battle reverberated through the ship.

To my surprise, I was afraid. I hadn't realized I could hate myself any more than I already did, but this newfound weakness was a good start. I'd also thought I was done apologizing, but I couldn't stop my next words from spilling out. "Dad, I'm sorry. For everything."

I checked that Jorin's cuffs were secure, handed my father the gun, and left the room.

The door sucked open behind me almost immediately.

"Wait," Dad called after me. "Come back."

This level had matching light fixtures, and they shimmered, unable to draw enough power from the backup support system to maintain a steady glow.

"It's no use, Dad. I can't find West for you."

He looked surprised.

"That's why you're out here, right? For West? Well, sorry to disappoint you, but I'm kinda banned from the Remnant for life. They hate me and want me dead, actually. But nice try. Thanks for playing. Now go home, and be glad you have one."

"He was always weaker than you, Char." He spit my name out through twisted lips. "He always needed us. But we weren't there anymore. First you, years ago. You never saw how he missed you. Then your mom, and—"

"But you were there!"

He shook his head. "No. Not since your mother—" he cut himself off, breathing a sharp, shallow breath.

I glared at him.

"Char—"

"STOP CALLING ME THAT."

My father choked, trying to find some kind of balance between his anger and his grief. "Charlotte," he said, more quietly. "She was my wife."

"She was my *mother*. I'm through with apologies. I'm through with second chances. We're way past that anyway. I no longer want you to forgive me. I don't want us to be a family anymore. Everything is broken."

"He's all I have left."

"*You don't want to know me*. So don't."

And then there was darkness.

Pure, inky, thick, black darkness.

And then there was a voice. As smooth as coffee, as beautiful as velvet. It held a million promises, none of them broken. But then, I reflected, Isaiah hadn't made many promises to me.

"ATTENTION, people of Earth, lost in space. The revolution is here. Allow me to enlighten you as to your current situation."

On cue, the lights blinked back on. I looked at my father, who was pointing the gun back into the room, presumably at Jorin.

"For years, my people—the people of the Remnant—have suffocated under the rule of your so-called *justice* system. And now, you, too, will suffocate."

*

251

Realization of what Isaiah intended to do next hit me like a storm in summer. I scrambled to retrieve the oxygen pack from under my shirt, shouting as I worked. "Dad! Your mask! Put on your oxygen—"

Then, I stopped. I couldn't speak, because there was literally *no air*.

I hit the green button on my pack, and oxygen filled my lungs. I rushed back into my father's room. He'd already gotten his flowing.

Isaiah continued. "For years, we've been without a voice. But the tables are turned, now. The day is coming when we will have equality. All of us. You too. So let me say this: We're winning. Matter of fact, we captured the Commander's strike force. Seems they couldn't find their way in the dark. But the darkness has been our home for a long time."

Isaiah paused.

"Here's the deal. The first battle is over. You didn't even know you were fighting, did you? But the war is just beginning. Now that you've seen what we can do, I urge you to write your Congressman, and tell 'em the Mole King sent you. Tell 'em you want equality for the Remnant. Full citizenship for everyone on board. A fresh start. Democratic elections."

There was a long pause.

"I'm joking. You wouldn't really want that, or you wouldn't have gotten where you are, with everybody else left to die on Earth.

"Instead, tell 'em you just want us left alone. From now on, the Remnant is a separate nation-state on board the Ark. When we're granted full access to the mainframe, we'll leave you alone. That's a promise. And I never break my promises."

With that, the system slammed back to life. Air hissed down from the wall panels around us. I shuddered, thinking of Isaiah's promises.

"Oh," Isaiah's voice continued ominously. "Here's one more promise. Until we get access, we'll shoot one captured soldier per day. Starting with the Commander's son."

My heart stopped.

I ripped the helmet off and looked back at my father, but he had returned to his bunk to shove the remaining helmet over Jorin's head. He'd been a little late, though, and Jorin wasn't conscious.

Or, more likely, Jorin was faking it again.

I stood in the doorframe, thoroughly confused about what to do. Isaiah had Eren.

Isaiah was going to shoot Eren.

If my dad had told the truth, West had taken off to find the Remnant. He probably wouldn't have left the bunk if he'd had no clue where to look. I would bet he'd found them.

Isaiah probably had West, too.

"He missed you," my father said, out of nowhere, still avoiding West's name.

"Why are you telling me this? Let me guess. You blame me." I shook out my shoulders, trying refocus. I needed to come up with a plan. A good one. But my father's words were distracting me. "I have news for you, Dad. I haven't spoken to West in *years*. Do you have any idea what that feels like?"

"There's a reason why you know that I blame you," he said quietly.

It occurred to me that, although I'd decided I was numb, West was gone. Our ugly, fragile, beautiful family had splintered again. The last link—the one between West and my father—was shattered. All this time, I'd been fighting to rejoin my family, but my family didn't exist anymore. There were, instead, the shattered pieces of the Family That Was, floating through space, detached and isolated.

I was cold. I was numb. I did not feel. I needed to think.

Above all, I wasn't going back to the familiar dance between us. Like I said, I was done. I fairly flew from the room. Let him deal with Jorin on his own. He'd have the connections he needed to make him either disappear or stay quiet, I imagined.

My father followed me into the hallway. "What am I supposed to do now? I don't have anything left."

I whirled around. When he saw my face again, my father made a sound like a sob. I felt my disbelief take over my face. I had never seen my father cry. The effect was how I imagined being sucked into space. There was no air, so I stopped breathing.

Everything in my chest burned with lack of oxygen. I was dizzy, detached, and nearer to dying than I'd ever been on Earth. I had no answer for my father, and none for myself, either.

My throat ached. I wanted to scream at him, but the pressure of space sucked my breath from my lungs and my words from my lips. I opened my mouth to *shout I HATE YOU* right at his face, but what came out instead was the last thing I expected to say.

"I can get him back." My voice was impossibly quiet. Calm, even.

"What?"

A shaky plan began to take root in my mind. I spoke slowly, deliberately. "West. I know how to get him back."

"Charlotte. I'm not asking you to do this." There was a note of concern in my father's voice I hadn't heard in years.

It was all I needed to be sure. My plan was suddenly as solid as a glacier.

"Of course you are." I gave him a frank look, and he had the grace not to deny it further.

I slapped his door panel and ducked back into the room. "Where do you keep your screwdriver? Never mind." I swept across the room and pulled a familiar metal box from underneath his bed. He'd always kept his toolbox there. "Some things never change," I said lightly.

He did not share my tone. "What are you *doing*?"

"Stand back, Dad. Way back. And pick that stunner back up. Do you know how to handle a gun?" I hurried to Jorin, who looked up, apparently deciding he'd rather see what I was up to than continue to feign fainting. I grabbed his cuffs and willed my hands not to shake. They obeyed me, so I looked a lot more confident than I felt.

"Charlotte, no. You can't let him *out*."

"It's the only play I've got left. I can't get anywhere near the Guardian Level without a guardian. Now get out. Don't come back to your room tonight."

"No. I'm—I'm not leaving."

I shrugged. This was among our stranger interactions, but I didn't have the energy or the courage to parse through everything at the moment. I needed all of both to keep from running away as fast and hard as I could, as every instinct in my body was pleading with me to do.

"Fine. Have it your way." I picked the lock on Jorin's cuffs with an ease that probably made my father blush behind my back, if he still cared enough to blush. The catch clicked, and the rivet popped out into my open hands.

Jorin stood slowly, not seeing any danger, but not understanding what was going on. I placed the cuffs in his hand

and extended my wrists to him. He looked down at them, eyes narrowed.

I sighed and took the cuffs back, then clapped them around my own wrists. "Now, Lieutenant Malkin. As you were saying. I'm under arrest. So take me to the Commander."

Thirty

Jorin's confusion melted into a dumb sneer, but he was only too happy to comply. He stood easily and gave a casual glance around the room, no doubt looking for more tricks.

For my part, I looked at my father one last time. He held the gun uncertainly, confused about where to point it and too unsure of himself to do any good with it. "Now, don't try any more funny business," he said to Jorin.

"He won't," I said. "Not here. The Commander's son's been taken. They're going to want to interrogate me for real this time."

My father looked slightly horrified and did not speak again.

Jorin gave him a long look before yanking me out the door by my elbow. I walked as gracefully as possible, and he continued to pull me off-balance as frequently as he could. It was a fun little game.

As we neared the end of the hallway, the calm blues and grays of the walls gave way to splashes of pinks, purples, and orange, which gradually melted into a mural. I slowed my pace, staring at the images that took form the farther we walked. The blue became an ocean that spread down onto the floor beneath us, teeming with dolphins, coral, and even a pair of scuba divers. The midsection grew into a mountain, which two climbers had nearly crested in the snow.

But the top of the mural was the best. The pale blue of the sky yielded to shades of purple and orange: an image of Earth's final sunrise. But the painter hadn't stopped there. Beyond the clouds, the atmosphere exploded into the majesty of space, covering every surface around, underneath, and above us. It was so much more than the star-speckled blackness I'd observed from the porthole in the Remnant. Here, the darkness was bursting with planets, nebulae, and even meteors, as full of energy as the ocean.

Sensing a theme, I found myself slowing further to look for the final pair of explorers before I found them: a tiny set of dots on a distant planet nestled among the stars. The planet appeared pristine and fertile, as rich with warmth and possibility as the one the meteor had ravished.

I stared at the new planet, transfixed, trying to read the dabs of paint and ink as though they might actually hold the truth about our future.

The mural was about hope. The abstract led to the concrete. Chaos and tragedy erupted into meaning and potential. It was our story, or the story that might yet be ours. We could never return to what we'd lost, so we would press forward. Our homelessness had made us a race of explorers. Someday, we'd become the builders of a new world.

Jorin yanked me forward, and I tripped over my feet, losing the game between us. I barely noticed when he laughed. It was precious, this potential of ours, and I found myself longing fiercely to protect it.

I kept my balance the rest of the way to the Commander's office.

I couldn't afford to trip again.

*

"Enter." At the sound of the Commander's voice, I shivered involuntarily, then steeled myself for what was next.

The heavy wooden door swung open, and I took in the pale walls and glass-like surface of the marble floors in an instant. The Commander's fountain did not bubble and change shapes, as before. Maybe he wasn't in the mood for it anymore.

The Commander himself seemed to have aged several years in the weeks since I'd seen him. He looked up at me, and I saw that the loss of his son was written all over his body. Even his uniform appeared less crisp. His shirt threatened to come untucked. His hair had fallen forward slightly. His face was more wrinkled than I recalled.

"Lieutenant." His voice was flat. "You've found her. Begin the interrogation. Keep her conscious. I'll be along shortly."

He waved, and Jorin pulled me back toward the door.

"Wait!" I said. I could have been the wind, for all the Commander acknowledged me. His face remained focused on his desk. Jorin pulled again, expecting me to stumble back, but somehow, I remained unmoved. The next time I spoke, the Commander would listen.

"Commander Everest, I can get him back."

He looked up. "Is that so?"

"Yes."

"And why should I believe you?"

I blinked. "I mean, I'm the reason you know about the Noah board being hacked."

"My dear, you would do well to stop flattering yourself. You're the reason the Noah board *was* hacked. I reviewed the security footage the moment the alarms stopped sounding. We hardly needed your so-called warning. My son could have done without it, certainly. It's a pity you didn't remain with the stowaways, for your sake. At least this way, I'll have the pleasure of seeing you die in person."

He massaged the bridge of his nose and gave another wave of his hand. Jorin moved toward me again.

My voice went up in pitch. "We want the same thing, Commander. If you've seen the footage, then you must know how I feel about Eren."

He stood, his face reddening. "I know my son was fool enough to fall for your act, but please don't mistake his gullibility for a family trait."

"*I can get him back*, Commander. Don't tell me you're not interested in hearing me out. Besides, if you're not afraid of being fooled by me, then what do you have to lose?"

He gritted his teeth and reseated himself slowly. "By all means, astonish me with your military acumen. If it works, perhaps I will spare you the discomfort of a few more days of your miserable life and move your execution up a week."

"Don't do me any favors."

"The plan, Miss Turner. The plan, or your interrogation begins right now."

I took a deep breath. "Can you contact Isaiah?"

"Who?"

"The King of the Remnant. Can you reach out to him?"

"King," he snorted at the wall. "And they said I over-reached myself." He shook his head and turned to me. "Why would I do that?"

"You need to offer him a trade. To get Eren back."

"You are as stupid as you are treacherous. The Tribune has refused to capitulate to their demands. They will not allow the Remnant access to the mainframe. Not even on my command." His voice lowered. "Not even for Eren."

"I figured that. Why would they sacrifice all their control just to save a few soldiers? They assume Isaiah will use it to gain control of everything and kick them out. Possibly try them for treason. But you have something else they want."

"And what would that be?"

I pursed my lips, then swallowed. "Me."

The Commander leaned so far back in his chair that he was facing the ceiling. "I have lost my patience with you, Miss Turner."

"They want to put me on trial for treason."

At this, he gave a short, mirthless laugh. "Don't tell me I'm going to have to start respecting them."

"He'll take the trade. Trust me."

"I will do no such thing."

"Commander, he's going to kill Eren. Unless you think he was bluffing?"

The Commander's frame sagged. He'd heard Isaiah's voice. Perhaps he'd recognized the calm, authoritative tenor of a man who'd made up his mind. We both knew Isaiah was as good as his word. He looked at me but spoke to Jorin. "I have done with this conversation, and with her. Take her away."

The holding cell was cold. Not just the air, but the bench and the floor were like ice against my hands and legs. Jorin pulled me off-balance before tossing me in, snorting quietly as I fell. He wore his cruelty as casually as his face, so I doubted he'd even thought about it. My only surprise was that he also tossed an oxygen helmet in after me. That was when I realized I'd won. The Commander didn't want me to die quite yet. Soon, of course, but not while there was a chance Isaiah would agree to the trade.

I was tired, more tired than I'd ever been before. My exhaustion seeped out into my blood from deep in my bones, poisoning my neck and arms with a paralyzing ache, clouding my brain, obscuring my vision. I did not attempt to stand, or even to lie on the bench. The whiteness of the walls pressed through my barely open eyes and into my skull for only a moment, then I let my cheek fall to the floor and allowed my lids to fall closed.

I don't know whether I slept. Certainly I did not contemplate my fate, which would have been pointless, or even that of West or Eren. My terror at losing either of them did little to slow the dampening of my mind into sleep. My terrible coldness was much more immediate, and even that had begun to recede as I lost consciousness.

No sooner had I lost sight of my discomfort than my cell door sucked open.

"Miss Turner." It was the Commander's voice.

I didn't move. I couldn't.

At length, he sighed. "Get her up."

Some moments later, I was upright. Not standing, exactly, but braced against Jorin. A small part of my mind was begging me to open my eyes, to see my way through the end of the game, but I couldn't be bothered.

"Have her sit on the bench. Wake her up. Gently, Lieutenant."

Jorin grunted, but he complied. Some other part of my mind found it strange that he did not otherwise acknowledge the command from his superior, but perhaps things were different in the Commander's highest ranks.

"Wake up, Miss Turner. Look alive."

A hand patted my cheek roughly. I opened my eyes just enough to give Jorin a withering glare, then turned to the Commander. He was his usual frowny self, and he spoke harshly. "The Remnant have agreed to the trade. We have a deal."

I wanted to reply, but his face slid upwards before my eyes as my body collapsed onto the bench.

The Commander spoke again, somewhat less angrily, but without any warmth. "Leave her. Monitor her. We make the trade in four days' time. Until then, Miss Turner."

I was fully asleep before the door had closed behind them.

Thirty-one

On my last day in Central Command, I thought only of West.

I did not think of Eren. It was unlikely that the Remnant would harm him in advance of the prisoner trade set to take place at high noon. So he was probably fine. But he was gone from me, permanently out of reach. Further thoughts of him were unnecessary and unproductive. And painful and warm. And frustrating.

And happy.

So I blocked him from my mind. Or I tried to, at least.

I had slept, mostly, since getting here, so the time had stretched and contracted in a senseless series of dreams and memories strung together by the rope of wardens and medics who visited my cell to hover over me, their faces a jumble of concern and kindness, and lately, of satisfaction.

I had dreamed endlessly of fox chases through my mother's formal dining room, where perhaps I had belonged more than I'd liked to admit, and a long, slow tango with a faceless man in a field of potatoes. I dreamed of birthdays at home, and the mess of blue icing in my mother's kitchen. I dreamed of her face at different times in my life, laughing, smiling, and straining to smile.

And of West. Always, always, I dreamed of West.

There were other dreams, too, of stunners and dead guards with dark holes where their eyes should have been and my father's disappointment, but these dreams didn't last. Whenever I cried out, a face appeared at my cell door, accompanied by a pinch in my side, and I swam frantically toward wakefulness even as I drowned quickly in the sweetness of oblivion.

The door of my cell slid open as soon as I was awake, revealing a pair of female guards who endeavored to brush my hair and clean my hands and face. I let them, model prisoner that I was.

Since my final conversation with the Commander, my belly had remained full. My wounds, old and new, had been tended by the finest doctors the human race had yet produced, and my back had been draped in a mountain of thick gray blankets. My fingers had lost the bluish tint of cold and hunger I'd grown accustomed to since my final days on Earth.

Central Command seemed unwilling to send me to the Remnant looking mistreated, on the assumption that it would affect the Remnant's treatment of its remaining prisoners.

They missed their mark, not that I planned on pointing that out. First of all, Isaiah would treat his prisoners fairly without regard to Central Command's actions toward me. I was more certain of that than of my own name. Second of all, I wasn't exactly a valued member of the Remnant. Isaiah would be true to his word. I would be tried for treason. I knew I'd be convicted.

I didn't know what would happen after that.

There was no future for me with West, either, but the time was fast approaching when I could say the things that had gone unspoken between us. Surely Isaiah would allow me that much. And then I would be at the mercy of the Remnant, and their tireless quest for justice.

I deserved their justice.

And so, when the Commander appeared about an hour after the guards had left, I went with him willingly. I had eaten well that day, meals of cheese and milk, cold roast and bananas, but I yet lacked the strength to spar with him.

When he told me, face impassive, that he expected me to appear before a team of cameras before and during the transfer, and not to make any decisions I'd regret, I merely agreed. I was mild, utterly tamed. I would proceed from this cage to another, much the same as ever.

I was not to mention any talk of treason, against the Ark or the Remnant, nor of my own hand in ending the battle between the sectors or recovering Ambassador Everest. My mind was made dull by the bliss of my body's recovery, and I did not question his motives.

"It is an armistice, Miss Turner, but it's a shaky one," he said, mistaking my blankness for contemplation. He'd pulled a thin metal chair into the cell from the hallway and seated himself before my bench. His hands clasped in his lap, and his leg was crossed knee-to-ankle. The effect was authoritative without being overtly threatening.

I looked at him, unable to decide whether I should consider his meaning or not. "Then you must have granted them access to the mainframe," I said, my voice plain.

He pursed his lips and matched my tone. "Not exactly. It seems they've taken it. Along with several of our citizens. Doctors, even a scientist."

"It was all a diversion," I guessed, my mind beginning to awaken. "The lights, the oxygen. Everything. I'm sure they always knew you wouldn't give them access. They must

have had other plans to... execute, during the blackout."
I straightened slowly. If Isaiah had had access to the entire
Ark, even for a few minutes, I was unprepared to believe he
had stopped at kidnapping a few high-value citizens. I knew
him better than that. He was capable of far bigger plans. I
lacked the energy, the grit, to guess what else he might be
up to. It wouldn't matter for me, anyway.

"So it would seem. The cease-fire won't last," said the
Commander. "We can't let them keep our people hostage.
Look at what happened on Ark Five. You may tell the King
of the Remnant to enjoy his victory, such as it is, for as long
as he can. But it won't last."

"I told you. They're trying me for treason. I don't exactly
have access to his inner circle at this point." We spoke to
each other without much emotion. It was the merest exchange
of information, and nothing more.

"My compliments to them," he said at last, and stood.
"See that you don't mention it to the cameras."

I nodded my assent and stood, limbs tight, while he rapped
on the door of the cell. It opened instantly, and the personnel
gathered at the door had a view of my furtive attempts to
stretch my arms and chest in the cramped space of the cell,
made smaller by the presence of the Commander. The cameras
crowded toward his face, which had transformed instantly to
that of a kind and competent leader. The perfect tinge of regret
heightened his look of determination, as if to communicate that
he didn't want to turn me over, but it was the right thing to do.

I yawned.

The cameras bugged in toward my face. The Commander's
hand was suddenly tight on my arm, and he started speaking.

"As a show of good faith, we have agreed to a trade for
the life of our own Ambassador Everest, who was captured

while leading a strike team behind enemy lines in an attempt to stop their attack on our life support system. In return, we relinquish Charlotte Turner, a high-value Remnant operative responsible for the attack as well as for the death of three guardians. It is with a heavy heart that I agreed to this exchange, in spite of my love for my son. Like you, I desire to see Turner face justice. But each life under my command is sacred, and you may rest assured that I will stop at nothing to win back the hostages they have taken. The battle may be over," he paused dramatically, "but we have only begun to fight."

The cameras snapped closed at his silent gesture, and he waited until the operators had dispersed before sending me out the door with Jorin. The Commander must have wanted to keep the way to the Remnant hidden from the general public. Jorin, exactly the same as ever, yanked me down the hall and toward the stairwell. I twisted my neck, popping it, trying to keep my mind clear.

His previous warnings to me proved unnecessary, since I never got the chance to speak. The walk to the edge of the sector was my first in several days, and as I moved, my mind began to awaken.

Surely the rest of the Ark, with their citizenship and dreams of utopia, had no reason to defect. So why the secrecy over the Remnant's location?

For that matter, why the lies about my value to the Remnant? The Commander knew firsthand I had betrayed them, and he'd almost certainly believed me when I told him I was wanted for treason. I chewed the inside of my cheek, slowly becoming frustrated with my lack of answers. I knew the Commander's real goal was to get his son back, and after that, to crush the Remnant. Perhaps he wanted to make me look valuable so that he would appear justified in making the trade for Eren.

So then, why would he exaggerate my crimes to the Ark? If he wanted to make the trade look like the noble thing to do, why not make me seem like a petty criminal, instead of some kind of cold-blooded terrorist?

This, at least, I thought I could answer. He was burning every bridge he could between me and the possibility of citizenship, and by extension, me and Eren. Eren was kidding himself if he thought his father would ever let this blow over, and now, neither would the rest of the Ark. I would never, ever gain citizenship. That meant that I would never be good enough for Eren.

Or my father.

I shook my hair from my face and continued to walk. None of this mattered. I had made my decision. I would win Eren's freedom and apologize to West. I would tell him that our father loved him and somehow convince him he belonged with the rest of the Ark. That I would also face charges of treason was a fair price to pay. I was, after all, getting everything I'd wanted since being locked away all those years ago on Earth. Except, instead of a fresh start, my story would have an ending.

Jorin pressed me through the door of the cargo hold, and I took in my last view of the bins. We were more than halfway to the end when his fingers clamped down on my arm like a steel trap. I stopped at once and made a grunt of protest, which I choked off when his fingers dug still further into my flesh, warning me to remain silent.

Jorin's eyes were wide, but not from fear. He was on high alert.

I looked around, wondering why we'd stopped, but heard and saw nothing.

"What is your game, silly girl?"

I wanted nothing more than a successful transfer, but I was hardly fool enough to think Jorin would believe me if I told him that. So I simply shrugged.

After a brief moment of consideration, Jorin pulled me forward, faster than before. And then, I heard it, too. The barest whisper of a shoe scuffing the concrete flooring, hardly making contact. Sneaking.

We were being followed.

No, not followed. I cocked my head and tried to make my feet quiet. It was harder than usual, with Jorin pulling on me. I pressed forward. I didn't need Jorin to encourage me to hurry. As we approached the end of the bins, my pulse raced faster than my feet, and my hands began their familiar tingling. Jorin was right. A new game was on.

We were not alone, and neither was the person tailing us. Jorin pulled me off our path, and we began to weave among the bins. I couldn't imagine who was tracking us. Not Isaiah. We were headed right to him, so he had no reason to come after us. Not the Commander, who'd sent us and expected Jorin to return with his son. And not Eren, who was still a prisoner. Baffled, I increased my pace.

At the end of two sharp turns, Jorin and I were moving more in unison, and I saw him give me an evaluating glance. As distasteful as his work could be, he was good at it, and his instincts tended not to deceive him. He decided that I had no part in being followed and loosened his grip.

As a result, we were able to move faster and more quietly. I wove around the bins, angling ever closer to the edge of the sector, following Jorin's lead, turning at the slightest suggestion of pressure from his enormous hand on my arm.

It wasn't fast enough. The closer we got to the edge, the more intruders I imagined.

"They know where we're going," I whispered to Jorin. He looked at me, his mind calculating our options. "They knew we'd be here. They'll be waiting for us when we get there."

Still we pressed on, and I began to see shadows shifting in the corner of my eyes. My growing trepidation gave me the speed I'd lacked since finding the Remnant. We were flat-out sprinting. I was as fast as ever, and profoundly grateful for the medical care and food I'd received over the past few days. Jorin, as usual, was slightly faster.

Also as usual, he was armed with a gun.

When he yanked me behind the corner of a bin, I couldn't help shaking my head at him. "You really thought you'd need a gun for this?" I said, panting slightly. "I'm flattered."

"You're up to something," he said.

"No, I'm not. But we'd be fools to go to the entrance to the Remnant right now."

He pushed his lips out, as if to say that my opinion meant little to him, then tapped a foot, thinking. His gun swung to point at me. "Fine. We go back. You first."

Another shadow moved nearby.

I lifted my hands, but the game was as good as over, and we had lost. By my count, there were four interlopers in our immediate vicinity.

Not counting the one right behind Jorin, with a gun pointed at his head.

Thirty-two

"Drop your weapon," said a voice.

Jorin complied, an ugly smirk on his face. "You won't get away—" he began, but was cut short. The man with the gun stepped forward to deliver a blow to his skull that sent him sprawling to the ground. I gaped at the stranger, but he offered no explanation for his actions. He stood, waiting for something. Or someone, as it turned out.

"I have no idea if you're faking that," came a new voice, "but be warned that we will shoot to kill if you move."

I looked around, wildly scanning the area for its source. "Who's there?" I said, trying to make sense of what was happening.

In response, the shadow itself seemed to move, rather than the man within it, pulling back, revealing his half-shaded form.

There, two steps before me, stood my father.

"Oh, Dad," I breathed. "What are you thinking?" I looked down at Jorin's crumpled form. "What have you *done*?"

"Don't worry about that," my father said, shaking his head. "He'll be fine, unfortunately."

"But you won't," I said, twisting around, trying to make

out the number of people in the shadows around me. "You have no idea who you've just—"

"I am not without my resources, Charlotte. Even up here."

I looked at him blankly.

He looked back, his face a mix of tension and some new emotion I hadn't seen there for a while. It took me so long to place it that when I finally understood it, I took a step back.

My father spoke first. "I don't know why I could never forgive you."

I made a strangled, laughing noise. "I can sympathize."

"It was my family, and I let it fall apart. But you were hard, Charlotte. And the harder I gripped you, the harder you got. It was never easy, knowing what to do with you." He paused, and a long, slow silence stretched between us. "My son is gone. I have no family left. Come back with me, Charlotte."

I could only stand there helplessly, shaking my head without thinking. "Dad, no. I still have to go."

"I'm sorry. I should have told you that sooner."

"You did. In juvy. Before the OPT left."

He grimaced at the memory. "Not that I failed you, though heaven knows I have my regrets where that's concerned. I'm sorry I didn't forgive you. That I blamed you for everything. Come home with me. I can make the Commander see reason."

Home. More than any other, this was the word I'd needed to hear. I clung to it like a dying man clings to the remnants of a sinking ship. It was all I had.

It wasn't enough.

"No, you can't," I said. "Don't underestimate him. He'd do anything for his son." I swallowed, about to say *and so would I*, but I wasn't ready to share that part of my life with anyone yet, least of all my dad.

He raised an eyebrow. "I've never been able to stop you before, and I harbor no illusion that I can make you listen to me now. I have learned, at last, not to tighten my grip any further. At least promise me you'll come back."

I smiled in spite of the growing tightness in my throat. "I'm through making promises, Dad. Besides, it doesn't work like that. I betrayed them."

"How do you know they're not going to kill you?"

I took a moment before deciding not to lie. "I don't."

He took in the weight of my words and looked, for the first time in my life, afraid. "Everything's going to be different now, isn't it."

I thought about West, the Arks, and our fragile little family. I thought about the storms we'd survived and the storms that were yet to come. I thought about Ark Five, vanished into the vastness of space. I dropped the smile. "I hope so, Dad. I really do."

I turned back toward the invisible door at the edge of the sector. I still didn't know how to open it, but I was sure someone was stationed on the other side awaiting Jorin's knock. Probably several someones.

"Wait! Charlotte!" my father said.

I stopped, hand frozen in a fist, poised to knock.

When I turned to look at my father, he caught me up in a hug so big I nearly lost my balance. "Charlotte—" he started, then stopped, and whatever else he'd planned to say died on his lips.

His arms grew tighter around me, pressing out my breath. I squeezed him back. A real home was more than driftwood in a raging sea, a final resort before drowning. It was a ship unto itself, fit to carry us through the storms and trials that lay between the shores.

"What did you say?" Dad asked.

I hadn't realized I had spoken out loud. His arms loosened, and I took the opportunity to fill my lungs with air. The door to the space between the sectors opened, and a patient face peered out at us. Adam. Shooting me hadn't affected his standing with Isaiah, it seemed. Not negatively, anyway. I knew there were more waiting behind him. I knew he was armed. This storm was hardly spent.

But I was ready. I had a ship, and I was not afraid.

I cleared my throat and met my father's eyes. "I will find West and bring him back here, and we will be a family again." I took a moment to weigh my final words. "I promise."

I left my father's arms and stepped forward into the darkness.

Acknowledgements

I'm grateful to God for his love and mercy. I'm also tremendously grateful for the following people, without whom this book would not exist in any form: Will Nolen, Morris Liddell, and Jenna Wolf.

For a writer, there is literally nothing in the world like finding out that someone else believes in your work. Thank you, Natasha Bardon. Thanks to Eleanor Ashfield and all the lovely people at Harper*Voyager* UK.

Thanks to the XO "Book" Club, for all the "books" we "read," the Book Aunts (Alex, Courtney, Elizabeth, Holly, Jennifer, and Jordana), Lesha Grant, Benjamin Morris, Ava and Liam, and Hal Liddell and the rest of my family (HI MOM!).

And thanks to my dog Miley, who is a very good girl.